THE SPARK AND THE DRIVE

THE SPARK AND THE DRIVE

WAYNE HARRISON

ST. MARTIN'S PRESS ≋ NEW YORK

Designed by Steven Seighman

Library of Congress Cataloging-in-Publication Data

Harrison, Wayne.
  The spark and the drive / Wayne Harrison.
      pages cm
    ISBN 978-1-250-04124-1 (hardcover)
    ISBN 978-1-4668-3735-5 (e-book)
  I. Title.
  PS3608.A78384S67 2014
  813'.6—dc23

                              2014000133

First Edition: July 2014

10 9 8 7 6 5 4 3 2 1

For the beautiful women in my life: Caye, Sabrina, and Josie

THE SPARK AND THE DRIVE

I SEE US PAINTING THE SHOP TOGETHER. I SMELL THE SHARP, gratifying blend of latex and gasoline. It's 1985, and Nick has offered me a hundred dollars to stay and help. "Walls only, three coats," he says, lugging eight gallons of platinum gray.

Into the first bay we pile disassembled pegboard, fan belts, hoses, wire sets. Nick orders a Meaty Supreme from Vocelli's, and when Mary Ann mentions beer I run out the side door to Lenny's Liquor Locker on the corner. I'm seventeen but formidable in my button-down Dickies shirt and dungarees; Lenny Jr. serves me even as I drop a hill of ones on the counter sign that says NO ID NO SALE.

We spread tarps, pry off lids, fill the roller trays. Nick spins on an extension pole and then rolls so fast a gray mist sprinkles his white Owner shirt. He overlaps where Mary Ann has edged and touches the ceiling a few times. Breathing hard, he drops the roller on the tarp and lights a cigarette, pondering the rest of the wall, the thirty feet of it left to paint.

Mary Ann smooths over his lap marks, and it's their quiet together that makes me feel safe. You hope for such assurance around your own parents, though mostly I remember my father's light jabs, my mother's retaliations, words that hook in and stay.

"I thought you were good at everything," Mary Ann says, on tiptoes stretching for the border tape.

Nick sees where he's gone over half the wall thermostat. He grins as when a random engine skip tries to outsmart him. "I get why Van Gogh cut his ear off."

"I like your ears," Mary Ann says. "Let's keep those. Maybe one of your big ugly hands."

And she doesn't move even when his choking hands come around her throat.

"Now you did it," he says. "Now you're in trouble."

When I look again at my own roller, fat gray drips have run down to the floor.

It's almost midnight when we finish the first coat, and Nick wants to speed up the drying. The tank of the waste-oil heater has been empty since spring, and I roll over the thirty-gallon catch from the oil-change bay and pump it into the heater tank. But the walls are tacky even after the thermostat hits ninety degrees.

"It's baking," Mary Ann says, fanning her face with a *Motor Trend*. "We're all going to bake in here." She gazes drowsily and finds the convertible Camaro that has been left for the weekend. "Well, hey there," she says, and walks over to it.

The Camaro is parked in the center bay, farthest from the wet walls, a rare '67 Rally Sport with hideaway headlights and chrome rally wheels. It was a ground-up restoration, and under a buzzing light panel, the cobalt blue paint is like looking into the polished ice of a glacier. The other muscle car shop in town passed up the job—a collector's car plagued by intermittent complaints—and I didn't blame them. Most mechanics come to accept that some cars just aren't fixable. But Nick's mind is boundless in its capacity for learning and wonder, and he has yet to open the hood on an unfixable car. I'm still hanging on to wonder myself, and it hasn't escaped my awareness that this is part of why Nick likes me.

Mary Ann pushes her fingers in through the Camaro's grille to pop the latch. She lifts the hood and unexpectedly turns to me. "Have you heard about the Pacific Coast Highway, Justin?"

"I think so," I say.

"It's where they make Porsche commercials," Nick says. "A lot of cliffs and hairpins."

"If you take a woman there in a convertible, she'll be putty in your hands."

"Sure," I say. "That was out in Oregon, right?"

"It's worth the plane ticket, believe me." She leans over the fender carefully, so that her tank-top shirt and jean rivets don't touch the paint, a careful yoga-like bend. Nick doesn't ask what she's doing, so I don't ask, and when he finishes his cigarette and walks up to the Camaro, I pace myself not to pass him. Together we look down just as she's pulling the speedometer cable away from the transmission.

"Voila," she says, leaning back, and the car is set to drive with no miles recorded.

From the bay windows a pearly light blooms out into the rumpled dark of the city. Deep in the backseat vinyl, I can feel the wind on a windless night as Nick eases out of the parking lot with the top down.

Wolcott Avenue opens to four lanes, and finding me in the rearview mirror Nick says what I've never heard him say before: "Buckle up." I dig for the lap belt and send the tongue into the buckle with a fortifying click before I can breathe again. With the clutch in Nick revs the engine twice, a perfect machine-gunning of the valves he's lapped and polished, and drops the shifter to second gear. When he dumps the clutch the sudden blast of air seems to be what throws me back, though of course it's the g-force, that awesome multiplier of weight, and then we're sideways, fishtailing. Nick chirps the tires in third gear and again in fourth. I know the police are out there, they're just not here, and after all the cars he's saved, Nick has surely earned immunity from traffic crimes. I whip around the backseat, anchored only by the waist, invulnerable and reeling with the sudden flush of complicity.

On Eden Avenue Mary Ann slides under Nick's arm. When he presses in the clutch she shifts smoothly through the gear pattern, and we ride over narrow hilly streets whose neighborhoods arise as odors in the treeless air—hot, dusty fire escapes and cigarettes from people out this late smoking on them, steaming aluminum fins of little AC units. Farther north, where the buildings are cared for, smells of cut lawn as we approach the quiet and leafy Waterbury Green.

I can hear the fountain before I see it, under the great brass horse, and above us the Basilica of the Immaculate Conception is spotlit from the ground. Mary Ann and Nick talk softly, their mellow tones a kind of tender anthem for the night. Then she kicks off her sandals, and as Nick slows the car she stands on the passenger seat, facing backwards—facing me. Her paint-speckled Sassons are threadbare at the knees, and his arm wraps around her thigh. Her face is radiant, her wind-strained eyes searching the night as if from the bow of a ship. On the balmy sidewalks, anyone laying eyes on her might fall in love. I crane my head back and find the Big Dipper canted as if to spill its potion over the gothic spires of St. John's on the Green.

"You try it, Justin," she says.

The speedometer needle is lifeless at nine o'clock, and I guess our speed to be an easy twenty or twenty-five. Nick feathers the gas so that it is no harder to stand on the tucked vinyl than it would be standing on an airplane. And we're aloft and banking softly. The air is cooling. We are in it and waiting for its slight gusts, and feeling the hum of the slow engine and driveshaft turning under our bare feet. Nick makes the loop again so easily we barely sway.

"What do you think?" Mary Ann says.

The word that comes to me bypasses my brain, is simply there from unthinking organs, and it is both for this ride and for the entirety of the summer.

Glorious.

But I'm shy with her and manage only a shrug. We take another lap with our eyes closed before Nick drifts us gently to the curb, and she floats down to kiss him.

The vision ends there, and I stay with it until the same bristle comes, the same bold dreams of transformation. I want to speak, to tell her the word she wanted, and to talk to them with the words I have now, as the husband, the father, the man at last. But the man can't change the boy, and anything I tell them they couldn't hear.

PART
ONE

1.

ROAD RAGE MAGAZINE, IN A COMMEMORATIVE ISSUE THAT mourned the death of the American muscle car—killed by the Environmental Protection Agency—ran a feature on Nick Campbell in 1983. The article was two years old when I started my internship, and I liked to reread it, framed and dusty on the counter, as I stirred powdered creamer in my coffee. I almost had it memorized:

> *Ten years after the EPA came down on Detroit like the church on Galileo, we still see no renaissance of horsepower on the showroom floor. With more repair shops catering to economy cars and imports, high-performance rebuilds and modification remain in the hands of a dedicated few. Recently, we sought out this dying breed of mechanic in the depressed factory town of Waterbury, Connecticut, and discovered one of the very best.*

The journalist hadn't identified himself when he handed Nick the keys to a cherry '68 Daytona. He asked for an overhaul that would boost factory output by thirty horsepower, a request that had gotten him laughed out the door at two previous shops.

But Mr. Campbell dreamed through a full orchestra of internal combustion cause and effect: shaving the cylinder head this much meant boring a carburetor jet this much meant extending cam duration this much, meant swapping these pistons for those, this intake for that—all of it drawn to a final composition in his head before I even signed the estimate.

The engines we saw were mostly small blocks, punctuated by a Tri-power GTO or a rat-motor Corvette—or, rarely, a true exotic like a Hemi Superbird. At seventeen, I was as dumbfounded as anyone to find myself touching these cars intimately, peering inside their complicated souls.

After two years in vocational high school, I understood the general repair mechanic to be the perfect masculine blend of strength and intelligence. Real men had a natural respect for mechanics, primarily for specialty mechanics, which we all were. Ray Abbot, in his fifties, was the oldest. He was frank and cagey with customers, though he held a deep, wholesome respect for their high-compression engines. He lived alone, was estranged from his kids, and lumbered on irascibly, scorning potential friends.

Bobby Stango had been hired on parole and was epitomized by a biker T-shirt he often wore in to work. TREAT ME GOOD, I'LL TREAT YOU BETTER, it said. TREAT ME BAD, I'LL TREAT YOU WORSE. With his pierced ear and handlebar mustache, he made even a starched-collar uniform look badass, pillows of tattooed muscle bulging against the chrome snaps. There was a willingness to fight that pervaded his words and gestures, even his laughter, and he gave you bear hugs if he liked you. I wondered if this were a natural disposition, or if prison had taught him what each day of freedom was worth.

And then there was Nick Campbell, who prophesied the rebirth of American muscle cars. He thought that on-board computers would revolutionize horsepower technology, and in my eagerness he saw a certain capacity for imagination, which was enough for me to feel anointed, to covet his life and believe that I could one day receive it as my own.

So when Nick's jobs started coming back for warranty work a year later, in the summer of 1986, I couldn't help feeling lost and forsaken.

The first few rechecks were only mildly incriminating. A cracked spark plug that might or might not have been factory defective, a missing screw that might or might not have been tightened. I convinced high-paying customers that they were normal breaking-in glitches, rather than shoddy work. But as word of Nick's unreliability began to spread, some of our formerly docile customers turned difficult. One morning a Ram Air Firebird, whose 400 engine Nick had beefed up with racing pistons, pulled right into the bays without a ticket. The owner was a fat, ruddy Italian named Mimo. In a black turtleneck and paperboy cap, he tried to promote a rumor that one of his relatives was connected, though instead of a cold-blooded mobster Mimo looked more like Dom DeLuise.

Nick, Ray, and I left our cars and approached the Firebird from different angles. Ray stopped to stretch with a fist in his spine, Nick lit a cigarette, and I tried to exude the same lack of urgency while Mimo got out and felt around in the grille for the hood latch. He stirred into the petroleum smell a sweet cologne that you couldn't get off all day if he shook your hand. "Something's leaking," he said. "I got oil drips all over my garage."

Instead of putting the Firebird up on the lift, Ray kicked over a creeper and rolled under the front end with a droplight. At this point we could still think that Nick's work wasn't to blame, that maybe it was condensation from the air conditioner and Mimo couldn't tell oil from water. We still had options. But when Ray pushed out from under the bumper he looked stricken, flat on his back and gaping at the chain-hung fluorescent light.

"What?" Nick said.

Ray sat forward and considered the blackened steel toes of his

Wolverines. "Drain plug," he said, softly. Nick looked at him with such puzzlement that Ray began to repeat himself, but Nick interrupted, "I heard what you said." He smoked his cigarette and sort of glazed over until, after a moment, even I hardly recognized him as the man who believed that cars could be great again one day.

"What's wrong with the drain plug?" Mimo said. "He didn't cross-thread it, did he?"

Ray bucked off the creeper on his way to the toolbox that Mimo had the misfortune to be standing next to. When I saw the chrome flash of a wrench I thought for a panicked moment that Ray might use it to crack open Mimo's head. "Hey Mimo," he said. "You got any naked pictures of your wife?"

"What?" Mimo said. *"What?"* His jowls flushed and he wadded his fat hands down in his pockets. "No, I don't. Jesus."

"You want to buy some?"

Mimo dropped his head and glared for a long second at a slick of tranny fluid in the next bay. "What is your problem, man?"

"My problem is a guy who pulls in here like he owns the place. A guy always coming in for more cam, more carb, more this, more that, thinking it's gonna make his dick bigger, and then don't want to pay."

"What's wrong with the drain plug?" Nick said.

Ray rubbed his oil-wet fingertips. "It's loose a little bit," he said, and as quick as I'd ever seen him do anything, he went back under the car with the wrench. Nick neglecting something so basic was inconceivable. Imagine leaving the house without putting on your right shoe.

Nick collapsed into a steel chair as Mary Ann approached with a bookkeeping binder pressed to her slender waist. By this point she and Nick had been on the rocks for six months, and I expected her to trudge past in her usual sad distraction, but the eerie quiet coming from three mechanics in the same bay woke her from her trance. She stopped short of the lobby door and turned. "What's wrong?"

Nick didn't answer, and I watched her helplessly, a look of rejection, or maybe resignation, in her eyes that I felt in my own stomach. Just as she was walking away, Nick said, "Do me a favor. Take Mimo out front and give him his money back."

"Whoa," Mimo said, a flattered, guilt-ridden knot of emotion now. "Hey, that's twelve hundred bucks. I'm happy with a discount."

"I don't give a damn what you're happy with," Nick said. He got up and threw his cigarette in the trash can, where any number of things could have gone up in flames.

2.

I FIRST MET NICK IN THE SUMMER OF 1985 THROUGH AN INTERN-
ship program with Northwest Vo/Ag High School. My shop
teacher, Mr. Harper, wasn't happy to find that I was the only one
who applied. He wanted to send Nick one of the engine wizards
of Northwest, but those guys either didn't have the academic
grades or they were constrained to family farms in the summers,
and I was it.

One evening at home, there was a knock on the door as I was
sitting down to dinner with Mom and April. Mr. Harper had come
by with a blown Ford 302 in the back of his truck and a bucket of
tools. I was supposed to tear the engine down and reassemble it as
many times as I could before June.

That winter and spring, swaddled in thermals and knit hats, I
rebuilt the engine twice in our garage. I didn't have the money for
a gasket and bearing kit to actually get it running, but when I spun
the flywheel around, the lifters rode the camshaft lobes, the crankshaft pushed the pistons, everything sliding and rocking exactly as
it should. I still didn't fully understand the engine, but I was gratified by the deep and complicated way it operated—imagining the
unfathomable timing of spark and valves, the constant grip of

vacuum, all of it contained in a seven-hundred-pound box whose sole function was to convert fuel and air into speed. I fell in love with the math of physical mechanics, the order, the predictability— always this effect to that cause—that was lacking from my everyday life.

My work on the 302 gave me a pretty good idea of all I didn't know about engines, so around the shop I told anyone who'd listen that I was just an intern. It mattered, especially with guys we called "the gearheads"—mechanics from other shops who hung around Out of the Hole on their lunch breaks. They came to pay homage to the cars they dreamed about when they were up to their elbows in skipping Omnis and dieseling Escorts. I was paranoid that they'd ask me something I didn't know just to prove how incompetent I was. Mostly they ignored me and sat in folding chairs talking about Nick as if he were dead and unforgettable. I'd overheard conversations like this:

"That time Marbles was going, 'They're going to kill me now. I'm dead meat.'"

"Yeah?" said the second one, wiping his mustache after wolfing a meatball grinder.

"He owed money, don't ask me to who. But he gets a race lined up behind the Oxford airport. Four grand. And then what does he do, the dumb fuck? Smokes the tires at a light and turns a bearing. Engine's toast. He pulls in here right at closing. 'I need that four grand,' he says. I mean, white as a marshmallow. And so then Nicky pulls in his Camino, yanks the three twenty-seven, and drops it in Marbles's Impala. The whole job in like three hours. I told him, call up Guinness. See what the record is."

"He win?"

"Fucking 'course he won. Nick's got that motor cherry. Four, four and a quarter horse. A lot better than Marbles had in his three fifty. Good second or two, I heard."

I couldn't help myself. "His name is Marbles?"

The first gearhead turned to me and looked annoyed. "Because of how he talks. He went through a windshield one time." Then he stood, belched, said to the other guy, "All right, I'm a good hour late now," and left.

The second gearhead was the less friendly of the two, so I wandered over to a restored Duster that Ray was working on. "What I miss is how they used to dress," he said to me, in his habit of greeting you in the middle of a conversation. He torqued a head bolt and ash fell from the cigarette on his lip. "Not the slut outfits you got today. I feel sorry for anybody who never pushed his face up under a poodle skirt. Get your teeth into a pair of them French knickers."

"Sounds like good, clean fun."

"Bet your sweet ass it was." He looked past me and straightened from the car, rubbing a shop rag between his hands as Mary Ann came over.

"I can't read this word," she said, holding in one hand a work order and in the other, napping over her shoulder, her baby son. It made me nervous to see Joey out here around scorching manifolds and poisonous vapors. I'd helped enough with my kid sister to know what a fragile thing a baby was.

Ray went to his toolbox and came back with reading glasses on the end of his nose.

"Actually, either of these words," Mary Ann said.

"Those words there? Those words, I believe, are 'carbon tracking.'"

"Where's the 'b'? Or 'k'?"

"They're in there, trust me."

She set the clipboard down on the Duster's fender and without waking Joey made the corrections. "Joey's going to have better handwriting when he's two," she said.

"Then he can take my dictation."

She stared at him candidly, and after a moment she shook her head as if clearing her thoughts. She caught my eye and winked. "Ray's what happens when you drop out of school."

"Be a doctor, kid," Ray said. "They got impeccable handwriting."

At this, Mary Ann had to smile. "You're just on fire today, aren't you?"

I tried never to bring my home life in to work with me, with one notable exception that happened not long after the night we painted the shop. Seated behind the old desk in the parts room, I called a girl named Kim Weatherall. She worked at a feed store in Levi, where I lived, and answered the phone, "Agway," in a tone of restless boredom, though after I said who it was, she perked right up. "Come on, man. What are you calling me at work for?"

I didn't feel like I had a choice. She hadn't called me, or been at home when I called her, for two weeks. I'd wanted there to be spark plug cases and carburetor rebuild kits around me when I talked to her. A mechanic in uniform was the right version of myself. In the splashed mirror over the tub sink, I saw not the unpopular kid who was sometimes afraid to get out of bed, but a man in control of things, my Dickies work shirt bearing the name of the most revered automotive shop in Waterbury. I'd hoped to be full of the confidence I knew I wouldn't have when I got home.

We weren't exactly dating, Kim and I. We trout fished together and rode her quad around her grandparents' property. In my Nova we imitated Eddie Murphy imitating Ralph Kramden. We'd had sex twice in a haymow. It was my first sex but not hers, and the hay gave me a rash on my knees; it was not romantic (though I'd brought candles) but stiff and determined, at times unfriendly. "Don't move," she'd said, pinning my legs down with her heels. "Already?" she'd said when I came. She wore her hair back with a ponytail hanging over the plastic adjuster of her red Agway cap, but I'd imagine how she would look in makeup and designer jeans. In any meaningful sense I barely knew Kim at all, but still it depressed me to imagine my life without her.

The call was short and toxic. I wanted to hear her break up with me and not mean it, and then in a tearful voice say she wanted me back. All fantasy. I couldn't keep us together any more than I could keep my parents together, any more than I could get the bearded farm kids at Northwest Vo/Ag, guys I admired and feared, to like me. Kim was another part of my life I had no control over.

"Cunt," I said, and kicked the bottom desk drawer in such a way that the knob handle punched into the top of my foot. "Cunt cunt cunt!"

Then I swung around in the metal chair and saw Mary Ann. She hadn't just come in. Her back was toward the lane between spark plugs and PCV valves, where from behind the center shelf she must've heard the entire phone call. Now she didn't turn and leave or speak. She was just frozen there with a big mystified look.

"I'm sorry," I said. "I didn't mean you."

"No, I didn't think you did."

"That's not even something I ever say. That word." I slumped forward. "I'm sorry. You were back there the whole time?"

She held up her inventory clipboard. "I should have cleared my throat or something."

"God." When I dropped my face into my hands my cap popped off and wobbled upside-down on the concrete floor. I was too drained to even get it. Kim had been my only hope that someone could eventually fall in love with me.

Mary Ann bent for the cap and then set it lightly on my head. She wore a powder blue polo shirt open to the last button, and from her tan throat came the faint aroma of jasmine. "She must've made you happy sometimes," Mary Ann said. "You might not see it right now. I wouldn't be able to, either."

I smiled, and somehow it brought me closer than I'd been yet to tears. I couldn't tell which emotions I should trust.

"There was a guy I dated in college," she said. "I thought it was pretty serious, but right before finals he dumped me. I was a mess.

He didn't have a record player in his dorm, so I sold back all my books early and got him one. And then I bought every Bay City Rollers album I could find." She shook her head, grinning, and sat on the edge of the desk and said that he wouldn't take them. But instead of returning the records and getting her books back to pass her exams, she smashed them in the parking lot. It was a generous, sympathizing story. Eventually he tried to get back together with her (this part was intended to give me hope, I thought), but by then Nick had cruised into her life and college was no longer in the scheme of things.

"He was into the Bay City Rollers," she said. "You'd think that would've told me something."

And I laughed because she laughed, though by then I was considering something else. A marriage like theirs, which had seemed to me to be ordained by the highest fate, and Nick wasn't even her first choice?

You didn't see a lot of beautiful women traipsing around with auto mechanics. The gearheads were sometimes tracked down by big broad-faced gals with wiry mullets and loose, manly laughs. I'd never seen Bobby's girlfriend, though I'd heard her yell at him over the phone, and it seemed impossible that any magnitude of hotness could offset her impulsive rage.

My logic for uniting my future wife with my future career was based solely on Nick's example. In the first meeting I'd conjured up between him and Mary Ann, she pulled in as a customer. Nick repaired her car, and though he tried not to boast she insisted that he describe the complicated process by which he saved her hundreds of dollars in diagnostic labor. He wasn't flirting, he didn't have to, and she fell in love in a shop bay. That was the proper order of things, and I'd calibrated my own fantasies by its plausibility: The girl, a little older, a junior in college, is smiling when I look up from her engine. She approaches the car timidly, her tan arms folded over a floral dress. "Can I watch?" she says.

But this new possibility that Mary Ann somehow stumbled

onto Nick during a moment of turmoil gave me pause, and though it was none of my business, I'd think about it for days.

I had a chance to prove myself to Nick on the last day of my internship, when a '75 Formula pulled in with a stalling complaint. It was a second-opinion job that had stumped all the mechanics at Sears Automotive, and as I spread the fender mats and attached the oscilloscope leads—battery, vacuum, tach., emissions—I should have been limbering my mind for the deductive marathon ahead. But instead I was rehearsing how I would tell Nick that I'd pinpointed the problem in the same uninflected voice he would use, as if there were no glory in it at all.

I'm sure it hurt their pride at Sears to send us these diagnosis jobs, but Nick was the local expert and either we would fix the car and they'd take the credit, or we wouldn't (to my knowledge, this had yet to happen) and they could be consoled by having frustrated the very best. As for Nick, he never gave a hint of feeling threatened. These second-opinion jobs were exactly equal to any other job, as he had shown today when he gave the Formula to me.

The previous mechanic had replaced the carburetor, to the tune of three hundred dollars, only to find that the engine continued to cough and stall. I had my four suspects—fuel, spark, compression, exhaust—and my anxiety rose with each one I ruled out. Nick, after all, had told me that I had a mind for abstract thought—he said that, and now I had to prove it.

I opened a toolbox drawer and propped inside it a chalkboard that my little sister didn't play with anymore. I wrote down each of my diagnostic steps as I performed them. I stepped back and pondered the board, was hoping for a revelation like mathematicians have in the movies, when Ray came by whistling "Carolina in the Morning" (not sincerely; when he sang it, as he sometimes did, he sang, "Nothing could be finer than to be in her vaginer . . .").

He stopped cold and stared at my chalkboard. "Son, are you re-tarded?" he said. Then Bobby Stango walked over rubbing GOJO up his arms. "What're you, retarded?"

"It's a second-opinion job," I said. Bobby skimmed the work order as he lathered off grease. Drips the color of storm clouds spilled off his elbows onto the steel toes of his work boots. When he smiled I felt myself brimming with unrealized greatness. He lit me a Marlboro, which he thought of as a luxury since I smoked Marlboro Lights. "I think our boy here just popped his cherry," he told Ray.

"He wishes."

But after an hour I hit the ceiling of my aptitude and was just groping around. When Nick walked out of the lobby, I ran over to my toolbox and slammed the chalkboard in the bottom drawer. I was wiggling vacuum lines I'd already wiggled, hoping to find a split in one that might explain the stalling, when he came up to the car. He stared calmly at the engine, his pale eyes, glassed as mine were from the fumes, flitting from component to component. Then he took a long socket extension and put his ear to it to listen to the intake manifold, glancing as he did at the soaring hydrocarbon count that registered on the emissions screen.

"Wet plugs in six and eight," I said. "I think it needs a valve job."

He nudged the throttle lever and brought the rpm up to 2,500. After a few seconds the hydrocarbons dropped to passing. I was baffled. Burnt valves are burnt valves at any rpm.

"Any vacuum leaks?"

I shook my head. "I ran propane all over. And the KVs look good. No carbon tracking."

Nick lit a Winston and walked over to my toolbox. Inside the lid I'd taped a card my little sister, April, had made, a cake and candles that looked like a blue cactus, over which she'd written HApE BERfdA JUsTiN.

"You're eighteen now?" he said.

I nodded.

"If you lived in Kenya, you'd be going on your first lion hunt."

"As long as I get a gun, not a spear," I said.

"They'd break eggs over your head in Germany."

"Here in America, your boss takes you out for Jäger shots."

He grinned. "How about dinner tonight at the house?"

I had to listen to the echo of the words twice in my head before I believed them, an invitation—albeit on my very last day—to enter and investigate his personal life. "Okay, sure," I said, and had to cut myself off to keep from gushing like a fool. I studied the KV screen again and ran another cylinder balance. I checked the ignition output and coolant level. Things that made no sense to check, I checked. I wanted to prove to him that I was better than the mechanics at Sears.

"Eighteen," I heard Nick say to himself. He was facing the hopper window behind the oscilloscope, squinting as if in the sooty pane he could see himself at my age. But his eighteen was impressive, the age at which he balanced and blueprinted his first engine—scouring every surface, boiling, polishing, then torquing every fastener to spec. It was the most exhaustive engine work you can do, a feat I was light-years from.

I advanced and retarded the timing until my eyes burned and I couldn't see the whirling slot mark on the harmonic balancer. I readjusted the idle speed and leaned out the mixture. I looked at the work order one last time and finally lowered my head on my forearms over the fender mat. "Goddamn it," I said. "It's unfixable."

Nick picked up a ball peen hammer, leaned on the passenger-side fender, and tapped the EGR valve. Something held by suction dislodged, the engine coughed once and almost stalled, and he revved it clean. When he let go of the throttle, the engine idled like glass.

We waited to see that the fix held. The engine breathed quietly, and in the afterglow of witnessing a miracle I realized that the job wasn't going to make me any money. An EGR valve was barely a seventy-dollar ticket, so my commission—I made that plus five an hour—would be almost nothing.

Nick looked over the paperwork again. He stepped up to the Formula, and with one precise smack of the ball peen he cracked the corner of the intake manifold all the way through. The engine began to sputter, and suddenly I was looking at a nine-hundred-dollar ticket. "It's on Sears," he said. "Happy birthday."

3.

THAT EVENING, AS THE DARK SHOP SIGN WANED IN MY REARVIEW mirror, I considered for the last time the caged windows of Braids Beauty School across the street, and over them the top floors of the Harris Circle Housing Projects, where I'd once seen a car on fire. I felt abandoned and helpless, incapable of uttering a farewell to this place I'd grown to love. In just two months' time, Ray had learned to tolerate me almost completely, Bobby goofed with me like a brother, and Nick and I were in the vicinity of a friendship I was sure would change my life if only we had more time.

Before we left, Nick had taped a repair plate to the back window of a '67 Valiant he'd resurrected, thinking he could get a few hundred for the car in the paper, and asked me to follow him home. At a stoplight he revved the Valiant's slant six, and staring wildly from my beater Nova, I let off the brake and tapped his back bumper. Reverse lights came on and he slammed back into me. We bashed into each other all the way to his house, prolonging a stunt only possible as a departure from a place where anything had seemed possible. I relished the shock on the faces of people who thought they were bearing witness to a bona fide accident. My last slam caught him at an angle and I heard the lens of my right front signal light tinkle on the pavement.

In his driveway we started laughing; as I scooped out shards from my signal light our voices softened to whistling puffs of air. It was wet, helpless laughter, Nick hitting a cackling high note and regaining his voice first. "The guy with the beard . . . in the Zephyr."

The side door opened, and Mary Ann came out of the house and started laughing herself. "You got him drunk?" she said to me. "Oh, my God. Say something drunk, Nick."

"I can't even look at this guy," he said.

I followed them up the front steps, trying to talk my voice clean: "All right, phew, God, all right."

Nick and Mary Ann lived in south Waterbury about three miles from the shop. The first time I saw their house, I'd gotten the address off a bill envelope and drove past expecting a big Victorian or something, a house commensurate with Nick's talent, but it was only a base-model cape, the kind kindergarteners draw—a triangle on a square with two shutter-less windows flanking the front door. I learned later that Out of the Hole was a failing inheritance from Nick's uncle, and that Nick had had to take out a mortgage to fix up the building, such as it had been, and buy diagnostic equipment. Still I couldn't help but feel that something was cosmically out of balance when a mechanic of Nick's stature should have to live so modestly.

We went first to the kitchen, a room that had nothing I could see of Nick: faded blue rooster wallpaper, dull-white linoleum, painted cabinets whose chrome handles, like the legs of the padded chairs at the table, were flecked with rust. The air, though, was conversely awake with cinnamon, clove, cedarwood, hibiscus, jasmine, lavender. Much later I learned these were Mary Ann's potions, essential oils that she wore to achieve certain moods in her day.

"Where's that Mugsy?" Nick said, and he walked to the counter, where their baby, Joey, sat in his bouncer seat. Father and son played peek-a-boo, Joey huffing and sputtering. He had a comb-over of fine hair and eyes of an indefinite color that watched you with more interest than you deserved—suddenly he'd lift his transparent eyebrows so that his skin didn't really wrinkle but dented like a balloon. I couldn't help remembering April, my little sister, at that age. She'd had those same eyebrows.

Mary Ann turned on the hot water as Nick leaned over the sink. Rather than Goop or GOJO, she took a liter-sized bottle of Castile soap and drizzled it up and down his forearms. It didn't surprise me to see the foam turn gray as she rubbed it in; Nick always washed his hands in the hurried way of a child who doesn't want to miss out on anything.

When she began to scrub his fingers with a nail brush, I had the anxious, envious thought that to be a mechanic of Nick's caliber you needed a wife as abiding as Mary Ann—not a circumstance in life you could exactly count on. She must've just taken a shower. Her wavy hair was falling over her face, black and sheen and smelling of spearmint. "I thought I'd get to see you drunk," she said to Nick, combing through the bristles of his forearm with the sprayer. With a dish towel she wiped a half-dried tear of laughter from his cheek and kissed him where the tear had been.

As she went to work on his right arm Nick opened his stance to lean more heavily against the counter. I'd never felt closer to him than earlier in the driveway, our eyes cried out with laughing, but as I watched his copper reflection in a hanging pan—smiling from the sounds Joey made, or from the steady rub of Mary Ann's fingers—it was as if he'd forgotten I was there.

Nick went out to the living room to answer the phone, and Mary Ann found me a dusty Heineken from the back of the refrigerator. When she yanked on a counter drawer stuck with the humidity, the crash of metal inside startled Joey. She took him out of the bouncer and held him to her chest as she fished in the drawer for a bottle opener.

We'd grown to be friends after that day in the parts room. Aspects of my personality that I hated—my sensitivity and inclination to overanalyze—were what she found appealing. Her family was three thousand miles away in Oregon, and except for Joey, she had only hard-talking mechanics in her life. She'd ask me what colleges I was trying for next year, and I'd say I was still deciding, though that was becoming less and less true. College was just an extension of boyhood, when boyhood was the very thing I wanted to leave behind. It was hard for me to put into words that I needed this visceral, spontaneous, unapologetic mechanic life to transform me into the man I wanted to be.

I asked her, in a light way that wouldn't be insulted by a no answer, if she wanted me to take the baby. She saw that my hands were clean and passed him over. As she checked the salmon I lay Joey facedown like a football on my forearm. His beanbag arms folded at the elbows, hugging and hanging on. He banged his mouth on the heel of my hand, and his warm toothless gums began to suck there.

From in the living room I could hear Nick on the phone, not really talking but answering "okay," and less than a minute after he'd come back the phone rang again. Joey started fussing. "Hey, Mugsy, hey," I said. "He's coming back." He didn't seem to like the nickname coming out of my mouth, and as he whirled his arms and legs like a water frog I began to swing him in a gentle arc.

"He's getting hungry," Mary Ann said, fluffing couscous in an open pan on the stove. She set down the fork and, with her back to me, lifted her breasts one at a time. A cool pain shot through my groin, and I backed away.

I widened my swing and found an angle that thrilled the baby but didn't scare him, a technique I had perfected on my little sister. His whole chest fit in my palm, and for an enormous second I felt him giggle without sound, only his little heart racing before he cackled in a long helpless convulsion that ran him out of breath.

"You don't have kids, do you?" asked Mary Ann.

"None I know of." I sensed in her grin that she thought this lame joke was out of character for me, and I blushed a little explaining about my sister, omitting the embarrassing truth about why my parents divorced before she was born.

Joey settled with my thumb in his sticky hands, and we could hear Nick in the other room. "They ought to do a real compression check. You can't trust a cylinder balance."

Mary Ann smiled in the direction of the archway. "Mister Popular," she said. She came up to me and rubbed the back of Joey's head. "So what was so funny before?" she said. "In the driveway?"

It was a strange moment. I could have told her about the drive, the mini crashes and the commotion at the intersections, but I wasn't certain how she'd react. I didn't want to get Nick in trouble. "I think I have to plead the fifth," I said.

She stared at me a moment, unblinking, confused, it seemed, that I didn't have any more to say. Then abruptly she looked down at her hands and brushed them together. "Of course you do." She reached for Joey. "Hey there, smooch monster," she said, and she kissed him on the nose.

The salmon, poached with rosemary and lemon, seemed to dissolve right into my blood, as if it contained nutrients I had been lacking all my life. It was thick and substantial, you could stab into it with your fork. Mary Ann said that Atlantic salmon had no flavor compared to the wild Chinook and coho in Oregon, but I couldn't get enough of it. We ate all three pounds, and there was baked kale with drizzled olive oil and rice vinegar and a little salt, crispy like potato chips, and this I couldn't stop shoveling in, either. "I want to show you something upstairs later," Nick said. "But eat up. There's plenty. Eat."

After dinner I followed him up to a stuffy bedroom crammed with boxes. On a card table pushed against the wall Nick turned on a portable computer, a Commodore SX-64 he had just taken in trade for a valve job. He turned it on, and after half a minute of the fan whirring and clicking, the screen began to lighten.

```
64 RAM SYSTEM.
38911 BASIC BYTES FREE
READY
```

Nick waved me into the folding chair, and I programmed an IF/THEN number guessing game. But instead of the "Great! You got my number!" response I had used in my BASIC class, I made it say "Holy shit! You're right!"

Nick guessed the number after three tries and played it again. He kept resetting it. Sometimes he got it in fewer guesses, sometimes it took four or five. He reprogrammed the game himself with different limits, and when he got the number he watched the effect without joy or disappointment. It didn't matter how long it took to win. He was trying to figure out how the system worked.

There was a floor-to-ceiling bookshelf on the opposite wall, and while he played I looked over the spines of Mary Ann's books on scented oils and Eastern meditation. I leafed through the end book—making lotions and diaper creams and lip gloss from things like olive oil and beeswax.

The car books were in chronological order on their own shelf, dating back to the first production car, the Oldsmobile Roundabout. Most of the books were on boring cars, Model Ts, curvy touring cars of the '30s, big-finned sedans that ran pathetic sixteen-second quarter miles—cars that always got in my way at the fairgrounds as I searched for the Chargers and big-block Chevelles.

There was also a book on Einstein, and on Daniel Bernoulli and fluid mechanics. Two books on thermo dynamics, a dictionary of terms. I opened one on physics and saw that he'd written word definitions in the margins.

There were footsteps on the stairs, and without turning from the computer, Nick said, "Let me go help put Mugsy down. Stay here."

While he was gone I looked in one of the boxes, unweaving the flaps to open it. It was all photo albums, and the spines, written in black Sharpie, said WATERFALLS. FLORENCE TO YACHATS BEACHES. NEWPORT BEACHES. MCKENZIE RIVER 126. I took out the one that said OREGON COUNTRY FAIR, expecting Ferris wheels and fireworks. The first set of breasts I saw made me sweat a little, and I kept one eye on the hallway. There were men in costumes with long colored feathers, girls in paisley minidresses and headbands. A guy in a top hat was juggling while riding a unicycle. More sets of breasts, some full-naked and some with ferns and rainbows drawn in body paint.

Because it was such a contrast, because conflicting images often infected my mind, I imagined Nick and Mary Ann walking nude under towering fir trees, Mary Ann dark and toned, Nick pale and doughy. He must've been only too happy to get the hell out of there.

I heard a stir in the other room and quickly dropped the album back into the box.

It was after ten when Nick turned from the glow of the computer screen, squinted at the clock on the wall, and said, "Jesus. You got a long drive." For the first time I truly regretted not living in Waterbury, where I would have made a habit of dropping by to see him after work. In that moment I sensed that he was regretful, too, and I rocketed through a series of outrageous ideas that began, what if?

He stood and leaned back against some boxes. He said, "Well," and I understood that this was our sudden good-bye. "Mary Ann's right," he said. "You'd better go to college. But if it ever happened that you take off a semester or whatever, come see me. Don't tell her I said so."

We shook hands and he walked me downstairs, where the TV

was on. Mary Ann rose from the couch and gave me a hug, and I shivered a little in my chest, but only after I was a few miles from their house, following a shortcut he'd told me to 84, did I turn off the radio and let myself freefall into the dizzying thrill of what he had said.

4.

IN THE AFTERMATH OF THEIR DIVORCE, MY MOTHER MOVED US to the comatose little farm town of Levi, where you might get stuck behind a tractor lobbing field mud, or a herd of dairy cows changing pasture. When you've had your license less than a year, every mile you clock without a wreck or a ticket is a triumph, but on those dewy summer mornings the twenty-two-mile commute to Nick's shop in Waterbury seemed not nearly long enough. It should have taken hours, if not days, to get from Levi to anywhere urban. Guys at my school said "nigger" and "spick" all the time because there were no blacks or Hispanics to set them straight. We stuck our arms up cows' asses for a grade (some didn't wear gloves) and were tested on how tightly we could pack hay bales on a rack wagon. Farmers were struggling, at least in Levi they were, the enormous dairy barns sagging into viney scrub like the ruins of a lost civilization, but in spite of the facts, the school sold the fiction that a local dairy could compete with the industrial farms in Vermont and New Hampshire, that a man could still make a living off the land.

That night after dinner at Nick's, I drove through Levi's downtown, which was a feed store, a gas station, an antique shop, a restaurant/tavern, and a post office/library, wondering if I belonged here any more than I had at the start of the summer. I'd planned to come back to Northwest with a full tank of engine knowledge such that my schoolmates would have no choice but to respect me, but now the plan began to fall apart under scrutiny.

I parked next to the town mail truck that was just a Subaru with the steering wheel on the other side, and got out to walk. As if to emphasize the start of school on Monday, I could see my breath under the one sodium arc light on the strip. Faint wood smoke hung in the air. As I walked the empty sidewalk an engine sang out from beyond the rustling corn, and I saw the truth as it had always been: Levi would never accept me. Even two years wasn't enough time. More importantly, I had no father—not one I admitted to having—and this was a serious offense in a town where sons are taught how to field dress deer and rock a truck out of the mud and chain saw logs without getting the bar stuck, all before high school.

I got back in my car and drove the two streets to our house, turned right at our lane, rocked over the bumps and ruts, and parked in front of a pine-wood swing set Mom and I had put together for April. I sat for a minute in the car. The east end of the yard leveled off to an aboveground swimming pool that had devolved into a waist-high vat of rainwater and slime bubbles. The pool needed to be dismantled and cut up somehow for a dump run on top of my Nova. In the darkness the hulking shadow of the pool rebuked me for neglecting my family these past months.

The next morning I went out and split firewood, waiting for the day to heat up before I dealt with the swimming pool. Some of the red oak logs were three feet across, and the dirt underneath crawled with roly-poly bugs and night crawlers. I'd been waiting to see if my mother's ex-boyfriend would come to take the wood back. She'd broken up with him a week after he'd borrowed a town dump truck to drop the wood off. He was a local cop who, after my mother dumped him, used to spy on us from across the street in his parked cruiser. Now I was running out of time if we wanted firewood for the winter, so fuck Sergeant Lou Costa. As it was I'd need to stack the wood crisscross to season, and still it might be too wet to throw heat.

It was good cathartic work. You could whale on the big slabs like you were ringing the carnival bell, your body calibrating each swing to the quarter inch, your aim deadly, the ten-pound maul head diving into the coin's width of a notch you made on your last swing. And sometimes the greener logs would open a swing too soon, leaving me panting and surprised over the split halves like a heavyweight after the knock-down punch, the sweat spraying off my lips hot as blood. The ladybug thermometer read fifty, but I could feel my thermal shirt clinging wet to my shoulders.

April liked to watch me swing the maul. The medium logs went after five strikes in the center, the sound of the fourth strike hollow like a bass drum, and I'd sing "Dinah, won't you blow," and April would return, "Dinah won't you blow your horn," which skipped a phrase, but gave her a line before the wood split, and I'd say, "Honk, honk," and she'd laugh.

I knew I'd have her for maybe half an hour before she'd want to go back in to watch *Inspector Gadget*. The limb logs I split one-handed, and she'd grab the halves and throw them in the pile, leaving pink threads from her gloves clinging to splinters. She wanted to try, and on a slab as big around as a manhole cover we held the little hatchet together and knocked apart kindling.

April hadn't been inside long when I saw my father walking across the rows of lawn clippings in his wingtip shoes. He held up a glass of water. "Can you take five?" he called.

I shouldn't have been surprised to see him. Mom had told him I'd decided to take time off before college next year. She liked to tell him the unpleasant news of our lives in a wry tone that implied his own culpability. "Oh, and by the way, Don," she'd say. I think also she wanted him to accuse her of neglectful parenting. If he had, she might have found the outrage to finally say what she'd held in for four years: You son of a bitch, why couldn't I be enough?

But Don never provoked her, and I think she felt helpless. He hadn't even given her an affair to hate him for, or the admission that he had fallen out of love when she still loved him. One day he simply changed into this whole other guy—or finally accepted his sexuality, as he put it. When he apologized for hurting her, the apology was laced with the faultless circumstance of having been manipulated by society to think he was straight all these years. After their phone calls, she'd pace the kitchen saying, "How does he sleep at night?" Then she'd collect herself enough to go up to her room and cry.

She'd just found out she was pregnant when Don stupefied us with the confession that he now liked men, and before she would have to explain a baby bump to the neighbors, Mom sold the house and moved us an hour north to Levi, where half the roads were unpaved, and where she saw in the harvest-season vistas the rolling farmland of her childhood.

I took the glass of water and drank so forcefully my throat made gulping sounds. Don picked up the maul, tested its weight. His hair was thick and wavy and he had color in his face, but I couldn't tell if he was thinner, if his lambskin bomber jacket fit more loosely in the shoulders. Whenever he drove out from New Haven to see me, I wondered if he was going to break the news that he had AIDS. It was Russian roulette for gays, everyone said so.

"Can I give it a go-round?" he said.

"In a tie?"

He looked at his clothes under his unzipped jacket. "One of my novelists has a reading in Hartford," he said. "He used to be a roustabout. He'd appreciate some sweat and calluses."

I set up a split piece that needed a second halving. He started from a kind of half squat, and when he swung it around, his necktie smacked him in the face, and his shirt came untucked, but he managed to hit the log about a third of the way in. The maul head opened the top of the log but stopped at the bottom strings of wood grain, so he lifted the maul stuck in the log—opening his stance for balance—and crashed it down so that it fell apart.

"Hit me again, barkeep," he said.

I set up a few easy ones he went through at a swing apiece, singing, "Shout now, with thunder/ Drove the Gaels under/ Cleave them asunder/ Swords of Valhalla!"

Then I gave him an ugly knotted beast that he bounced off of twice. "Now you're just being sadistic," he said. His next swing stuck enough that he could let the handle go and it stayed there. He wiped his hands together.

"All done?" I said.

"Are you going to walk on my back when I throw it out?"

"April might."

He patted his forehead with a handkerchief. "She's adorable. She gave me a hug upstairs."

"She's like that with everybody."

"At least I'm everybody," he said, tucking himself back in. "So no SATs, Mom tells me." While I set up another log he said that college wouldn't be like high school, if that's what concerned me. I regretted the times I'd called him to complain about my miserable experience at Northwest. My classmates had no regard for a private-school transfer who showed up the first day in an Iron Maiden shirt and acid-wash jeans, who didn't know two-stroke from four-stroke, who scored lower than every girl at backing up a hay wagon with the school's Super A. Don had offered to let me live with him and start back at Milford Academy in the fall. But then he moved into Stuart's big colonial (Stuart, the psychiatrist) in New Haven, and it scared me to think what I might witness in that house.

At school I learned to be invisible, which essentially meant overcoming impulses of joy and curiosity, and I'd also discovered the weight room. Hardly anybody at Northwest lifted weights—they could stack the military press just from farm work and spent free periods in metal shop welding push bars for their pickups—and in the wall mirror I watched myself grow. When I finally declined Don's offer I felt good about myself, embarking, as I saw it, on a manhood of my own making. Don was disappointed, I heard it in his voice as I heard it now when he asked if I thought I'd still be interested in college after a year off. "A lot can happen in a year," he said. "You'll start making good money. You'll get an apartment, right? Have dinner out, vacations, new clothes. How's it sounding?"

"How do you think?"

"But then the sabbatical's over, and it's a two-room dorm and a meal plan."

"Maybe I'll have a career started."

"Most people change careers," he said. "What kind of openings are out there with no degree?"

"So then I go back to school."

"With credit card debt. Maybe a Mrs. Bailey. A Justin Junior."

"Remember Richard Elvin?" I said. Elvin was one of Don's fiction authors at the agency in New York.

Don closed his mouth and watched me for a moment. "Rick," he said. "He's got a collection coming out this spring."

"You called him a genius."

"Well, he hasn't exactly set the world on fire yet."

"I know a genius," I said. "I worked for him all summer." My strength had come back, and my swings were fluid, the steel handle shooting electric current all the way up to my elbows.

He waited, but I couldn't get my words right. I'd thought the point would be glaring, but now it eluded me. "A genius mechanic," he said, finally. "Mom told me. He's the opposite of me, is that the appeal?" And then after half a minute or so he grinned: "I like your tactics. Keep quiet until I make an ass out of myself."

"So only your kind of genius counts?" I said.

"What if you majored in business first? Then go all in. Open a shop like your friend. Maybe at that point I can come up with—"

I swung into a log I'd been avoiding, three feet in diameter and crooked with knots. A big hit buried the maul head halfway in. I tried to stomp on the handle and missed. My teeth jounced. "Fuck," I said.

"Don't hurt yourself, son. Take a break."

I picked up the hatchet where April had dropped it. Don stepped back, his eyes wide, the fear in them swelling me up as I walked past him to the swimming pool. I took a one-handed golf swing with the hatchet and it felt like striking the side of a whale. The hatchet broke the plastic and slipped out of my hand into the rip. Instantly green water sprayed in an arc that reached the halved logs five feet away.

Don lurched and stumbled, threw up his hands in surrender. "I'm sorry," he said. "You win," and he scrambled back up the hill.

5.

I LIKED TAKING THE SEVEN HILLS ROUTE INTO WATERBURY, WIND-
ing out the narrow county roads, Weekeepeemee to Quassapaug
to Bunker Hill, which rudely became South Main, and driving
along the banks of the Mad River, where I'd once seen Mary Ann
jogging along the crumbling sidewalks, probably the only jogger
in the history of those sidewalks. Porchless triple-deckers were set
right up against the street, and then you were dodging potholes
under the carcasses of old brass factories, ten-story hulks of dull
brick and what looked like silos, train tracks running into the heart
of their darkness. The lower windows were empty of glass, and
sections of brick wall caved in as though someone had taken a few
swings with a wrecking ball, said, "Why bother?" and left. On the
other side of the street were private detached garages carved into
hillsides, and their angry little houses leaned over brown rectan-
gles of front yard.

Past the 84 overpass, Wolcott Avenue ascended to a brief crest
from which you looked down at the treeless west side, the low,
vandalized retaining walls bulging over the sidewalks. Parking lots
spilled out in crooked oblongs from discount shops and Greek din-
ers and package stores, and sagging electric lines led to the farthest

stoplight, which harmonized the three-way traffic in front of Out of the Hole.

It was my last Christmas break before graduation. Four months ago my internship ended at Out of the Hole, and I couldn't wait until summer to know if Nick was serious about hiring me.

One tight parking spot was left in the front lot, right up on a telephone pole, and thankfully the bay doors were fogged up so they couldn't see my six-point parking job. Outside, I walked past a metallic blue Barracuda, a candy-apple Firebird, a ragtop Challenger. Even seeing them parked was, by the artistry of their designers, like seeing them move—burying their speedometers or laying rubber up a city block. Long hoods and short decks, elevated rear fenders and wide racing stripes. They looked like resting dragons. Acting according to their nature was illegal, and on public streets they were hunted by the law. They were the bullies, the badasses, and, for a short summer, my very close friends. Already I felt estranged from them. Surely someone would yell at me if I went over and opened a hood. Their absence from my life I experienced as a physical oppression, and I had to stop suddenly and take a breath.

I hadn't paid attention to the woman standing in the cold smoking a cigarette until I saw that it was Mary Ann. Walking toward her I thought to razz her about smoking (she'd gotten on to me about it before), but she was glancing vacantly at the passing cars, or at the cleaners across the street, as if she didn't know where she was.

When I was only a few feet away, she turned and blinked at me. "Justin," she said. The fleece-lined jean jacket she wore was unbuttoned, though she was trying to hold the front closed with her elbows. "How's school?"

I shrugged, feeling more like a stranger than a friend. "We're off now. Winter break."

"God, it's cold," she said, stepping the cigarette out among the other frozen butts. She looked in through the lobby window, and vaguely embarrassed I asked if Nick was around.

With the panel doors closed the bays were humid, and the air was choked with hydrocarbons. Through watering eyes I first saw Ray, who wore a Santa hat and was occupied with a carburetor float. "It's beginning to feel a lot like syphilis," he sang to himself and didn't notice me.

Nick was in the third bay, staring at the ground as another man, a customer, spoke to him excitedly, opening his hands, his fingers, laughing. In the slow course of bringing a cigarette to his lips, Nick saw me, jutted his chin once, and looked away. Suddenly aware of my enthusiasm, I stopped by a trash can, and he didn't look at me again. As if I had other business I turned abruptly and found Bobby shooting a timing light under the hood of an Olds 442.

He came around the fender and gave me a bear hug I only pretended to resist. He said that Tina at Carquest kept asking about me. "They got *Rocky IV* playing at the Six Plex," he said. "You should take her to that."

"She's got a boyfriend, Bobby."

"That cat with the poofy hair? What's his name, Fifi?"

He got us a couple of Dr Peppers out of the machine. The taste of it, so crisp your eyes watered, was the taste of working here, of having earned your first break after the morning rush.

We lit cigarettes, and Bobby was showing off a new air wrench when Nick walked over. Nick grinned quickly, awkwardly it seemed, and the handshake was an afterthought. When he asked about school just as his wife had, I wondered if she'd found out that he'd offered me a job. I spoke indifferently about school in the hopes that Nick might pick up on my fading enthusiasm and realize he'd squandered my attention. I wanted him to think that I was going to be a mechanic whether he hired me or not, that I'd be his loss, but he only stared at me a moment, nodding almost imperceptibly, before he glanced down at the engine.

"Needs a distributor," Bobby said. "Advance springs are shot. The points are pointless."

"HEI?"

"That's what I'm thinking."

I looked at Bobby, my only hope—if I lost him to the job, I'd be left to wander after Ray—and suddenly remembered that Bobby's girlfriend had been eight months pregnant when I left. "Was it a boy or a girl?" I said.

Bobby grinned. "Kill it, would you?" he said to Nick, who went around to turn off the engine. Bobby handed me a creased three-by-five picture cut smaller, which he pulled out from where the bills were in his wallet. "Rowdy Randy," he said, and then a little more seriously, "After Randy Rhodes, is who we were thinking." The baby had a crown of blond fuzz and big ears. Cute, I thought to say, or adorable, but they were strange words to use in the bays, and I'd have to follow it with a lame joke that he must resemble his mother. So I told him congratulations and held the picture for Nick to see, only Nick was gone.

I leaned to look around the car but he was already out of sight, in the parts room or the lobby. "I'm an asshole," Bobby said. He tossed a ratchet into a rolling tool tray, where it crashed into wrenches with the sound of glass. "You heard about Joey? A month ago. Not even a month."

I don't remember handing the picture back, but Bobby was looking down at it, explaining SIDS, which he said was when a baby dies for no reason. "Even the doctors don't know shit."

"You mean he died? Joey died?"

He pushed open the back window and spit down to the excavated gravel lot two stories below.

"I should go say something," I said.

"Man, there's nothing to say."

A few minutes later I walked out to my Nova. From the parking lot I could see into the lobby, where Mary Ann was batching service orders and Nick leaned on the counter beside her, giving one-word answers over the phone.

A month, Bobby had said, just a month. It was no time at all.

I got in my car but couldn't turn the ignition. In my mind, I saw April die, and I was staggering around in a wasteland of cold light. When I looked at the lobby again, Mary Ann was outside having another cigarette. I got out of the car again, but then froze when I was ten feet away, as if I had just run to jump into water before getting a look at how high I was.

I came up to her slowly, and she saw me and started to nod. She looked away and exhaled smoke. "I kind of wish people would stop finding out," she said. "That it could just be after." She bent to pick up a flattened paper cup. "Most of the time," she said, but then didn't finish. I followed her to the Dumpster and lifted back the metal lid so she could drop the cup inside. And then she started picking up trash behind the Dumpster. It was ankle-deep back there, blown in from all over the city to a kind of wind eddy between buildings. We picked up newspaper pages and hamburger wrappers, straws, cigarette packs, plastic bags, as well as shop trash that had fallen out when the Dumpster was overflowing. There was so much, we would've needed snow shovels to make a real dent in it, but I didn't think about what we were doing, more than to believe in easing a nervous breakdown with small bursts of insanity.

"I feel like I'm just waiting," she said as she worked. "The morning's got to end, then the afternoon. I don't know how people say there's not enough time." As randomly as she'd started picking up, she quit it and went back to the lobby door. I thought about hugging her, but she wasn't crying yet, and I expected her to if we hugged. When I said good-bye, she said, "Okay," and before she turned and pulled open the door she brightened for a moment, but then lost expression again, as if she knew it would hurt to smile.

6.

MY HANDS WERE STILL IN THAT RAW, RASHY STAGE, UNUSED TO the solvents and grease, when Nick's jobs started coming back as rechecks. It was a few weeks after I'd gotten my diploma, in June of 1986, and Nick had just hired me as an apprentice mechanic. I sensed already that his gifts might be fading, but I tried to prolong his greatness by intercepting the cars and sometimes, while he was washing up, by popping the hood on a job he'd finished and double-checking his work. But over time, covering for Nick changed me, allowed me to see him as human and fallible.

I was dragging a trash barrel loaded with spent oil filters out to the Dumpster when a Monte Carlo pulled in overheating. I'd stopped twice to squeeze blood back in my hand, and had it not taken three tries to get the barrel over the lip, I wouldn't have been outside to see the car pinging up the small incline from the street.

Two days earlier I had shuttled the car's owner to his janitor job at the Naugatuck Valley Mall. The Monte's interior had been spotless and gleaming with Armor All, a faint smell of ammonia radiating from the windshield. We barely spoke on the ride—his English seemed to embarrass him—and staring at the bronzed baby shoes hanging from the rearview mirror, I decided that he was a hard-working man, the father of very unspoiled children.

I hated to see him come back now.

"Edwin, right?" I called, deserting the trash barrel on the sidewalk to intercept him. He took another step toward the shop before he turned. "I need Nick," he said.

"I can help. What's up?" It was a nervous question—we could both hear the coolant hissing from his engine—and he shook his head once and continued on toward the bays. After he was inside I jogged over to the Monte and opened the hood. Jesus Christ, one of Nick's screwdrivers had harpooned the top of the radiator. I reached into the sugary-smelling steam, thinking only to hide the evidence as pin-sprays of antifreeze seared the living shit out of my wrist. Wagging my arm around for the slight relief of moving air, I took out a rag and unstuck the screwdriver, then kicked it under a neighboring Dodge while the last dregs of coolant streamed out of the radiator.

Edwin came out with Nick two steps behind, dragging a kinked hose that he handed to me. I poured the cool water over my wrist as Edwin looked down into the engine compartment. I said, "It looks like a rock might have kicked up and—"

"Why you took it out?" Edwin said.

Nick sawed through the top hose with a kitchen knife. He threw himself under the car and cut through the bottom hose, the last of the steaming water trickling over his hand. As he stood I cooled his hand for a second before he took the hose from me and jammed it into the thermostat housing. "Start the car," he yelled, and Edwin hopped in. The engine sucked the water into its canals and jackets and expelled it onto the pavement, where a foaming stream ran down to the curb.

Nick looked in the window and checked the heat gauge. "It's got to be running, or those heads'll warp."

Antifreeze had sprayed onto the fenders, and I got a bucket of soapy water and some clean rags to wash it off. When the engine had dropped to operating temperature, Nick shut it off and I used the hose to rinse off the fenders, spilling more of the cool water over my burning wrist.

"I trust you guys," Edwin said. "I ask around where to take my Chevy. Who's the best."

Nick started to unbolt the radiator, Edwin watching him as if he didn't know quite how to manifest his disappointment. When Nick went to his toolbox for a swivel socket, I stepped into the painful beam of Edwin's glare. "Would you mind waiting in the lobby?" I said. "We'll come get you when it's done."

His eyes on me were like things hot to the touch, shimmering as they squeezed and let go, squeezed and let go. He seemed to be two men inside himself, and finally it was the reasonable one who triumphed and didn't take a swing at me. He said something low and in Spanish before leaving for the lobby as I'd asked him to.

Nick did a terrible job bandaging me. He cut off the gauze in the shape of a musical note and taped my wrist as if it were a package he was mailing to China. His blisters were bigger and whiter than mine, and I taped the back of his hand carefully, keeping pressure on the gauze to flatten air pockets.

"He said there was a screwdriver," Nick said.

I ran the last strip of tape and he pulled his hand away. Every response I could offer had pitfalls I wanted to think through, and finally he said, "Jesus," and walked away. I followed him into the lobby, ready to say that I never saw any screwdriver, but each second that passed shot the moment farther out of reach.

Rather than asking for a shuttle, Edwin took the bus back to work, and Mary Ann had one other customer in the lobby. I went over to the window ledge, where the coffee maker, cups, creamer, and sugar packs were arranged on a cafeteria tray. Nick poured a cup and watched out the window as a black Suburban pulled in with a car trailer in tow. A man in sunglasses and a white sports coat got out and started undoing multiple covers over what looked to be a yellow Corvette.

Across the counter from Mary Ann, the customer started to laugh. He was dressed in a Hugo Boss jacket and electric green T-shirt, and he could have passed for Italian except for his accent, which he seemed to be parodying. "If I don't do dis, I do someting else. You got to have dis," he said, rubbing his fingers to indicate money, "to have dis," and he curled his fingers back to the lapels of his jacket. "If you don't have dis, you have natting. Natting." I guessed he was Albanian.

It took a few seconds for me to understand he was flirting with her. Our repeat customers knew she was Nick's wife, but the new ones, who never saw her holding Joey or showing Nick affection— bumping or tickling him, or just being aware of him in the room—these customers you couldn't really blame. Though Mary Ann didn't have feathered and blow-dried hair, wore almost no makeup, and used essential oils instead of Poison or Obsession, she was pretty in the West Coast sense, which was the seventies, rather than the eighties, sense. You became attracted to her by small surprises—her almost bronze eyes, the terra-cotta freckles that dusted her nose and forehead. On her finger she wore a band of colored bars that didn't look like a wedding ring if you didn't want it to.

I poured my coffee and looked back to find Nick staring, frozen, at the Corvette. I didn't understand. Corvettes came in all the time. The car covers were mostly off by now, and I could see enough of it to have a reasonable guess at the year. It had a flat back window, which meant older than '77, and a front bumper, which meant older than '73. Third-generation Corvettes began in '68, so it was between a '68 and '72. Finally, and I was proud of my detective work here, there was no fender flare, which appeared in '70, so we were looking at either a '68 or a '69.

The car also had a strange black stripe squaring off the hood. I'd never seen one like it. If Chevys had stripes they were usually the two fat Super Sport stripes over the trunk and hood.

"I order tave kosi," the customer was saying to Mary Ann. "You will like the tave kosi. Dis, I guarantee."

Rubbing her fingers, Mary Ann said, "You don't have dis for dis"—pointing at the paperwork—"you get dis"—making a fist. She turned to see Nick, who was only six feet away from them, still watching the Corvette outside. I don't know what words could have been as malicious, as unloving as his indifference to an awkward situation that could have easily been cleared up.

"Or any menu you pick," the Albanian said.

"You're asking me out to dinner?" Mary Ann said, still watching Nick. He was a photograph, his thumb touching two fingers as if he were holding a tiny teacup in front of him.

"No lamb, no problem," the Albanian said.

She turned abruptly. "Why not? My husband doesn't seem to have an opinion."

It took the guy a second to register, and then he held his hands up. "I kid, I kid," he said. Mary Ann looked down and began punching numbers on the calculator.

"I'm a dick," the guy said, his accent gone. "Let me get out of your hair. I'm sorry. I'll come back." Nick still had his back to them, so the guy approached me. "I apologize," he said, and stupidly I shook his hand.

I started to leave with my coffee black, hell with the sugar, but as I glanced back I saw that Mary Ann had closed her eyes and was pressing one of her temples. "Nick," she said, but he was lost. She dropped her hand and stared at him with surprise and fury, a look that precedes someone saying, with full contempt, "Are you kidding?"—in fact, I thought for a moment she had said that.

After a long second she turned and went down the hallway to the office. In the humming quiet, what drew me back to Nick was the small sound of liquid running onto the carpet. His cup was turned over on an end table, the last of the coffee beaded over the cover of a *People* magazine. "You should talk to her," I said, and he turned suddenly and bumped into me, causing my own coffee to splash out onto my shoe. His eyes were startled and seemed not to recognize me. I moved out of his way.

I got paper towels from the bathroom, and when I looked through the front window, Nick was pacing by the car trailer with his hands on his head, like a witness fresh on the scene of a gory wreck.

When I came back out to the bays, Ray was alone in a folding chair with an Arby's Big Boy on his thigh. He was staring contemptuously at a *Smokey and the Bandit* TransAm in his bay. "Are you telling me I have to get up for this shit box?" he said.

I looked at the car, black and gold and all weighed down with ground effects and spoilers. The hood was opened, but that was all, no diagnostic leads clamped on. Ray preferred his own five senses to any oscilloscope. He read spark plugs like a mystic reads tea leaves and could tell you the octane of a gasoline by tasting it.

The TransAm's engine was choked with hoses and vacuum lines for smog control. You couldn't even see the spark plug boots. I leaned over and started loosening the wing nut on the giant air cleaner, singing, as I did, a line of "Eastbound and Down" from the movie.

"It's a real shame what you got for cars," Ray said. "Your generation. The music's shit, too. Now it's the law I got to wear a seat belt?"

He went on like that and worked himself into a coughing fit, after which he spat something terrible into a trash can.

"What's the deal with Nick and Mary Ann?" I said.

"Aw Christ. Hell. Don't ask me." He walked away, and then came back. "All I know is if you're going to call it quits, do it young. Me and Bonnie stayed married for the kids, and what the fuck good did that do? All they ever seen was fighting." He spit again into the trash can. "My boy's out in Ohio someplace with a warrant out. Ginny's got that big Polack, can't even feed his kids.

Meantime, I'm fifty-two. I want company, I'm supposed to go dance the jungle boogie? You laugh. Just wait, your time's coming." He chugged his Dr Pepper and produced a great explosive burp that caught him off guard. "Jay-sus," he said and glanced up the aisle between bays. In a sudden low voice he said to me, "Don we now our gay apparel."

I ducked out from under the hood as a man in a mauve polo shirt and pleated pants walked up to the car. "This one's mine," he said. "I just picked it up." He looked a little embarrassed. He'd had to have heard Ray's belch. "From that place Chachi's, on 69."

"They give you a money-back guarantee?" Ray said.

The man smiled as if getting a joke, but Ray didn't say anything else, and the poor guy laughed awkwardly. "Nobody does that," he said.

"What do you mean it hesitates?" Ray said.

"Not really like a bog or a skip. She asked me that out front. More like I'm towing something. It doesn't pick up like you'd expect." He gave Ray a chance to answer all that he'd said, but Ray stared at him vacantly.

"I remember when I was a kid my neighbor had this Super Commando—"

"Okay, let me stop you right there, chief." Ray stood and threw away the last two bites of his sandwich. "A big Mopar and this you got here have zero in common. Zero."

The guy looked at me, and I rolled my eyes in a weak show of camaraderie.

"You ever want to break the speed limit in this boat," Ray said, "yank out that smog motor and invest in a four-bolt small block. End of story."

I went back to get the work order for the Albanian's car. At the pegboard I was reading over his complaint when, from the lower-level parking lot outside, I heard gunshots. I ran to the open window. Two stories below, the yellow Corvette was parked in the middle of the dirt lot and Nick was walking around it, creating a perimeter, it seemed, between the car and the old tires and hoses and oil drums and trash unrelated to cars that had ended up in the weeds. After a moment Bobby came out of the Dungeon hauling out buckets of the rusted bolts and engine parts littering the bay.

When I got down there Nick had his hands buried in his pockets and was slightly bent over the open hood, his mouth moving. I hurried into the Dungeon. "He's out there talking to himself, Bobby," I said.

He handed me a .22 Marlin rifle. "Here, I'm not supposed to be around these things," he said, speaking with a cigarette in his lips. "You see a rat, blast his ass. Nuke the little cocksucker."

He brought out two more buckets while I stood dumbfounded between the damp fieldstone walls, the mortar black with mold, until a rat the size of a fireplace log ran past me. By the time I thought about the rifle I was holding, it had disappeared behind a broken Hibachi. Then Nick was beside me. "Get something to cover that," he said, pointing at the little scratched Plexiglass window no bigger than a cereal box in the bay door. "Find some cardboard. Here." He handed me an ancient roll of duct tape from a workbench and then hurried back to the Corvette. All the cardboard was rotten, but I was able to cover the small window with strips of duct tape alone.

"The 'Vette needs an overhaul," Bobby said, returning to the small bay for more buckets. "You and Nick are doing it down here and don't tell nobody. If they ask upstairs, you're scraping asbestos out of the ceiling. That way they'll stay out."

I was only frustrated a few seconds longer, because it had to be some kind of joke. Bobby was big on jokes. He'd charge a points condenser with eight thousand volts, pick it up with rubber-handled pliers, and toss it to you. He'd glaze a toilet seat with WD-40 or paper the inside of your locker with hermaphrodite porn.

I leaned the rifle against an old radiator and lit a cigarette as I followed him outside.

"No fuck-ups on this one," he said, as he passed me again. "You watch him whenever his hands are on that motor, you hear? After it's done, we get a few pictures to prove it."

"Prove what?" I said, kicking around a foot of old radiator hose.

He dropped the buckets and shook blood back into his hands. "It's a ZL-1," he said, turning to the Corvette. "King of the hill. The fastest production car America ever built."

I exhaled smoke with a wry laugh. "Right."

He looked at me, annoyed, and I wondered what the hell the joke was. How could a Corvette be faster than a Hemi Superbird, for instance. Or a big-block Cobra? Except for the side pipes and high-rise hood, this yellow one looked like any other Corvette. It had Florida plates that said EVEADE.

"Is that a vanity plate?" I said. "It's spelled wrong."

Bobby ignored me.

"What is it again?"

"ZL-1. All-aluminum four twenty-seven."

I laughed again. "All aluminum. Does it fly around and shoot laser beams?"

He started back for the Dungeon, the veins in his neck standing out like waxed extensions of his mustache.

"How many are there?" I said. Since I'd been here, we'd worked on a convertible 'Cuda, one of two hundred and fifteen, and a '67 Z/28, one of seventy-three.

"Two," he said, and I realized he thought I meant how many buckets did he have left to bring out.

"How many ZL1s, I mean."

"I just told you. Two."

"This car is one of two?"

"Careful you don't ding the paint," he said.

7.

THE CAR WAS OWNED BY A TALL REDHEAD NAMED EVE MOORE.
Though I associated true redheads with tomboys, suspenders, freckles, bare feet like Huck Finn, Eve wore a sun hat and a white dress that looked like it was silk, over which she had tossed a light aqua sweater, the color of her eyes, that had only one tiny button at the neck. Her hair, shoulder-length, looked expensively maintained—each strand coated to slide individually so that the cumulative effect was a movement like water when she turned her head. As she got closer I smelled an understated perfume that made my scalp tingle. She was the kind of woman I instinctively looked away from, reading any interest she might show as mockery and steeling myself against her smile.

Eve had asked us to pick a restaurant and to not worry about prices. Nick didn't care where we ate, and of course I didn't know any fine dining in Waterbury, so after some discussion Ray and Bobby decided on Tia Juanita's, where the house wine came out of a box and they charged for a second helping of chips.

Bobby rode with me to the restaurant, and I speculated on how a woman so young could own such a car. I thought she was an actress—I was pretty sure I'd seen her on episodes of *The New*

Mike Hammer, and maybe in *St. Elmo's Fire.* Bobby just let me go on and on and was grinning when I looked at him. "I mean, what's a car like that worth, you think?" I said.

The number he said so astounded me that for a second or two I wasn't even driving my Nova, as if I'd fallen asleep, and I woke to find Bobby's hand nudging the wheel back from the center lines.

Bobby started playing drums on the dashboard. "She don't lie, she don't lie, she don't lie," he crooned, rolling the backs of his nails over the vents and flicking them against the window for a cymbal when he got to the payoff: "Cocaine."

"She told you that?"

"She's rich in Miami, bro. They got a meeting in New York tonight. Look at that big Dago she's got opening her doors." He drummed some more.

Not until the six of us were standing by the stucco arch in the foyer, waiting under the knotted strings of paper shades as the waiters sang "Happy Birthday" to a fat kid in a giant sombrero, did I really take a look at Dennis. His eyes drooped like a boxer's (though it might have been Bobby's calling him a Dago that made me think of Sylvester Stallone) and he was stocky with short, moussed hair that was the same black and ivory as his herringbone blazer. When Eve spoke to him he leaned in attentively, nodding with his brows lifted, and after she finished he turned and offered a brief reply I couldn't hear, before returning to a spine-stiff military stance, hands clasped in front of him.

Bobby had told me what the ZL-1 was worth, and who else had that kind of money? I looked around and imagined men with Uzis splattering blood all over the cheap frescoes and mosaic table-tops.

Dennis left his blazer on when he sat, which made me think there was a shoulder holster under it that contained maybe a Bren-10 like Crockett wore on *Miami Vice.* But when he leaned forward to take a menu, his jacket opened, and I saw that all he was hiding was patches of dark that spread from the armpits of his shirt. I ordered a Negra Modelo like he did.

The day was fast turning into the strangest of my life, and every next minute distanced me from my innocent past. Five years ago I was at Milford Academy in my blazer and tie, and now I was here, watching in a daze as food was ordered, was brought to the table; we ate and drank.

I don't remember what was talked about until Dennis broke his silence. He leaned toward Bobby and said, "Back in my knucklehead twenties, I did a job for some disorganized people that cost me twenty-eight months in North Dade. I say so because I notice how you got your arm around your plate."

The dangerous moment came when they watched each other, each man frank and undaunted, and even after Bobby nodded there was a long, uncertain second before he spoke. "They got me on a stretch up here just about like that. Twenty-six months."

Dennis leaned back from the table and sipped his beer, and when I saw that his inquiry was finished, I said to Bobby, "Tell them how you did it."

Bobby set down his fork and tried to laugh it off with modesty that was only half genuine. "I'd like to hear it," Eve said, and she held him with her big pale eyes as if no one had ever interested her as much.

Bobby looked away first, dragging a forkful of enchilada through his guacamole and leaning over for a bite. "Well," he said, wiping a napkin over his mustache, "looks like I got the floor now. So back in my 'knucklehead' twenties," he said, and Dennis gave a polite laugh, "I realized that about twice my paycheck was going into drink and drug. I had a girlfriend was working at the Howard Johnson's in Hopeville, which is out of downtown, but not too far. You can't see the parking lot from the street. It's where a lot of secretaries and their bosses like to go for a nooner. It's sort of famous for it."

Bobby left out that everyone called the hotel "Blow-Jos," and that he'd keep his story clean for a woman gave me the strange feeling of laughing inside. Often Bobby seemed remote and a little dangerous, a former taker of bad pills and a drunk, a former thief and convict, a current biker with biker friends, and whenever I saw a recognizable behavior—due to manners, in this case—I felt that we weren't so different, that whatever made us different wasn't more than the random matter of life experience.

"A guy I knew ran a chop shop over in Bunker Hill," Bobby continued. "'I'm always getting guys bringing me Town Cars and Audis,' he tells me, 'only I can't unload 'em. What I need is Hondas, Camrys, Escorts, like that. Joe Lunchbucket rides.'"

"Because who gets high-end parts from a chop shop?" Eve said.

He opened out his hands in affirmation. "So I've got Melanie keeping her eyes open for couples that show up, no bags. Cash. They try to leave the make and model blank on the form, but Melanie tells them they'll get towed. So when she gets a good one, she puts 'em in front so they can't see the parking lot from their room. Then she gives me a call. I slim-jim it, hammer the steering column. I'm out in a minute and a half. Leave my own rig in the lot, pick it up later."

"Oh my God," Eve said. "It never gets reported."

"Or if it does, they say it got took from work, or from Bradlees or somewhere. By the time it even comes over the radio that Camry's in fifty pieces, VIN numbers ground off. And I'm out the door with a tax-free grand in my pocket."

Nick and Ray were finished eating, and Nick lit a cigarette. Eve gave Bobby a chance to chew his food, but she never stopped watching him, and the way she just barely squinted made her eyes seem enchanted and capable of extracting all your secrets.

"You miss it?" she said.

"What, jacking cars?" He grinned, his forehead shining. "Nothing too severe. You get cocky, and in the clink you go. I keep that in mind. But I think about walking out of that place with my money, and knowing the car's their problem now, and I wasn't going to get caught. All you keep saying to yourself is, 'It worked. Holy fuck, it worked.' Yeah, that I miss."

Though drugs were never mentioned that night, I couldn't help thinking that these were serious felons, and I found myself putting on an act of casualness, shaping the ash of my cigarette on the rim of my plate or faking a yawn when I was certain they could all hear my heart banging like a Super Ball in a jar.

"You know what I'm good at?" Eve said, settling back in her seat after Dennis had lit her Benson & Hedges. The question was put out to all of us. Nick sat back and watched her, and even Ray looked earnestly curious, as if he'd never given a wise-ass answer in his life. "I understand customer demand," she said. "It sounds simple, and it is simple. Miami right now is the place to have your midlife crisis. All you see are hot rods."

"Everybody wants that bad B-body they couldn't afford in high school," Nick said.

"Go fast and go American," Eve said. "Three shops in South Dade specialize in Ferraris—thank you, Don Johnson. But when I wanted someone I could trust with my Chevy big block, look how far I had to come."

Nick stared at her a few moments—Mary Ann, I thought, would've killed to have his attention like that. And as if it had just materialized there, I noticed the stucco wall mural behind the booth: a hulking Aztec warrior carrying a sleeping princess over the desert. "There must be a few decent shops down there," Nick said.

"But I wanted a genius. You know, Joe Meretti doesn't shut up about you."

Any last doubts about her line of business dissolved with the mention of Meretti. Not even thirty, he owned a Hemi Challenger, a Hemi 'Cuda, and a six-pack 440 Charger. He wore a gray fedora when he came to the shop, and was always stepping out to make a call at the pay phone on the corner.

"A month ago, I bought six bays in Coral Gables," Eve said.

"I'd like to turn it into a specialty shop. It's virgin soil for good muscle car mechanics."

"You let me know when you start hiring," Bobby said.

"I will," she said, her eyes intent on him as she paused to smoke her cigarette. "Bobby, I'm hiring. I need a crew. I want all of you. I see the potential for a franchise, two or three shops in the next ten years. Dade County alone."

"You mean you're taking old men, too?" Ray said.

"No old men," she said. "But I want you."

And now Ray, remarkably, looked away and blushed. He scooped up his bottle by the neck and fell back in his chair. "She's one of a kind, this one," he said to Bobby.

But it was Nick, shaking his head, who awakened us from our reverie of white beaches and speedboats. "Wouldn't last ten years."

Eve set her cigarette in the ashtray. "Okay. Tell me more."

"If I opened a shop that fixed record players only, how long you think I'd stay in business? And you can still buy a record player. The last muscle car came out of Detroit in 1973."

"Fuck you, EPA," Ray said.

"The war on smog," Eve said. She looked at Nick again. "So, tell me what you're thinking."

"It'll happen again," he said. "With computers and fuel injectors. Maybe some kind of intercooler system. You'll get low-emission horsepower."

"Ah, bullshit," Ray said. "I don't care what kind of computer you mash on a nine-to-one smog motor."

"You sound like you'd rather be in the design room at GM," Eve said to Nick, and he laughed, picturing himself, I thought, leaning over a draft table with a pencil behind his ear. "Once the science is there," he said, "somebody's going to have to modify it. Your computerized Firebird comes out of the factory with three hundred horsepower. The guy who owns it wants four hundred. How're you going to get there? You can't bore and stroke, or so long emissions. It's going to be technology. Computer chips, sensors. Guys that only know carburetors are going to be dinosaurs."

"But when motors aren't mechanical, you won't need mechanics," Bobby said.

"You'll need technicians," Nick said.

Eve slid a manicured nail under the cellophane of her cigarette pack. "Tell me what a lasting specialty shop looks like."

"You take in muscle cars now. You school everybody on computers—they're already getting certified at GM. Start fooling around with computerized engines. Figure out how to modify them before anybody else, and there's your virgin soil. There's your million-dollar franchise."

Eve picked up her Tom Collins and lifted it to Nick. It wasn't really a toast, though I felt the impulse to pick up my glass. Before I could, she said, "And let dinosaurs go extinct."

Gone from the night was any semblance of reality, and the future seemed limitless as we stood outside watching the black Suburban pull into the warm exhaust smell of East Main Street, when ironically it was Nick, the one I most associated with the abstract, who brought Miami back down to earth. He turned to the three of us, gathered under the bird shit–stained awning, and said, "Not a word to Mary Ann."

It was going to happen. Nick was going to reinvent the American muscle car and redeem himself. He was already making plans for Florida, the most grave and radical of which was that he wasn't going to bring his wife.

APRIL WAS STILL UP, POUTING IN HER TIME-OUT CHAIR, WHEN I came in through the kitchen door. I took off my boots and walked into a fizzling puddle of Sprite by the stove. "You could have warned me," I said. She wanted a hug, and I bent down to her. "You're all sticky."

She peeled her arms from around my neck. "Because I shaked it up first, like you did."

"That was outside. Where's Mom?"

"In here," I heard, and followed the voice. The lights were off in the living room, and the last speckled dusk drew back from the windows. At the far end of the couch she was still dressed for work, an elbow on the armrest and her temple in her palm. "I had one nerve left, and guess who found it."

I took April upstairs for her bath and then untaped the soggy bandage from my hand while she played in the tub. One of the blisters had popped, and the skin bunched like wet tissue, while the other blister was at its waxy peak. April gently rubbed her bubbles on my hand and then kissed it, and I laid my cheek on the cool enamel. Bath time was a constant in my life, her urgent little voice tinny on the water, the humid perfume of Pert and Ivory, and I felt my shoulders drop as if they'd been unhooked.

Early one morning a few months after April was born, I found my mother facedown on the living room floor. Liquor was new to her, and I woke her trying to lift her legs, thinking I could carry her up to her bed. She got off the floor saying, "Your father blew it. No, he'll come back. Hands and knees, you watch." A few days later, I came in from the garage and saw the empty cocktail glass as she lathered April in the kitchen sink. I tried to project a sense of delicacy when I offered to start giving April baths for a bump in allowance—I was fourteen and saving up for a car. Mom was relieved. "You're my rock," she said, and she called me Rocky for a few days, until I told her to quit.

Now April shot at me with her rubber squeeze tomato.

"Keep it in the tub."

"Did you know Mommy has a fuzz booty? When she goes potty."

It took me a second to get what she was saying, and when I laughed she said, "What's so funny?" in a slow, dramatic way that she must've learned from TV. "Sometimes I get a fuzz booty."

"No, you don't. You have to be a grown-up." And finally it struck me that I was considering a move fifteen hundred miles away. The sense of doubt washed over me so strongly that I fell into a laughing fit to escape it, laugher that made my eyes run and caused April to stutter and howl in that genuine way kids do when they see adults laugh.

Mom was asleep on the couch when I came downstairs. I took a long drink of her Tanqueray and tonic and was just heading back upstairs to bargain with April—another book if she could go to sleep with a kiss from just me—when the phone rang. I picked up in the kitchen and was shocked to hear the voice of Lou Costa, the cop.

"You miss me yet?" he said.

"Hey," I said, wishing I hadn't picked up. "Hey, Lou."

"She around?" he said, and I told him she was sleeping.

"Double-check on that, would you? She said to call around ten."

I looked out the window at the dirt turnaround across the street where he used to spy on us from his cruiser. Then I returned to the living room and took a closer look at Mom. She was on her side with her legs curled up, snoring softly on a corduroy throw pillow that would leave lines on her cheek. For a moment I watched her mouth tighten and slacken in what looked like an uneasy dream. When I touched her she jerked forward, almost falling off the couch, and in the moment before she realized where she was, I saw on her face a look of true horror.

"It's okay, Mom," I said, gently as I could. "You're safe. You're home."

9.

THE NEXT MORNING I LEFT THE HOUSE A LITTLE AFTER SUNRISE.
When I got to the shop, Nick's El Camino was already parked in front of the bay door window I'd covered in duct tape. He was inside pouring hydraulic fluid into the reservoir on the old frame lift. Blood-colored drips fell onto his boots and the brown concrete slab. He was the only one there.

I could smell burnt cordite from Bobby shooting rats on Saturday, or from Nick shooting some this morning. Black dirt spread across the floor from each damp wall, and the ten-by-fourteen slab seemed to float like an island in a bottomless sea. A foul tub sink canted forward on metal legs, and in one corner a shower curtain hung in front of a steel toilet, the kind they have in bus stations. On the ground a damp box with orange mushrooms growing on the edges lay melting into the toxic dirt.

I'd picked up coffee and donuts in Watertown, which was exactly halfway between Levi and Waterbury, and Nick sipped his tall regular as I stood on the lift arms so he could raise me up and test the lines. Mornings at the shop we came in fresh and clean and caffeinated, smelling like Irish Spring, but even with comb lines still in his hair Nick looked old, his skin dull and chalky, eyes red-rimmed, his smooth-shaven jowls pulling down. It was like getting a glimpse of him in his sixties, before his stubble surfaced and leaning over fenders put the blood back in his face.

We lifted off the Corvette's hood like the front plate of a bomb and then put the car in the air, the lift wheezing and groaning. I held my breath until the first pins locked, so that even if a line blew it wouldn't fall far—these pins clicked in every foot or so. While Nick drained all the fluids and started disconnecting the transmission, I taped paper floor mats, white-side up, onto the top and bottom trays of five rolling carts. I wrote "TOP END" on one tray, "PISTONS" on another, and so on.

When the engine was disconnected, he lowered the car and wheeled over the engine lift. The aluminum 427 was supposed to weigh a hundred pounds less than the cast-iron version, and I could feel the difference as I pumped the lift. I worked it steadily, an inch at a time then a break to see that nothing was snagging or scraping, and then another inch, the front springs creaking until the car sat high in the front, like a funny car gunning out of the hole at a track. In the ten minutes or so it took, Nick's hands caressed every surface of the engine to check for clearance and to keep it from swinging.

I felt a great release, as if my body were a taut cable suddenly given slack, when the engine was safely bolted to the stand. I lit a cigarette and touched the strange glazed metal of the block. I couldn't tell if it was cooler or warmer than cast iron, but it was certainly different, like some new element just cometed down from another planet, and I was afraid to get any grease on it.

There are two kinds of grease. One comes from a grease gun and has a new sheen and a mild varnish smell. The other kind, the common kind, is caused by oil seeping through valve cover gaskets, oil pan gaskets, half-moon gaskets, rear main seals, all of it blown by the fan and by driving speed as a petroleum vapor that thickens in the air, and what it leaves on your skin smells like gasoline—which is, of course, a derivative of oil itself. You don't realize that until some gas splashes in your face and eyes and doesn't burn like acid but has a warm, slick feel. This second grease, grainy with bits of road sand and dust, coated every horizontal surface of the Dungeon, where we began to disassemble this rare engine of immaculate design.

Nick suffered me as I took bolts from where he set them down and sometimes right from his fingers, to make sure that nothing was lost between engine and the parts tray. I understood that doing the job right was more important to him than his pride, and this is perhaps the single attribute that distinguishes a great mechanic from a good one. I invaded his space to touch what he touched, sometimes brushing the rough dead skin of his forearms, where any fine hair had long ago been worn away and only pig bristles stabbed out, forearms twice the size of mine from the pull-and-push strength of car work.

Nick had wired in an intercom receiver and it crackled before Mary Ann's voice came through: "Green Cordova coming down for a recheck."

Nick finished torquing the last engine stand bolt and walked over to the intercom. "I thought I was getting left alone down here," he said into it.

"He was throwing a fit," she said, and there was a second of silence, of waiting, before she released her button with another crackle.

Nick and I stepped out the side door as the car pulled in, a two-ton tank that slid to a stop in the gravel. A black man with a shaved head got out, and Nick asked what the trouble was.

"Get in and smell."

Nick leaned in the open window and then came around the front to pop the hood.

I don't know what would've happened if the engine had gotten hot enough. What you see in the movies is all hype—even shooting into a gas tank won't make it explode. But there was a small surge of panic, an impulse to run for a fire extinguisher, when I saw the fuel line dribbling over the intake manifold and a brown ring of evaporated gas.

Nick took a screwdriver out of his shirt pocket and got a full turn and a half out of the fuel line clamp. The guy was incredulous, laughing bitterly and then walking away with his arms folded, shaking his head, whispering what I think was, "Christ, God." Before Nick handed him eighty dollars out of his wallet, the guy told us, "I hook up cable TV. That's my business. That's my livelihood. You think I don't go through every one of them motherfucking channels before I pack up? That's dependability. I don't want to get a call that motherfucking HBO went out right when Holmes is putting the jab on Spinks."

After he was gone I followed Nick back into the Dungeon, where he picked up a half-inch wrench and started loosening a mounting nut under the carburetor of the Corvette. He was out of shape, and the machine of him took long sucks of air to operate, and as I listened to his whistled breathing I understood there would be no more mention of the Cordova or of how Nick had neglected a detail as significant as a fuel line. He seemed to have come to the fatalistic resolve that his rechecks were inevitable, and I worried that Miami was doomed. All the juggling I'd been doing in my mind to take Mom and April down with me, and now it felt decided. No Miami. And he might be finished here in a year or two.

We worked our ratchets on either side of the 427, and when we had the massive single-intake manifold off, we flipped the engine over and started unbolting the oil pan.

For a while I couldn't shake the self-pitying thought that the end was coming and it all was avoidable, such a waste. After what felt like an hour I asked, just to have words going, how Nick had first gotten into engine work.

"My old man used to bring home junk motors," he said. "Three oh twos. Three oh fives. We'd do rebuilds and then he'd put them in the paper."

"Where'd he get them?"

"He ran a boneyard in Oregon."

"Was he a good mechanic?"

"When he was sober, he was. Let me get that swivel."

I passed it to him and couldn't think of anything else to say. In a while, he asked if I was going to come by his house to pick up the two-ton floor jack he was getting rid of. "Wednesday," I said.

"I told you where the key is, right? There's a torque wrench you can have, too. An old dial one."

The headache of bad sleep I'd been fighting came pounding back. I'd been doubling up on cigarettes to fight it, and now I felt dehydrated. I went over to the tub sink, where the spitting flow ran orange, and waited as long as I could before I leaned over and sucked at the blood-tasting water.

"I'm not going," I said when I came back.

He handed me the oil pan bolts he'd taken off on his side. "You're not going where?"

"To Miami, Nick. Whenever it happens."

We lifted off the oil pan and started peeling the gasket off the bottom of the engine with our fingers. "It wouldn't be like here," he said. "You'd get ASE training. You know computers."

"I know WordPerfect and Donkey Kong."

"More than these guys know," he said. "More than I know." He handed me a single-edged razor blade. He'd explained that we'd need to use these rather than the steel gasket scrapers to avoid gouging the aluminum. It was small, tedious work, half an inch at a time.

"Because of that Cordova?" he said after a while.

"Here at least you have a reputation. Nobody's going to know you down there. What if we don't get any business? It's a big deal for me. You already moved across the country. I've never lived out of Connecticut." I stopped myself when my voice shook, and we worked for a few minutes in silence.

My hand throbbed under two Band-Aids, and I gripped a screwdriver to choke the nerves with contracted muscle, which was only temporary relief—I knew the pain would come back two- or three-fold when I let off. During a mindless stretch of loosening machine screws, I thought how I'd burned my hand for him, how I'd just admitted that moving far away scared me, and what was he giving back? They were ugly thoughts, thoughts I knew I wouldn't be proud of as soon as the hurt subsided, but right then they were the truth.

"What's it like?" I said. "Like you're thinking ahead and then you miss a step?"

"I'd tell you if I knew."

"Talking might help."

He dug gasket out of a channel with his thumbnail. "I forgot to tighten the fuel line," he said. He wasn't trying to be funny, but I stopped working and stared at him as if he were. He crouched to blow off the chips of cork gasket and blue sealer, the dull white-silver aluminum spotless where he'd worked. "What do you want me to say?"

I was poised to remind him exactly what was at stake—this car was one of two, she'd come fifteen hundred miles—but I saw how easily the points could erupt into melodrama.

"Maybe it's something else making you forget," I said. "Like from some other part of your life."

"You sound like a shrink," he said. "I just start talking, and no more rechecks?"

"What could it hurt?"

He looked off at an orange stripe of ooze on one of the field-stone walls, possibly thinking of a way or two that talking might hurt. "You saw it on *MASH*," he said. "Hawkeye can't stop sneezing until he remembers he got pushed in a lake when he was a kid."

I had to laugh because it was true, and I felt an opening. But then he said, "All I know is I never got pushed in a lake."

When the gasket was removed, we turned the engine sideways. Nick started unbolting the main bearing caps while I cleaned up the intake manifold.

"When my little sister was a baby," I said, "she had this fever like a hundred and five. We had to take her to the hospital. She was lying in my lap. She needed a drink, but we didn't have her bottle, we forgot it. She lost her voice she was so thirsty. Her eyes were all pink. Her fingers were burning up. I thought she was going to die, it was like I was seeing it happen. I mean, this baby, holding on to my finger."

We were both sitting on milk crates now with the engine between us, and I could only see his legs under the exhaust ports. The legs were still.

"We get there, and my mom runs into Emergency with her. I'm just sort of wandering around between cars. I remember being in this Chinese restaurant all of a sudden, and the hostess was talking to me. Your brain just shuts off. All I could think was, she's not coming home again. She never even said a word yet. She never walked. She never did anything wrong. If she didn't make it, I don't know what I would have done."

I had to get up. I went over and leaned against the bay door, where I stared at the ground and smoked half a cigarette. When I came back to the engine Nick was frowning at the bearing cap, turning his coarse-toothed Snap-on ratchet so slowly you could count the clicks.

"That's what I mean," I said. "Just talking, okay?"

He lit a cigarette.

"Why don't you try it?" I said.

"What do you say we quit playing Sigmund Freud and get back to work."

I told him I needed coffee and went outside, where I picked up a bald tire and ran with it over my head, hurling it finally at an old radiator. The radiator folded over at the site of impact, its brittle fins crushing in with the sound of stepping on shells. I was panting. Emotions for me were infectious, and the shock I felt going back four years to that car ride with April, that shaking dread and superstition that thinking about it now could somehow make it happen again, all these feelings translated easily into fast hot anger.

My hand was throbbing again. From the gravel under-story parking lot I looked up at the backside of Out of the Hole Automotive, a two-level building that had once been a brass mill with a foundry right here in the basement. The brick was pitted and round on the corners, the mortar cracked under a sagging wooden roof. It seemed to be standing only by Nick's magic. If he could just get his shit together, someday we'd laugh about this place, not only the building but this lowdown city of Waterbury, remembering the slumming days as we polished our ratchets in Miami, surrounded by the best diagnostic equipment drug money could buy.

I called him an asshole and paced around. I told myself I'd been using him all along, that I wouldn't be his friend except for his genius, because more than anything that was what I felt as I paced the dusty parking lot: used.

Up in the lobby Mary Ann was calling in a parts order, and I went over to the coffee maker. She put her hand over the receiver. "I thought you two were unavailable."

I held up the coffee cup but didn't trust my voice. She finished the call as I was stirring in my third packet of sugar. "What happened?" she said. I realized what I must've looked like.

"Did he say something to you?"

"No, he didn't. That's kind of the problem."

"If he's rude, you don't have to put up with it," she said, and I was pulled into her eyes, gold-flecked and more fiery than I'd ever noticed. I could only feel myself nodding as we shared for a moment the same broken heart.

"I know he likes you, Justin," she said. "And I know how it is when you're in his spotlight—you feel big—and then when you're not you feel so small." She looked down and pushed papers across the counter, ending the moment abruptly, as if she was afraid of what she might hear herself say.

10.

TUESDAY WAS THE DAY THAT TIME FORGOT. NICK AND I WORKED until noon upstairs while the engine block was being boiled and resurfaced at McGreggor's, and after lunch we slipped quietly through the side door and down to the Dungeon.

I had the rolling trays in order, and as we worked I wheeled them over one at a time and handed Nick tools and parts, often without his needing to ask. There was no clock or radio, and only a dim line of daylight along the bottom edge of the bay door indicated that it wasn't yet night. I couldn't measure progress by time and the hours took on an abstract quality. We didn't talk. The reassembling demanded all of our concentration, and we entered a higher plane of exactness and discipline. If we worked this efficiently upstairs, our dependability and attention to detail would've been world famous, though the stress would've killed us young, the sense that metal was crystal that couldn't be bumped or scratched, certainly not dropped.

The second sandwich I'd brought caused a dull pain in my stomach, either because I ate it too fast or I'd gone too long between meals, roast beef and Dijon plunking into a pool of raging stomach acid. Nick didn't eat. He'd brought in a coffee maker, and only Folgers and cigarette smoke entered his system. He was at the height of his powers as he pieced together these ultra-high-performance parts, his mind transcending the needs of his body. I mean, my spine felt like it was on fire, and I was seventeen years younger and in shape.

It was slow, steady, un-glorious work. It was evenly painting Loctite over bolt threads and then keeping them free of grit, closing your eyes to get them to catch, and a full three turns before using a ratchet because good luck retapping aluminum if you rushed and cross-threaded. It was ignoring pain. Nick worked as if it didn't matter if we ever got to hear it run. There was no future but only this thin steady bead of gasket sealer, this gentle, silent seating of valve to port. It was genius broken down to small observable moments, no action or acclaim, just don't rush, don't rush.

Before we lowered the engine in, I splashed my face and did some jumping jacks in the back lot. Outside the sodium arc lamp buzzed in the full dark over Nichols Street, the windows upstairs reflecting the weak blue security lighting. All I knew for sure was that it was after eight because Lenny's Liquor Locker was closed. I'd been prepared to stay, had told Mom not to expect me until late, but my body was approaching full exhaustion, a striking thing to feel at eighteen.

I took my place behind the engine lift, opening the valve to release no more than a pinhole hiss of pressure, and when the engine was in place we tightened bolts, plugged in harnesses, and connected lines. Nick used the bathroom for only the second time since we'd come down. There wasn't any coffee left, and I sat on a milk crate with a cigarette, hoping to pull another ten or twenty minutes of consciousness from the nicotine, but then I opened my eyes and Nick was standing over me holding my cigarette, his hand on my shoulder. "Help me get the hood back on," he said. "Then go on up and crash in my office."

It was just after midnight, and before I lay down on the vinyl couch I opened the phone book. She answered on the third ring. "I need to ask you something," she said, "and I don't want you to think—"

"Mary Ann, it's Justin."

She was quiet, then cleared her throat from a distance. "He's not coming home tonight, is he."

"We couldn't find a stopping point. Nick wanted me to call you."

"Would you mind interrupting him to deliver a message?"

I closed my eyes. "Okay."

But then she only sighed. "He didn't ask you to call."

My eyes still closed, I could only wait for her to keep talking or hang up. "What would you do if you were me?" she said.

"I guess wait and see."

A few seconds passed, and then she laughed an exasperated laugh.

"I'm sorry," I said.

"Don't be. I knew that's what you'd say."

Thunder rolled as I dove off the bow of a lightning-struck ship and onto the low shag carpet. I stood and paced around the office, picking up things to bring myself out of the world of dreams.

Coffee was on in the lobby, though the door sign was turned to closed—it wasn't even seven yet. Out in the shop the Corvette was holding a big choppy idle in the first bay, the massive camshaft lobes I'd held now pushing against the heavy valve springs. Nick was adjusting the mixture on the bottom of the carburetor. He revved it only minimally and the sound was how the world would end at low volume.

Nick straightened from the fender. "Sleeping beauty," he said. Remarkably he didn't even look tired. I asked if he'd taken it for a ride yet, he had, and if he'd put the pedal down, he hadn't. A rebuilt engine needed about five hundred miles of easy driving to seat the rings and bearings—we told this to customers all the time,

and it was always a small heartache for the guys to baby the cars on test drives, never tasting the fruits of their work.

But how could you climb behind the wheel of such a car and not put the pedal down? Eve was coming tomorrow morning, and after that, who knew? It seemed worth it to risk scoring a cylinder or spinning a bearing and then having to rebuild it just to find out what a car like that could really do.

He killed the engine, and I helped disconnect the scope. Over the ticking cool aluminum he handed me a postcard from the White Mountains of New Hampshire. I didn't understand.

"Don't believe the name," he said. "None of them mountains was white."

The saddle-back seats pulled you down at the hips as if in preparation for a blastoff. You had to reach up for the radio dials, and a mile under the dashboard your heels pressed heavier than your toes, the glove box level with your chest. The emergency brake at your elbow had a gun handle like a bomb hatch pull in a warplane.

New Hampshire and back was enough mileage to break in the engine and then some, but Nick was still babying it with me. He pulled onto I-84 and then onto Route 8 South. He told me to watch for cops, but then he barely broke the speed limit, the engine humming low as he slipped in the passing lane and eased by an early commuter. I have to admit I felt relieved, as you did as a child when the carnival ride you dared yourself to get in line for stops working through no fault of your own. I'd held the lungs and muscle of this engine in my hands and had a pretty good idea of what it could do.

It sounded great at low rpm, deep and gravelly and implying—like the husky voice of a rock singer—that it was capable of an outrageous scream.

"Harley-Davidson wants to trademark their sound," Nick said, evidently reading my mind. "That po*ta*to-po*ta*to. They only use

one connecting pin for two cylinders. It's a waste of compression. Inefficient as hell. That's how come Bobby rides a Triumph."

"I didn't know you knew about bikes," I said.

"Engines. Think what the two of us could do if we only cared about noise. How you could shape an exhaust valve. A combustion chamber. We could invent a new V-8 sound and get rich."

I nodded, a little flattered to be part of his daydream.

"But you know you wouldn't do that. You're not working on a church organ. When you get done with a rebuild, you want that thing to *go*. Who waters down horsepower on purpose?"

"No mechanic I ever knew."

He grinned and then turned to look at me for a long second. "You did good work," he said. "I think we got it perfect."

We got off the highway after five exits, and then idled up the overpass and onto the entrance ramp headed back north. Merging onto the highway Nick started winding the engine. When he punched the gas in third I thought we'd been rear-ended by a train. He shifted to fourth at sixty and the awesome car chirped its tires, and then we were coming off the ground. This wasn't my imagination—Nick, who never drove with two hands, grabbed the wheel at ten and two, joggling back and forth to no effect at all.

We passed between bedrock cliffs and the side pipes echoed like jackhammers—I caught myself lurching for the floor. The highway wasn't wide or straight enough for our speed. Nick, when I glanced at him in horror, was saying words I couldn't hear, his eyes wide and moving, looking awestruck and like death was the last thing he expected. It didn't seem right that his hair wasn't being blown back.

Up ahead a panel van cut into the fast lane, and if it had been me driving we would've died in flames and pieces, but rather than swerve Nick switched lanes so gradually it was more of a lean, like on a motorcycle, until the gray smoke that was the van disappeared and he swayed back. And then our exit was coming up and he let off on the gas. The five exits north seemed to flash by in less than a minute. It felt like we were barely moving, like I could open my door and step out, and I wondered if something was wrong with the engine, if he was going to have to stop in the breakdown lane, but when I looked at the speedometer we were doing seventy-five.

"How fast was that?" I said, mainly to let him know I hadn't had a heart attack or anything. We were on the exit ramp now. Tears were in his eyes as he stopped the car at the bottom of the ramp, and he dropped his face on the steering wheel. He was breathing hard, and I reached over to put my hand on his shoulder when he started to speak.

"Intercoolers are what it's going to take," he said. "Grand Nash intercoolers, in line with turbos and port fuel on V-8s. More cold air in the cylinder and a computer mixing gas. Carburetors are gone, cam shaft fuel pumps are gone. No slop. A sensor wherever air goes through. Make it clean. Metered. Exact." He ripped up the emergency brake and got out of the car pronouncing furious words I didn't want to embarrass him by getting out and hearing. He circled the car with his hands up in his hair.

At the shop, Nick slept from late morning through the afternoon in his office. I was adrenalized enough to work the full day, which was fortunate since the scheduling of jobs at Out of the Hole was engineered around Nick's only taking off Sundays. I did eight tune-ups and ten oil changes by myself. I barely saw Bobby and talked to him only once, while we were washing our hands, when I tried to tell him about the drive in the Corvette. But words are never enough for an experience like that, and all you've got is your pauses and whatever lame adjectives you can think of. Bobby shook his head, grinning. "Once in a lifetime," he said, and then we were back out spinning ratchets, scarfing lunch over a fender. It would occur to me only later, as I was walking out to the parking lot for the next job, that Bobby must've been hoping to go for a ride.

11.

AFTER WORK I DROVE TO HOG WILD, A LOW WINDOWLESS WATER-bury tavern in the last strip mall before the warehouses and empty casings plants on Freight Street. Parked among Harley Sportsters and a few Softails, Bobby's Triumph was backed up to the sidewalk curb.

The heavy Gothic-arch door pulled open on a dim room under a tin-stamp ceiling whose spinning fans you couldn't feel. There were wooden chairs with cut-out handles in the backs, deer heads and coats of arms and dart boards, and in one corner a red-felt pool table. Bumper stickers were taped to the mirror behind the bar. LOUD PIPES SAVE LIVES. HELL WAS FULL SO I CAME BACK. I SUPPORT POLE DANCERS.

Southern rock played on a jukebox I couldn't see through the crowd. There were a lot of guys who, you could tell, didn't give a fuck, who wore bandannas like pirates and had handlebar mustaches and week-old stubble. You felt far from the law in here, and though sidestepping in the cigarette smoke was disorienting I stayed aware of my distance from the door.

As I walked the length of the bar searching the tables someone got me in a headlock, and I resisted only for one second—that resistance of instinct—and went limp in the hopes that it was only Bobby, and of course it was, horsing around.

"This is the guy going with me," he said, and then I was tucked at his side and walked to an empty stool, where he asked the next guy over to shove down. Bobby introduced me to men in Levi's and engineer boots, some in leather vests, all with y's at the end of their names. I pulled off a number of the three-point handshakes he'd taught me, and half terrified—it was like being in a mead house after a battle—I said almost nothing and tried not to smile too much.

"What're you in work clothes for, dummy?" Bobby said.

I came up close to his ear. "To look older."

Bobby took a drag from a cigarette going in the ashtray. "Richie," he called over the bar. An older guy with a braided ponytail looked up from the drink he was pouring.

"My man here is twenty-five."

"The fuck do I give a fuck?" Richie said.

Bobby clapped a big hand around the back of my neck and said to Richie, "This is who's going to be in the picture you get from Miami. Me and him and a motherfucking marlin."

We split a plate of nachos at one of the tables across from the bar. Though he was only drinking O'Doul's, Bobby was drunk on a dream. We'd spend New Year's in Key West, rent a cigarette boat, get me a bike and cruise the Everglades.

Bobby lit a cigarette and leaned back singing an Allman Brothers verse an octave or two lower than Dickey Betts. I sipped my beer and looked at Jim Morrison's famous mug shot from New Haven hanging over the cash register.

"So, it ran pretty good," Bobby said.

"I'd kill myself in a car like that," I said.

"Man."

"He needed sleep, Bobby, or he would've taken you out."

"Bro, it's cool. You earned it." With his cigarette in his lips he air-guitared a fast riff.

"How come he doesn't want us to tell Mary Ann?" I said.

Bobby looked at me. "You want me to guess, I'd say he don't want her to come."

"You think that's a good idea?"

He shrugged. "Maybe they're no good for each other. My brother-in-law quit screwing my sister, but then she caught him beating off with her panties. Weird shit happens."

"At least he's got somebody," I said. "Who's going to take care of him down there?"

"The single life's a son of a bitch."

"Maybe if they had another baby."

Bobby shook his head. "He got cut."

I stared at him.

"Fixed," he said. "No toothpaste in the tube, man."

"He told you that?"

"I drove him to the clinic," Bobby said. "When Mary Ann's sister was here. I thought it was a fucked-up plan. What, a week after they lost him. But he did it, he wouldn't say why. I don't think she even knows."

The story didn't seem over, but he swung around because the talk was getting quieter, and then the crowd in front of us sort of parted around an angry blonde holding a little boy. It took me a minute to realize that this was the baby in the picture Bobby had showed me. Robbie? Ronnie? Randy—that was it.

Bobby slid off his stool. "What're you bringing him here for?"

She handed the boy out to Bobby. "You're only moving down there to get out of visitation," she said. "I'm not a moron." She spoke for everyone in the bar to hear. "He's yours tonight. I've got plans." She was almost to the door when she turned back and called, "Bye, baby," and blew a kiss to the boy.

Randy locked his hands around Bobby's neck. I guess he was about a year old. "Hey, bud," Bobby said. To Richie he called, "Get me some of that apple juice."

A one-year-old at a bar. The idea that anyone might object

didn't occur to Bobby, and there was, consequently, nothing wrong with it at all. Three years of being told when to turn out his light and when to eat, shower, shave, and shit had probably cemented this libertarian spirit as soon as he was released. Though he joked often and was dedicated to his sobriety, chugging near-beer among all these alcoholics, Bobby was fiercely suspicious of the laws of society. He was the kind of man you could imagine dying over a minor principle. From his example, I saw myself in a few years acting on what I wanted, heedless of, and fully ready to accept, the consequences.

Later that night he set Randy on the pool table. The boy jumped when the clang happened and the balls came cracking down. Bobby racked, and we shot lightly while Randy scraped blue chalk over his knee.

From one of the nearby tables a giant in height and muscle and fat—a man who could've filled a doorway and destroyed it by lifting his elbows—called over to us, "Naw, man. He'll piss on the felt."

"Calm down, Larson," Bobby said. "You know what a diaper is. Your old lady wears 'em."

12.

I DIDN'T EXPECT MARY ANN TO BE HOME WHEN I CAME BY FOR
the jack. I parked behind her Malibu in the driveway and found
the garage key under the second brick, where Nick said it would
be. The garage was a separate little building in the narrow side
yard. Under humming fluorescent lights I walked around two
refrigerator-sized Snap-on boxes and stripped engine blocks three
to a stack against the back wall. Nick's last project had been a '66
GTO he'd gotten for twelve hundred and flipped for eight thousand, and there was just room enough to fit a car, though I wondered if he'd ever find the energy for side work again.

It started to rain as I was putting the jack and torque wrench in
my trunk. I hopped in but felt Nick's key still in my pocket, and as
I ran it back the rain came to a crescendo, big drops splashing up
from the cement, a sudden current rushing in the eave gutter over
my head. With my back against the door I lit a cigarette and
watched the house until the rain let up. I looked in the windows
for Mary Ann, realizing too late that I should have knocked to let
her know why I was here, in case Nick hadn't told her. I thought
about going up to the house, anyway. I didn't know how I would
say it, or if I'd be able to, but I saw one last hope for Miami—if she

only knew about it. Maybe it could be a new start for them. And I'd heard that vasectomies were reversible, or maybe they could adopt, or maybe they could just be enough for each other.

The rain slowed and I snuffed out my cigarette. On the steps to the kitchen door I had to dare myself to knock, and I waited in the spitting rain, juggling thoughts that were in the end irrelevant. She never answered the door.

Walking back to my car I heard her before I saw her, her exhales sharp and arrested, her face flushed a deep red as she turned in from the street. Lifting and dropping of her feet seemed to help her vacuum in the air, and she slowed to a wide-gaited walk right past me. Hands on her hips she came back nodding, gasping, "Hey," and then pacing back. She was soaked through her tie-dye T-shirt and shorts.

"How far did you run?"

She shook her head, panting. "What time is it?"

I didn't own a watch. "About two, I think."

She wiped her wet forehead with her wet forearm, her sweat indistinguishable from the rain. "I left at eleven thirty." As she walked up the stairs she pulled from between her T-shirt and sports bra a necklace ribbon holding the house key.

I'd never done much jogging—four-minute rounds on the heavy bag was the closest I came to aerobic exhaustion—and it always amazed me how serious runners could take themselves near death and be half recovered in ten minutes. In the kitchen she drank a full glass of water, still breathing heavily through her nose. I smelled her warmth and the quiet made me anxious. I told her I'd come for the jack, which she didn't seem to know or care about.

"I meant to thank you for calling the other night," she said. She set down the empty water glass and leaned back on the wall. Her face was still red, her wet hair pulled back tight in a ponytail.

"Did he tell you about the Corvette?"

I was surprised when she shook her head. I'd thought it had been a safe question to ask. Already I'd told Mom and April and even Don about the car, and I would have told many others if Nick hadn't told me not to.

"As a matter of fact, no, he didn't," she said. "We didn't really talk at all. Not today. And if not today . . . Today or never, right?" She smiled, and when she turned her face up to the ceiling I saw that she was fighting back tears. I didn't understand. She was standing on one sneaker with the other pressed against the wall, so that her knee, bloodless white, pointed at me. I pictured the wet shape she would leave on the wallpaper when she stood away from it.

"I got up with him. I followed him in here, back to the bedroom. He changed clothes. He brushed his . . ." She pushed the heel of her hand against her forehead. "He wouldn't say anything." There was a calendar push-pinned to the wall across from me, and I looked at today, July 26th, but the square was empty. What was today? I couldn't ask her. Somehow that would be a betrayal on par with the betrayal of Nick's not talking to her. July 26th. Exactly a month before my birthday.

It struck me a moment after I thought the word "birthday," and suddenly I was breathing through my mouth, the air burning cool on my tongue. I dropped into a chair at the table. I took off my hat with the sensation that it could suffocate me. One year old, he would have been. When I looked at her she had drawn her arms around, hugging herself. I said the only thing I could say immediately, the thing on my mind. "Nick should have stayed home today."

She began to nod, her lips curled, and with her arms still in place she started to cry violently. Her body couldn't give up more air or water, I thought in the second before all thought turned to instinct, and I went to her. Her lips were drenched and she opened them to breathe and pinched them closed and shook her head no, but I knew that the no wasn't for me but for Joey leaving her and for Nick leaving her, and I took another step before she pushed herself off the wall. I caught her, staggering, her arms around me. Her heat came through my shirt, and her sweat was so flushed through as to have no smell except for the faint baby powder of her antiperspirant. She wanted to be off the ground—I didn't realize this until her leg came up around my leg, buckling it so that I staggered and tipped over with her onto the kitchen floor.

I was able to throw my weight and take most of the impact on my elbow and shoulder, and I started to ask her if she was hurt, but she kept her face hard on my collarbone, holding me against her with all the shaking strength she had left. My shoulder on the floor was taking most of our weight, but I stopped feeling it as the pressure of my embrace seemed to be slowing her down, deepening her breaths.

We lay there on our sides on her kitchen floor. Time was measured by how settled she became, how close to settled, and the wet that was her wetness all over me was cooler now, and when I closed my eyes my sense of smell heightened—pine, maybe, and the weak shampoo of her last shower. The ball of pressure on my back was her hand, I realized when she opened it, and her fingers spread over my spine. The sensation of her pressing fingertips caused a movement in my testicles, and I recognized with horror that I was getting hard, and then was fully hard, the length of my cock mashed against her thigh. When I pulled back, she made a sound and the hand that had been on my upper back sank down, and with this as leverage she slammed her hip back against me.

Before my mind turned off for some immeasurable time, I knew that I would feel remorse, which was an old reflex that usually kept me out of trouble. But the gigantic wrongness of what we were doing was only in words. It was nowhere in her touching me, her warmth and softness, her wanting to, though strangely I felt the sin of what Kim and I had done a year earlier without love, the contrast of those two sticky gropings in the hay dust with now.

In a slow lucid moment, I let my body determine what was necessary. This love. Mary Ann. I'd resisted letting myself know her because I was afraid I could love her. The way she looked, the unexpected things she said, her courage after Joey. Had there been an opening to talk now, I would have said the kindest words. I would have been selfless, better than myself.

Yet it was because we weren't talking that I felt briefly awakened, if not in the Buddhist sense then as if a film, a residue of some kind, had been peeled away. I wasn't looking behind or ahead. My mind was in fact empty and I was my body, following the light, no matter its source. The truth was there, and it said that a moment I lived inside of could never be bad.

The snap opened and the zipper spread, and when she squeezed me a flaring pain ended, a crushing weight was removed, and there was no stifling the groan from deep inside. She laughed a nervous, encouraging laugh, and I came in a burst of heat that must've gone straight up her bare arm and onto her shorts and maybe the floor. I couldn't look down at it, couldn't look at her, closed my eyes, and when she rolled back from me I reached down to close my pants, feeling the warm disgusting glue of myself, but she said, "No, God." She knocked over one of the kitchen chairs swinging around to throw off shorts and panties together, and then she rolled back and pulled my pants down to my knees with one clean yank. When she straddled me I was hard still and became harder inside her.

On top of me she pulled off her shirt and the sports bra. She reached for my hands and brought them up around her sides so that I could feel her smooth ribs, and later I would think about this positioning of my hands—she even spread apart my fingers—as a kind of preparation for the moment when she tipped forward and kissed me.

13.

NICK WAS SLOUCHED OVER IN THE SWIVEL CHAIR BEHIND THE old Gunlocke desk, and I couldn't stay away from him. At first, it was just out of needing to know if Mary Ann had said anything— I'd staggered from her house yesterday with no idea about the future—and then it was out of wanting to tell him what I'd done.

But getting us anywhere near that conversation was complicated by a bizarre circumstance: Eve hadn't come in yesterday morning to pick up the Corvette. It was parked in the Dungeon, its exotic fenders scarcely concealed by the terry-lined cover. We had no phone number and her address on the work order was just a P.O. box in Miami.

Nick shook his lighter trying to get it to work. "No phone call, nothing," he said, as if all the worry had occurred in the last five minutes.

I set down the spark plugs I was gapping and came over with a lit match. "She said they were staying at a Hyatt. The Grand Hyatt, I think."

"I called over there. They never checked in."

"I'm sorry," I said, and I had to keep myself from saying it over and over. I went to the door with my spark plugs but turned back. I just had to be around him.

"Now I got this car down there," he said, knocking ash over the floor, "this famous car waiting to get stole."

Lying awake last night, I'd tried to convince myself that Nick was bad for Mary Ann, and that in ways I wasn't fully aware of, she was bad for him. But now I couldn't get beyond seeing Nick as my friend, and I was in a mood to talk like friends at the same time I was afraid that silence might turn into accusation. I knew I was a coward, uncertain of myself at an age when I wanted my personality to be set in steel.

In the months before Don finally left us—he'd been erasing himself for years by then, working late or attending readings in the city, poring over manuscripts on the weekends—I would tell myself that at least he wasn't like some fathers out there. He didn't hit me or insult me or embarrass me in public. But when I was facing any of the thousand crossroads of my childhood, when I was called on to tell the painful truth, or to stand on principle, then I felt only jealous of the kids who had fathers they looked up to. So I'd compiled several men into a role model of my own, and now the stoic Charles Bronson wanted to remain silent, while the morally complicated Don Johnson wanted to hear Nick say that he didn't love Mary Ann.

"It's like having a padlock on the *Mona Lisa* down there," Nick said. "Anybody with a pry bar could jimmy that bay door."

"But nobody knows it's a ZL1," I said. "Right? I didn't tell anyone. And I know you didn't. Does Mary Ann even know?"

When Nick looked up at me, I couldn't read his stare. He was wise to me, and now that I'd said her name . . . Suddenly he turned and threw himself over the desk, pounding the parts room window in a deranged expression of his full hatred of me.

But no. On the other side of the glass, Bobby was taking a work order off the peg hooks. "No cherry-picking, Stango," Nick called. "Take it in order."

Bobby cussed, put back the second work order, and took down the first. He came in to the parts room and set it on the table. "What the hell am I supposed to diagnose?" he said. I looked at the work order. A 1982 Corvette. Check engine light. Black smoke. Hesitation.

"Course it hesitates," Bobby said. "It's got a Tonka Toy motor."

Nick took down one of the new computer books he'd bought at Carquest and handed it to Bobby. "See what you can figure out."

"I figured it out when it pulled in," he said. "Low compression and a shitload of wires."

"It's a D and A," Nick said. "Hook it up to the scope."

"Rally rims and a spoiler do not a muscle car make."

Both of us were shocked—at least I know I was—when Nick grabbed the book out of his hand and gave it to me. "Here," he said. "Go see what you can figure out."

Bobby came over when I had the Corvette hooked up to the scope. "He's serious," I said. "He wants us doing computer cars down there."

"Down where," he said. "I look around, I don't see Eve coming back." Bobby thought she was dead. He knew a mid-level manager for Fat Tony Salerno in Harlem, who said there was a whole graveyard of out-of-town drug dealers at the bottom of the East River.

The engine was choked with vacuum lines and wiring harnesses. In the center of it a large plastic cover read CROSS-FIRE INJECTION. Bobby shook his head. "Best of luck."

But then he kept coming over to see what I was doing. "So you just ask the computer what's wrong?"

"That is the plan."

"One robot talking to another robot. Neat."

I took the air cleaner covers off the two throttle bodies. "It's like dual carbs on a Hemi."

"That," Bobby said, "is about as unlike dual carbs as a pair of bowling balls. Where do you adjust the float? Where's the choke and the mixture screws, smart guy?"

I sat in the driver's seat and read through the diagnosis section twice. It was almost funny what it was telling me to do. I found a paper clip on the ground and straightened it into a V. Under the dashboard was a matchbox-size ALDL connector with twelve cavities. Just like the manual said, I ground the A cavity with the B cavity using the paper clip, then turned the key. There came a clicking from under the hood, and the check engine light started to blink. One blink. Pause. Three blinks. Then one again, three again. Code thirteen. "Holy shit," I heard myself say.

"It's the oxygen sensor," I told Nick.

"You sure?"

"I'll check resistance, and then yeah. A bad sensor can make it run rich."

He went over to the book and moved his finger down the page it was open to. I was about 95 percent sure I was right. "It was a code thirteen."

"I believe you," he said. He came back over and leaned on the opposite fender. As I was discovering beyond any doubt that it was the oxygen sensor, Nick said, "You're in it."

I looked up from my ohmmeter, caught off guard and suddenly looking him in the eye, which was the last thing I was ready to do. He watched me with the admiration of a father grooming his son to take over the family business, and I knew that my voice would break if I opened my mouth.

"Wouldn't matter if the place was burning down around you," he said. "You're working it through. Seeing the patterns, what's causing what. No surprises. It can't be any other way than what you're thinking. You're in it, partner." He clapped my shoulder and I had to look again at the quivering dial on the ohmmeter, my face hot, my sinuses melting. I'd been waiting all morning for Mary Ann to show up, but I was suddenly glad that she hadn't, and that I couldn't see her and that she couldn't see me, because I felt, for the first time, angry at her. I couldn't have said why, because it had nothing to do with the mind.

Nick asked what I was making, and after a moment I was able to tell him.

"Starting this week, you're up to seven percent commission on top," he said. "Computer work's fast and expensive. That's better than a raise."

14.

BACKING OUT THE CORVETTE, I GLIMPSED MARY ANN THROUGH the big window as she arrived for the day and set her purse behind the counter. From the low bucket seat I watched like a stalker, feeling lost to myself, thinking the words "crime of passion" and how that was only a way of rationalizing the crime. What was I now? What was she?

I expected her to look like a victim, adrift and betrayed, but instead she wore the expression of any other day, glancing around behind the counter at the work she had to do.

I parked the Corvette and went in with the work order. The lobby was empty, and as I came up to the counter she said, "Good morning," in a sweet way, and the indescribable thing we had done was in the realm of the possible. All I had to do was seem capable of containing it.

She smiled and glanced down at the counter. "Nick didn't do last night's deposit, I see." And, my God, that she'd allowed my hands over her soft breasts, that her hands had told mine to squeeze, and that she'd kissed me with even some shyness in the backward order of my already being inside her. I was seeing her body and our messy lovemaking on my third try, when I was able to last and she made the sounds of letting go and I let go inside her.

Unlike my own, her eyes were bright and not swollen; already I'd been in the bathroom trying to wash out the bloodshot with tap water, which made it worse, and then pressing a cold Dr Pepper can to the under-eye bags, which did nothing at all.

"So how are you?" she said.

I couldn't hide my amazement at the question. "I'm not sure."

She zipped up the money bag and the wrapped change made a thud where she dropped it on the floor. "That can wait." Then she looked up at me with a sudden smile. "So what are your plans for lunch?"

I fell on her over the front seat and jammed the gearshift up to first with my shin. The backseat would have been more practical, but I was ready to snap off the steering wheel and throw it out the window before I broke from her long enough to climb over the seat. My cock felt harder than any bone in my body when she took it in her warm hand. Under her cotton dress I found that she was as ready as I was.

I stopped to open my shirt because you couldn't really see my upper body muscle with it on. Then I was tearing at a studded condom package with my teeth. "What are you doing?" she said. "I have my diaphragm in." She knocked the little red package out of my hand, and I hated to see it go. In the bathroom at Chevron I'd put my quarters in the Ultra Ribbed slot, between Ultra Thin and Extra Sensitive. I would've picked No Feeling At All, if that had been an option.

I thought that Nick could probably last with Mary Ann. He could look at her phenomenal face, her sexy lean jogging body, and not feel daunted. It seemed to be a passage of manhood to deaden yourself to the unspeakable beauty of women.

"Are you safe?" she said. "I'm safe. I guess we should've discussed that yesterday." She kissed me. "I trust you, Justin."

She'd done an extraordinary thing since I'd seen her in the lobby—she'd put on eyeliner. I could suddenly recall the very few times she'd worn it. I don't know what the occasions were, but now I was the occasion. My God she was hot. I was pumping in her hand before I realized it. "I'm sorry," I said, agonizing for a final allowance.

"I want this as bad as you do." She reached down to disentangle one leg from her panties.

It wasn't long, seconds, before I was thrusting with all my strength. I had to pull back and out and close my eyes, hold my breath, let the still release of the air reset the timer. As we began again and found our rhythm, she didn't make sex sounds or really let her hips answer my thrusting, but only breathed in lapping rhythm with our slow dance. When she finally did start to move I tried to pull back again but she held me there, and with her first soft, "oh," I was done. I pressed my mouth down on hers and let go. Then all I could do was hold still, like an invalid, pressing down on her until her eyes rolled back, and I watched her face, watched everything it did. She settled and sighed, and when she looked up at me she smiled with such sweet thank-you, her face flushed, her eyes sleepy and wet.

Only minutes had passed since we'd parked, and we got out of the car at a place that looked like the day after the Apocalypse. Sections of concrete parking lot jutted up like broken ice on a pond, and rusted and peeling chain-link fence opened on mini temples that had been caved in or knocked apart.

It was the remnants of a Waterbury oddity called Holy Land, USA. I'd read that in the '60s a hundred thousand people every year made the pilgrimage here, some from overseas. Its name had even issued from the Pope's holy mouth, I forget why, but now it was just a bizarre *Road Warrior* vision of the Bible. Crosses were covered with spray paint, nearly every statue decapitated. The Ark of the Covenant lay half charred and upside-down under the archway for Eden. According to the *Waterbury Republican,* the park was a haven for junkies and gangbangers, and I noticed for the first time the cluster of low-riders parked on the opposite side of the lot.

She wanted to take me on a little tour, and we still had some time. I'd told Nick I was going for a test drive and then to Popeye's Chicken, where there was always a mile-long line at the register. In a skipping Dodge Dart I'd followed her Malibu out through neighborhoods of turn-of-the-century mansions that were three-family houses now, with round parlor rooms and wraparound porches, and up Pine Hill to a world that was sacred and terrifying.

Through the parking lot she led me around fire pits and glass and rain-puckered porn magazines. Past the broken cinder-block wall of a former gift shop, guys with black bandannas were spray-painting crowns over the Ten Commandment tablets. They weren't bullies but the murderous badasses that bullies modeled themselves on. Relaxed among the wreckage, they seemed to arise from lawless places, one of them baseballing rocks out into the biblical city with a stick. They were Latin Kings, and according to the paper, they'd left bodies in this very park. They called each other Angels with the unsettling implication that they weren't afraid to die.

I avoided eye contact and smiled at nothing. Though I couldn't think of a single word, I strained to give the impression that Mary Ann and I were deep in conversation, and also that I was the last person who would ever report a crime. Someone laughed and I couldn't swallow. With her olive complexion, Mary Ann could have passed for Puerto Rican, and I saw the danger that holding her hand and being white might put me in. I was afraid enough to let go, but I didn't let go.

In my periphery I saw one of the Kings stop moving. Then a voice full of gravel: "Yo," and in a black Yankees cap he glided up on us. He was squinting so hard one eye was almost closed, as if aiming a gun, only the gun would come up sideways. They pointed them sideways to break convention, or to say this is my hand, too, this gun is my hand and you're so close I can't miss, as easily as I can slap you I will shoot you.

"Hold up," he said. "You know about Buicks? I got an eighty Regal. It does this shit like ting-ting-ting, like castanets, you know?"

My brown-and-khaki Out of the Hole uniform. It got me into bars and liquor stores, and now it was saving my life. I looked at Mary Ann, who was waiting for me to speak. "I think he means pinging," she said.

I found my voice and asked what kind of gas he used.

"High-test only," he said, and I was stunned by both his somberness and the understanding that this outlaw, this "soldier of the street" according to the paper, used the same grade of gasoline as the CEOs who brought us their muscle cars. With a slight dip of his head, a faint bow of respect, he asked if I could take a look. I allowed myself to smile when I was walking behind him, giddy with a resurgence of faith in my profession. Automobiles were like a great species among us, more vital and abiding than most people in our lives, yet only a handful of us fully understood their complicated language. Even gangbangers were humbled by the ailments of their cars.

The radiator was low on coolant and I showed him a leak at the thermostat housing. From out of a Newport pack he handed me a joint, and though I'd never tried pot I thanked him, as if he'd tipped me in ordinary currency.

Mary Ann laughed about it when we were alone again. She took my hand and I was sure of nothing, a moment gone wild because it wasn't a casual crossing of the hands but a lacing of fingers that pressed that softest of skin. It was just that everything was working in reverse, and only now was I realizing that she liked me, despite all my fervent denials.

She led me along a path that must've been a lawn at one time, though what grew now grew out of magazine pages, cigarette packs, McDonald's wrappers, broken glass, plastic bags. The weeds looked mutated they were so big, and there were briar bushes and poison ivy and tamarack trees that didn't know where they were, flying a ripped flannel shirt like a flag, the leaves yellowing underneath, other limbs broken by a tire, a rusted tricycle. And the crawling and flitting bugs didn't know where they were either, hovering down to a rose petal that was really a torn Doritos bag.

There was a stucco table with stucco benches in a clearing where gravel and concrete kept the plant life down. You could imagine a family having lunch here long ago, but now half the table had been broken off, its rusted chicken-wire skeleton showing underneath. When I lifted a damp newspaper off the bench on my side, two firey centipedes came to life and I knocked them away.

"Last Thanksgiving, there were guys in army jackets up here," she said. "Vietnam vets. They made a fire and had a turkey cooking on a spit. It snowed, remember that?" She looked around as she described the flocked buildings, the vets using the park for cover in a snowball fight, and it occurred to me that Thanksgiving was only days after Joey died. I looked around through her eyes of mourning, imagining a kind of comfort she'd found in all the wreckage.

Rather than looking like a tiny burrito, the marijuana joint was carefully rolled into a funnel shape. The wide end was twisted into a fuse and the narrow end had a small tube of cardboard wrapped inside, to keep the contents dry from saliva, I assumed. I turned it lightly in my fingers, appreciating the street skills of criminals.

"What are your plans for that?" Mary Ann said, and my surprise at the question embarrassed me. I didn't know anything about this illegal twig in my fingers. At the age when I would've been open to experimenting I transferred to Northwest, where pot smoking, with its associations of laziness and pinko Democrats, got you labeled a burnout. I closed my mind to the few stoners and learned how to hustle laughs from the farmer kids with slit-eyed Cheech impersonations. ("Fifth time I'm late to work dis week, and it's only like Tuesday, man.")

I gave her the joint and lit it with my lighter, and like the song says she smiled before she let it go. I'd never actually watched someone smoke, and when her eyes softened and glassed over with almost sexual delight, I let go of four years of prejudice in a second or two. Her eyes were lighter than I'd realized, gold-flecked with the early afternoon sun, under eyebrows that were thick and exotic—foreign, though she was half Klamath Indian and more American than I was. Her nose wasn't wide and flat like a girl I knew who said she was Cherokee, but thin and straight-edged and delicate. But it was her eyes first and the close, unselfish way she watched you.

"That's not bad," she said. She hit from the joint again, and I tried it when she offered—a puff diluted with air that took me right to the brink of coughing. I gave it back and waited to see what happened.

Across from us, the Real Photograph of Jesus Christ was sun-faded and shellacked with grime, but the Hitler mustache and swastika earrings stood out in a throbbing gold. At the top of the hill behind Mary Ann were three crosses, white in the sun. Jesus hung on the middle one, his body missing from the waist down, and for the time I had an odd sense of piety up here. "My mom works at a church," I said.

"Does she?"

"It's Methodist."

"Are *you* Methodist?"

"No. She isn't either. It was after they got divorced. She went one Sunday for service and came back with a job."

After a third toke she tapped the end of the joint and set it on the table between us. "I hope she found some answers," she said. "Or peace of mind, at least."

I looked past her, to the surrounding neighborhood of triple-decker houses with TV antennas sticking up, to where the I-84 lunch-hour traffic had loaded up the exit ramps. In between billboards and rooftops flashed the green leaf canopies of distant hills.

"Not really," I said. "You can't just plug into it. You think you can, but you can't."

Mary Ann smiled easily, the pot working the way it's supposed to. "You can ask me anything," she said. "I promise to tell the truth."

"If you want me to pretend nothing happened, I will," I said.

"Is that what you think I want?"

"I don't know. I'm not sure what Nick means to you anymore."

"I know what he means to you," she said. "And if *you* want me to pretend nothing happened, I will."

I nodded cautiously. Her look was soft and didn't challenge me to say anything, but long seconds passed when I was afraid to speak. She scraped moss from the rutted tabletop with a flake of stucco. "You can never predict how you'll be," she said. "My sister came out. She was with me every minute for a week. But Nick went back to work. Back to his cars. He should have had people around him and he had machines." She looked up at me and sighed. "I know, Ray and Bobby and all his minions. I don't mean them, I mean real people. And I'm sorry to sound cruel. I should've closed the shop. But that's the only part I blame myself for. I said I'd give it a year. But what's it costing? We don't touch anymore. We don't talk. If you asked me what he wants from his life, I honestly couldn't tell you. The man I've lived with for seven years."

As she said all this her voice drew taut and at times was tearful, and the sudden wash of emotion both stunned me and made me feel close to her. I put my hand over hers. Words seemed weak now, and there was nothing I needed to know.

"So that's what he means to me, Justin. Less and less."

Everything she said was so far removed from what I'd expected to hear that I felt dizzied by it. Suddenly I was in the rarefied place of sitting across from her while she seemed to want to prove something to me.

She made a circle of her thumb and forefinger and sent the burnt-out joint spinning into the weeds. "You want to stay friends with Nick," she said. "I don't blame you. I think it's sort of noble, actually." This she said without sarcasm, and I thought about love and loyalty, how one can get in the way of the other, and it felt like the secret to the good life was in making the two compatible.

We stood and held hands. As we walked back toward the cars there was a laugh from nearby, a woman's laugh, and Mary Ann stopped and turned. From inside the Beit Shearim Catacombs a light flickered. It went out and that was all—no voices, no sexual sounds that I found myself listening for, imagining a couple looking by matchlight at themselves lying in the cave.

"I like how it blurs together up here," she said, and I understood that blurring to mean the holy and the unholy, the right and the wrong.

PART TWO

15.

EVE DIDN'T SHOW UP FOR THE CORVETTE THE NEXT DAY, OR THE day after, or the day after that. The mood around the shop darkened as the idea that she and Dennis were really Jimmy-Hoffa gone evolved from an outside possibility into a likelihood. Talk went around about calling the police, but what would be the point? The killers were certainly contract pros who got to be that way by not leaving evidence, and all that would happen, the cops would confiscate the Corvette and auction it and keep the money.

I was mourning the Miami dream for my own reasons. Surely if Eve had come back Nick would have told Mary Ann by now that he was leaving her. And in that time of selling the shop, selling the house, they each would have moved into their own apartments. Would Nick hold it against me if I started seeing her before the divorce went through? I even let myself think, wouldn't he be grateful I was there for her?

On the eighth day Nick disappeared after lunch, and I found him in the Dungeon. The chamois-lined car cover was off the ZL1, and in front of the car Nick was slumped on a milk crate like a string puppet set down. Antifreeze drained out of the radiator into a catch pan. He noticed me with a casual glance. After a moment he said, "Imagine being the guy that breaks in and gets his hands on this sucker. Doesn't even know what it is."

"What're you doing?"

"I can't sell it without the title. Whatever I can get for the engine is it."

I went in the passenger side and opened the glove box, but it was empty. "Over there," Nick said, jutting his chin at the workbench. The vinyl envelope contained the registration and insurance card. Eve Moore. No address and the same P.O. box as she gave on the work order. I wondered if her last name was really Moore. I got out and came around to the front of the car.

I don't know how the idea came to me, just from staring at the car, I guess. "You think anything could beat it in the quarter mile?"

After work that evening I stayed in Waterbury, waiting to meet Nick. I had dinner at a Greek diner on Franklin, walked around Kmart for a while, and then got carded at the Scoreboard, so I went through the new McDonald's drive-through window. Sucking on a milkshake I watched the light stream of traffic. About every third car on Wolcott had its headlights on.

Nick was waiting in the Corvette when I pulled into the lot at nine thirty. Seeing him down low in the awesome car, I realized I had been doubting all along if he'd show up, and now there was a burst of shivering anxious energy, of myself in charge of the night, as I pulled up to his window.

"If she asks," he said, "you and me are finishing up that Charger. That okay? She doesn't want me out racing."

We could've gone 84 to 63 to 6, three right turns into Levi, but instead I took him over the Seven Hills and through the rolling farmland, from Breakneck Hill to White Deer Rock, glancing at his headlights as I held a casual speed so that he might find enough peace in an untroubled drive through the country to reflect upon his intention to leave Mary Ann—the course he'd made inevitable, I thought, when he got the vasectomy.

In Levi I pulled into the parking lot of the Arco *ampm,* the only place still open in town except for two restaurants, and Nick parked beside me. I told him to wait in the Corvette while I went inside.

Walter Maze was working the counter, as he had every night shift since years before I moved to town. I used to revere him, the keeper of tobacco and *Hustler* magazines who used to sell some of the Northwest kids beer. Then a few months ago I'd stopped in and brought a six-pack up to the counter. "You got that wrong," he said, and as if a mask had come off I saw him for what he was, an inbred in his late thirties, still cashiering at *ampm,* still with his folks, balding, hollow faced, a monster truck on his cap though he drove a '72 Gremlin—a rust box with a bumper sticker that said I LIKE TO SNATCH A KISS AND VICE-VERSA.

I hadn't come back since, even for gas.

"Anybody out at Wickersham's tonight?" I asked as I paid for a pack of Marlboro Lights.

His eyes skimmed the aisles behind me before he opened the register. "Probably," he said, which was code for yes. If nobody was there, he'd say, "Doubt it."

There was a story behind the quarter-mile racing at Wickersham's. When Sheriff Reynolds was new on the job ten or so years ago, he engaged in the high-speed pursuit of a Ford Galaxy full of teenagers who had been drag racing on the Route 6 flats north of the high school. The chase ended with the Galaxy plowing into another car at ninety miles an hour where Rail Tree Hill intersected 317. Legend had it they had to go in with a cherry picker to get bloody limbs out of the trees. Four dead. His first month as sheriff.

Reynolds knew he wasn't going to stop the kids from drag

racing. At Northwest they learned how to trick out engines, and in the evenings after their farm chores, they went out to the machine shed to work on their own hot rods. Reynolds's brother-in-law, Al Wickersham, owned a section of farmland that was cut by Peacock Lane, a half-mile stretch of blacktop paved and then abandoned by a developer in the '70s. Nobody used it except hunters in the fall, who continued after it became a single-lane dirt road at the base of Sawpit Hill. Reynolds put out the word that as long as there was no other racing around town, he wouldn't send his deputies out to Peacock Lane, though it was understood that Wickersham would keep an eye out and report any trouble. By the time I went through Northwest, Wickersham's (it was cooler than saying "Peacock Lane") came up as often in conversation as Arco or the drive-in in Wolcott.

I'd been there a few times in the daylight just to see it. Start and finish lines had been painted in reflective white a quarter mile apart, and kids patched and resurfaced the asphalt as it was needed. It was actually one of the smoothest stretches of road in Levi. They'd even put in a telephone pole with a streetlight hanging over the start line.

When Nick and I arrived that night in the Corvette, having left my car in the Arco parking lot, a bonfire was going on a stony crust of mud behind Wickersham's alfalfa field. I saw backlit silhouettes tipping bottles that were bigger than beer bottles, and things that weren't logs were getting thrown in the fire, sending up sparks.

In the dirt turnaround I recognized Tim Heller's Charger and Mickey Burke's Monte Carlo. "That's one of them," I said to Nick, in answer to his earlier question about which cars to take seriously.

"The Charger," he said.

"It's got a four forty Magnum."

"One four or three twos?"

"Just a four-barrel, I think. The Monte's got a four fifty-four."

Nick didn't seem interested in the Monte, and neither of us bothered to mention the other cars—two smog-era Firebirds and a Nova that was a year newer than mine. Nick slid the shifter up to neutral and slowed. "Just pull up?" he said. I nodded, and as Nick began rolling down his window the smell of bonfire conjured the same jittery dread that had crippled me in high school. Three guys came over and blocked our way as if it were private property, and Nick eased to a stop.

Billy Motts wore canvas suspenders over bare skin like he had on the first day of school, when he dropped on one knee in front of my desk and jabbed a hand at me to arm wrestle. He was missing a finger—that nub of flesh still had some small, clammy movement—and beat me after half a minute or so, though I'd been afraid to try all the way.

Except for a glimpse around town, when I usually turned to avoid the potential embarrassment of waving and not having the wave returned, I hadn't seen anyone from school in more than a year. "A lot of these guys are dicks," I said. I don't know what response I was trying to elicit, perhaps just that he have more awareness of his words and gestures, but his expression didn't change at all. He was staring at the cars.

When Tim Heller started looking over the front end of the Corvette, I saw that Nick had removed the 427 emblems from the hood.

Nobody introduced themselves. I'd made a fool of myself at Northwest when, still in the mind-set of Milford Academy, I'd walked up to a circle of them trying to kick a hacky sack with steel-toe work boots and said, "Hey, guys, I'm Justin."

"Big block?" Heller said now.

A long moment passed before Nick said, "I'm not used to having to say."

Motts laughed. "Fuckin' A. He got you, Heller."

"Yeah, but you got Brainiac," Heller said, and God how I despised that nickname. I thought of how in school, by the myth of familiarity that a nickname implies, I'd fooled myself into believing that these people would someday be my friends.

"He knows what I got," Heller said to Nick. "You're one up on me."

"It's a big block," Nick said. "Four twenty-seven."

"Nitrous?"

Nick shook his head.

"I can smell it," Motts said. "Giggle gas smells like rock candy." A guy I didn't know, standing suddenly beside Motts and holding a bottle of Bacardi, said, "You're a fucking goon, Motts," and Motts spat his snuff juice and said, "You laugh like you got rubber bands on your balls." Motts looked at me, grinning, and with no choice except to take his side I grinned back and dared myself to speak. "You guys having a party back there?"

"Anderson's old man croaked," Motts said. "Everybody brought shit to burn."

"I wouldn't of burnt a good fishing pole," the guy with the Bacardi said. "Reel and everything. Like a reel's gonna burn."

They set the race at three hundred dollars. Since the Corvette was lighter than the Charger, I would ride with Nick while Heller raced alone. Nick agreed to the condition reluctantly and looked a little irritated when the guys explained the fairness of it, which was all pool-shark strategy. Nick didn't know it, but his attitude of not giving a damn about making friends was going to make him friends. From his wallet he counted out twenties and fifties. Motts came to his window and as he took the bills he said, "That first red oak after the finish line, start laying on the brakes. You got around a thousand feet before it turns to dirt, and then it's your fucking funeral."

A kid who'd been a year or two behind me, sipping a Sam Adams, called over, "You know what that Chevy cross is for?"

I looked at Nick. "I think he means the bowtie."

"It means you're getting crucified," the kid said.

Nick started the car without seeming to acknowledge the comment, but the word "crucified" sent a chill through me. It suggested death, and death is what there was out here. You could smell it rising from the pavement, that vinegary haze of drying rubber, and in the strange chemistry of fire smoke and carbon monoxide. In seconds I would look into the face of death as the too-dark dark of the woods rushing toward us at speeds in the triple digits. It was the dark of pre-civilization, where cars didn't belong, gnats and mosquitoes exploding in the two puny cones of headlights, and the end of everything in the shimmering tree trunks if Nick didn't find his brakes in time.

But then, cheating death was the whole appeal. That was why in the cafeteria at school, where conversation topics rarely lasted longer than a few bites of pizza, where you were a sucker if you cared too much about anything, the races at Wickersham's were timeless talk. Year after year, freshman through senior, it made the most unexcitable guys blush and stutter.

Eavesdropping from another table, I'd heard about the close calls—fishtails at the start, locking brakes at the finish, stupefied raccoons scampering out in between—and was amazed that no one had ever been killed out there. But tonight it seemed a little less by dumb luck than by design that wrecks were minimized. There were two rules pertaining to safety, though of course the rationale was explained as keeping the cars in one piece, which was a more manly concern than not getting hurt. The track had to be kept clean. To this effect there were two push brooms nearby, and when someone mindlessly flicked his cigarette sparking onto one of the lanes, he was slapped across the back of the head and told to get his ass over there and pick it up. The second rule was that if you were there to race, you stayed away from the keg. Sheriff Reynolds had donated a Breathalyzer for this reason, and everyone took a blow on it before money on the race was even discussed.

Motts used the fanned-out bills as a flag, and when he brought it down there was only thrust. Nick jumped forward and eased off, letting Heller up to the front fender with a lazy shift to second, more concerned with the illusion of neck-and-neck than with winning. Most of the race, my door was even with the back quarter-panel of the Charger, and in the last seconds Nick bumped ahead to win.

After we stopped, Heller came running over to us. Instinctively I slid my elbow over and locked my door.

"Goddamn it, that was close!" Heller yelled. "I missed third a little, did you hear it? That was fucking inches." He started laughing. He might have been hollering that he'd won.

On the drive back to my car, Nick handed me a hundred dollars for thirteen-seconds' work. "You plugged us in," he said and glanced at me. "You don't mind taking their money?"

I couldn't say no emphatically enough.

"They your friends?"

"Just guys from school."

Nick shifted gears, and then he did something unlike him, something Bobby might do. He reached over and patted me on my thigh. It wasn't a hard pat or a soft one, but exactly the right impact to say to hell with all of them. "They're goofball hicks," he said, and it was the most insulting thing I'd ever hear him say, making me ashamed of all I'd ever done to try to win their assholing approval. He squeezed my thigh once and took his hand back.

"Was it enough money?" I said.

"It's plenty."

We both needed cigarettes, but he didn't want to smoke in the Corvette, so I directed him to a wide shoulder by a suspension bridge over the Pomperaug. We got out and leaned over the iron railing, looking down at the moonlit water as we smoked. "We could have taken him by a second or two," Nick said.

"Jesus."

"It's an embarrassment for a car like this to be in their company." When his ash fell, his gaze followed it, but you couldn't see where it hit the water. We stayed on the bridge longer than I'd expected, Nick lighting a second cigarette and a third. And then out of nowhere he said, "You know what they say is proof we'll never make a time machine?"

I watched him for a moment. "A time machine? Like H. G. Wells?"

"Figure it out," he said. "You're smart. What's the proof it can't be done?"

My mind was blank, and then the answer was just there. "Because nobody ever came back from one."

He nodded. "If they figure out how to do it, we'd see somebody come back. There was a NASA guy in the sixties doing research, but the funding got cut. Just like when the EPA said no more high compression. Could you imagine what kind of horsepower we'd be seeing today? Or if NASA kept going with time travel. What good does it do anybody, we landed on the moon?" Animated now, he leaned over the bridge rail.

"There's a rock ledge down there," I said, afraid that in his mania he might jump.

"There's a way it could happen." He flicked his cigarette away, and in the same second it hissed in the water he had the pack out of his shirt pocket and was getting another. "It's going to be about gravity. Figuring out how to make it and concentrate it. A passage of some kind. But the thing everyone gets wrong is, you won't be able to go back to any different time than what you already lived. And you won't know you're reliving it. You just will."

"I don't know what that means, Nick."

"Say they get it so you can go back to an exact year. An exact day. You want to go back to Disney World when you were ten, or the night you lost your cherry. You step into that passage and you're there again. But you don't know you went back. You'll live your life exactly like you did all the way up to when you go into the time machine. You have to, or you get the paradox. You'd maybe kill your grandfather by mistake. And you can never *not* get into it. It always ends the same way. It has to."

"What happens to you after you go into it? Where does your body go?"

"It just goes. You disappear. You don't live after that second you step in. But you live forever. Get it? You keep living that ten or twenty or fifty years over and over. You got cancer? You got six months to live? You got tragedy? Get in. Go back to the best part of your life forever. Isn't that better than a flag on the fucking moon?"

16.

ON MY DAY OFF I GOT A ROLL OF QUARTERS AND CALLED MIAMI from a pay phone. I half expected to hear Lieutenant Castillo's lifeless voice say, "Vice Division," but it was a woman who routed me to a detective after a five-minute wait. I told him I had information on Eve Moore, and there was a silence. I wondered if they were putting in the trace. "Do you know who that is?" I said.

"Yes."

"She's a drug dealer, right?"

"Can I have your name?" he said. I dared myself to wait, and then in a sharper, less friendly voice he said, "Who is this?"

I hung up the phone.

Ironically, the mystery was solved with the help of Don two nights later. Not long after Eve disappeared I had called and asked him to save me his *New York Times*. It was a random shot, and I'd forgotten all about it until I came home to find ten newspapers on the front stoop under one of Mom's decorative stones. It was in the "Metro Briefing" section four days after they were supposed to come back for the car.

I read the article aloud the next morning in the locker room. "A man and woman found in an abandoned panel van parked on

East 13th Street were identified by police as Dennis Faverau, 44, and Eve Moore, 31. Mr. Faverau had been arrested for burglary and Ms. Moore had been arrested twice on drug-related charges. An autopsy determined that both victims had been shot. Anyone with information about the deaths are asked to call the Crime Stoppers hotline—"

"They wanted to send a message back to Miami," Bobby said. "Else the bodies never would of been found."

"Jesus. God," Ray said and dropped onto the bench where we pulled on our shoes. "I figured, maybe . . ." He shook his head at the ground. Nick slumped on the wall. Bobby fell into a kind of child's squat and brushed the concrete floor with three fingers. Ray held his face in his hands.

"They say where she was shot?" Nick said. I shook my head.

"It was pros," Bobby said. "Head and chest. Had to be."

"Then maybe she didn't suffer too much," Nick said.

"If she told them where the car was, they would've been here already," I said. The way Nick looked at me made me feel insensitive to have thought of that, but it was just that I was twelve hours ahead of them in dealing with the news.

We all felt helpless that day, but Ray took it the worst.

After lunch he kicked over an antifreeze bottle that left a running splatter like green blood on the wall. Then diagnosing a Mustang GT he half-shouted, "Work, you whore." All the bay doors were open, and in the parking lot the Mustang's owner flicked his cigarette away and came inside. I intercepted him.

"What's with that guy?" he said.

"Air compressor's on the blink," I said. "Grab yourself some coffee. He'll come get you soon."

When I came over, Ray didn't look up from the Chilton book. The radiator fan was ruffling the pages. "When it won't set codes, what do you do?" he said. "You go wire by wire on every shitting little sensor. It's guesswork. Switch this, see what happens, switch that. Bullshit. I'm done. I'll go sit behind a counter at Carquest."

"Let me see," I said.

"You go ahead. Fuck it, I'm getting out when I can still remember real cars. Real motors. Not this dicking around pricking wires."

"What's up?" said the owner, behind me all of a sudden.

Ray straightened from the fender. "I want you to see something, now," he said to the guy. "Take a look over here. You see all these little idiot sensors everywhere?"

"Ray," I said.

"They can't take the heat and short out. Here's what's making it stall. It's this thing." He jiggled a sensor on the side of the fuel injector. "No wait, it's this thing. Hang on, it's really this."

He let go of a harness and swung his hand around, and with a sickening ding of fan blade two of his fingers came off at the knuckle. He held the hand in front of him as if he didn't understand what it was, the bones emerging white before blood sprayed from them with the pumping of his heart. In my peripheries the shape of one glistening finger lay by his boot, but I couldn't make myself look at it. He squeezed down over the stumps with his left hand as the fan sprayed his blood back at the car. The last thing I saw after Ray was carried off in the stretcher was Bobby Windexing the bottom of the windshield.

In Mary Ann's car I stared down at Ray's finger, gray now where it wasn't splotched with grease, the nail chewed to the quick. I felt tested and proven. After the moment of panic I'd picked up the finger and even considered washing it, but then I thought I might lose some of his nerve endings down the drain. We didn't have ice so the finger was lying on a can of Dr Pepper, cold out of the machine, in a gallon Ziploc on my thigh. The middle finger had been sucked in the fan and exploded into the radiator fins. With mixed feelings I realized that just that morning I'd seen him flip the bird right-handed for the very last time.

It wasn't cardiac arrest but unstable angina brought on by trauma and forty years of smoking. The prognosis was good, and the doctor congratulated me on my job with the finger, which they were sewing back on. Ray would have to stay overnight for monitoring. I'd called his ex-wife in Hartford, and she was on her way.

One nurse said we could see him and another said we had to wait. I didn't care. Time had stopped and I was getting paid to be here with Mary Ann, my sudden lover and friend. The accident was tragic but not for us, and though we cared about Ray he wasn't family, so we weren't sedated with grief like the other couples in the ER waiting rooms, or moping in prayer for an end to suffering like the children of very old people, or confused and miserable like the uninsured sick waiting for one of the urgent-care doctors to see them. We were temporarily stranded, unneeded, smiled at by nurses and ignored by receptionists with phones pressed to their ears.

In the cafeteria we sat among the hospital staff, who were eating from trays or sipping coffee in their light green smocks. I was still jittery with the feeling you get as you pass a gory wreck on the highway, the sense that it easily could have been you, that impulse to change your ways and be more deserving of the unknowable quality of luck.

Mary Ann and I glanced around quietly as the room filled with late lunch and early dinner patrons. At one point she was engrossed in a conversation barely audible between the cashier and a woman in teddy bear scrubs. I couldn't guess what Mary Ann was thinking, but her expressions ran a short spectrum from despairing to hopeful, and then she looked away, turning with apprehension when people stood up, as if they all had news for her.

"I hate hospitals," I said.

She turned, startled, though I'd been careful not to speak loudly. She said my name and for a moment seemed confused. "It's hard to believe you're so young." Then she looked out at the wide, doorless exit to the bright hallway. "Can I take you somewhere?"

she said. Admittedly I was unnerved, and I asked if she wanted to finish her coffee first.

"You're very protective," she said.

"What do you mean?"

"With the customer. You helped him sit down. You asked if he wanted water. How many guys were out there—five or six? And nobody else thought to help him."

I sat back a moment. I was receiving images and sounds from the past hour as if they'd happened to me years ago. Yes, the gearheads weren't worth a damn. I'd brought the customer a folding chair after he'd just watched his engine disfigure Ray, but I didn't remember asking him anything.

"The last time I was here I was in labor," Mary Ann said. "And I was thinking just now that I couldn't see his face. He crowned . . . they have a mirror on the ceiling, but he wasn't looking up. He was facing Nick. And then Nick said he was beautiful, and I started crying, and that just tightened everything up and out he shot, the rest of him, in one push. A fastball, Dr. Field said." She smiled and touched her cheek where it was suddenly wet. "God, am I crying?" She dabbed napkins at her face. She seemed nervous and a little embarrassed, and I tried with my own smile to ease her worry.

In the maternity ward I shuffled beside her, ready to turn back at her first hesitation, but with her arms folded tight against her ribs, turning at every sound, she pressed on. The long window was coming up, and suddenly I remembered Nick asking one of the ambulance drivers which hospital Ray was going to. I'd expected Nick to take the bag from my shaking hand and follow them, but then he asked Mary Ann to drive me. In the middle of everything—Ray had just been loaded up, the customer was crumpled over holding his pale face in his hands—Nick had taken the time to find out what hospital, when Mary Ann could have asked, or I could have. There were three hospitals in Waterbury, and now I tried to understand what possible reason he could have for letting her go to the one where only a year before she'd given birth to Joey. There were no good answers.

Seeing the babies through the fingerprinted window, she was teary and laughing. I thought of April, how before she could speak she seemed to pulse with all she couldn't say, as Mary Ann seemed to pulse now in her urgency.

I looked in. Some of the babies were black and some were white, but they all had the same big eyes, the slits too long on the sleeping ones. Their heads were half-deflated balloons and you couldn't tell what final shape they'd take. They were girls and boys only by the colors of their hats, wrapped like burritos up to their necks, eight of them, most sleeping, one crying, one who seemed to have perfect vision as he watched his quivering hand.

Mary Ann pulled me close, her fisting hand untucking my shirt at the side. I remembered looking in April's window at Mercy four years ago and making my melodramatic fourteen-year-old's promises to stand in as April's father. Their needs were enormous and dire. Take care of us, they said.

A large black woman in teddy bear scrubs came down the hall reading a clipboard. Mary Ann let go of me and pushed back from the window. The woman saw us over her glasses. "Girl?" she said. She opened her arms as Mary Ann stepped toward her. "I thought I told you the rules in here," the nurse said as they hugged. "You bring that baby when you come by."

"He's with a sitter," Mary Ann said, in a voice so even it shocked me.

"Well, go get him," she said. "I can wait."

Mary Ann laughed, or tried to, and I looked down and stared hard at the floor. "We're visiting a friend," she said.

"How old now?" the nurse said.

"One. He just had a birthday."

"Nick and Mary Ann," the nurse said, remembering their names, and then looked at me. "Oh, that Nick," she said. "Had to be right up in her business. 'What's this, what's that?' Dr. Field said one more time and out. Lord, I never seen her threaten before."

After the doors closed on the elevator and Mary Ann and I were being pulled up to a random number I'd pushed, she released a pent-up breath and shuddered. "God, it felt true," she said. Then she turned and lurched and for a second time in as many weeks she cried in my arms.

On the seventh floor she held on to me, and we walked like we were just learning to walk, like the spinal cord patients in rehab, up to a wall of glass that gave us the Union Clock Tower against the hills of nowhere towns like mine, and it was there in that ginger dusky light that she looked up at me as if I were someone she could love.

When we finally got in to see him, Ray was weak and giggling. He wanted me to throw one of his nitroglycerine pills at the wall to see what would happen. His ex-wife had arrived, a thin woman with a small lined mouth that looked angry even when she smiled. She went out to "have one" as soon as we got there.

More drugs kicked in and Ray looked peaceful, like he was going to die, though the doctor had assured us that he wouldn't. He was plugged into an oscilloscope whose screen wasn't a whole lot different from the one we used for cars, but with only one blip instead of eight. I realized that he had never panicked, even when he was on his back on the cold concrete, the blood pooling, his heart shorting out. This was, I could determine now that the scare was over, the way a man ought to die—without fear or complaint.

"Hey, toots," Ray said to Mary Ann. "You been crying?"

"She was worried about you," I said.

Ray grinned and said, "Listen. You know what that Saint Peter's telling God right now?"

"Keep him alive?" I said.

"He knows I get up there, I'll just raise hell and kick a chunk under it."

Mary Ann smiled and rubbed my back, and Ray looked at the two of us together with a Buddha smile, as if he knew everything was going to turn out all right. "Except for this, I notice you been happier," he said. And then he looked at me. "Kid, they got a 7-Eleven down the street. Go get me a can of Kodiak. Wallet's in that drawer."

"I got it," I said.

He looked at Mary Ann. "No smoking, the fuckers," he said. "They never heard of cold turkey making you have a heart attack? I seen it happen."

When I got back with the snuff he was asleep. Mary Ann stood at the window, looking out at a glass building glazed with the lowering sun. Ray's ex-wife was watching Phil Donahue and I gave her the snuff as Mary Ann got her purse. She was smiling as she walked up to me.

"What'd he say?"

"Good things about you," she said.

17.

WE PICKED UP CHINESE BUT FORGOT TO GET MY CAR, NOT because we were talking but because we were thinking, at least I assume she was, both of us smoking quietly in her Malibu as a low sun melted between buildings. At a vague point in the afternoon, or at several vague points, I'd gone from feeling shocked by her affection to feeling entitled to it. Now I was conflicted when a guy across from us at a stoplight, who at first looked to be admiring her car, tapped his horn and blew her a kiss.

"God, grow up," she said, and as I was clenching from the disrespect it showed me—I was her husband for all he knew—Mary Ann reached over the shifter and took my hand.

"You okay?" I said.

She nodded but took a moment to speak. "Right after he was born, he was so fragile. I used to think sometimes, 'What if?' It's hard to trust their little bodies to keep running. If it happened, I knew I'd never, ever get over it. And then it was like that, but after I don't know, a month, two months, you start being the same as you were before. Eating the same food, laughing at the same things." She turned into the driveway and parked behind Nick's El Camino.

"It seems like it didn't happen. You're the same and you don't know why."

"It makes sense."

"But Nick isn't the same," she said. She smoothed two fingers over her bottom lip as she stared up at the house.

In the kitchen Nick sat across from me at the tan Formica table, his head framed by the doorway to the room in which, on the braided rug, I had given Mary Ann the first orgasm I had ever given anyone other than myself, a moment I never fully stopped thinking about. Though I should have been starving I could only stab at water chestnuts with my rubber-banded chopsticks. It was a warm evening and the windows were open, the night breeze thinning out the house smells, which were mainly the wheat smell of hardwood floor and the faint, foreign perfume of Mary Ann's aroma oils.

"He was all right until the ambulance left," Nick said, telling about the Mustang's owner as he turned lo mein noodles on a fork like spaghetti. "I don't know what happened. Soon as it got quiet he sort of collapsed. I almost called nine-one-one again."

"He didn't expect to see that," Mary Ann said.

"On top of a refund I gave him fifty for the pants."

Mary Ann let go of her fork and laughed bitterly. "Who cares about pants? Who would give a fuck about pants?"

"Another reason I don't like them out in the bays."

"What happened after that? After he fell?"

"We got him up," he said. "Bobby sat with him until he could drive."

"Bobby."

Nick sighed and looked at the tabletop. "I was busy."

As Mary Ann stared at him, I felt myself dissolve from their awareness until I was afraid of what I might bear witness to. "I want to know something," she said.

Nick sat back from the table, away from her.

"Tell me exactly what you felt today," she said. He said nothing, and after a moment she leaned forward with such urgency I thought she was getting up. "Tell me. Just say it. Pity? Compassion? What? Annoyance? Don't think. Just say what you felt."

"You weren't there," Nick said. "Maybe if you were, everything would've been different, but you weren't." His voice remained steady and without heat. It was the indifferent tone my father used when my mother tried to guilt-trip him. Nick's marriage was over, I saw that now, and through no fault of my own. But I was all for letting it die quietly. I hoped that Mary Ann wouldn't say anything else.

Nick pushed his bowl away and got his cigarettes and a saucer from the middle of the table.

"It's like there's something missing in you," she said. "Compassion? Is that it?"

By now I was holding my breath, hoping the evening would mark the end of their time and the beginning of ours—mine and Mary Ann's. But I wanted it to come gradually, predictably. That seemed within reach, and the words I said to Mary Ann in my mind were these: Lay off a little. You don't have to fix him anymore.

"You never talk about it, Nick," she said. "Is that supposed to be macho? Because I think you're just scared. It hurts and you're afraid to say it. That's really sad. It's pathetic. You're pathetic." And out of nowhere she was the outraged woman I was afraid she'd become looking at all those healthy babies behind the glass.

Nick had one hand opened on the tabletop as the other flicked ash onto the saucer. He sat crooked and tapped the cigarette filter like a machine on a slow cog.

"Tell him what you would have done," Mary Ann said.

I looked up. How long had she been watching me? How long had I been commiserating with Nick?

"Me?"

"After you got him a chair. After you showed him that amount of pity. If you stayed instead of Nick—tell him."

Nick wouldn't look at either of us, and I tried to force any words that would come. But after a moment, Mary Ann knew I had nothing to wait around for. She stood from her chair and walked out of the kitchen to rooms at the back of the house.

I poked at a tiny corn on the cob with the chopsticks, and after a few minutes Nick mashed out his cigarette. "They give him any kind of prognosis?"

"He'll be okay," I said. "He doesn't think he wants to come back to work."

"I was scooping meat out of a radiator," he said, "is why I didn't go sit with the guy. I wasn't going to make Bobby do it."

Earlier I'd planned on Mary Ann taking me back to my car, but she never came out of the bedroom, and so it was Nick who drove me in his El Camino. "You think anybody's at Wickersham's?" he said as he pulled in behind my Nova.

It was summer, and the chances were someone would be out even when it wasn't Saturday, but I told him probably not. He nodded gravely and stared off, but he perked up when I reached for the door handle. "You feel like going for a drive?" he said.

"I'm pretty wiped out." I wanted to be in my room, where I could turn off the light and think about what had happened in the past four hours, just play it all from the beginning.

"I didn't know if you wanted to talk," he said. "I talk better when I'm driving." He leaned forward and closed his eyes. "There's that skip," he said. "You feel it?"

"I don't want to talk about cars."

Nick settled back into his seat, staring at the gauges. After a time he said, "I wish I knew what to say to her. I don't ever know what she's thinking."

"Why did you ask her to go to the hospital?"

"You weren't in any shape to drive," he said. "Bobby and I had the car to clean up. I figured, as long as it wasn't where they took Joey. The one with the morgue."

I was stunned for a moment. This hadn't crossed my mind, and it redeemed him at least from the worst thoughts I'd had—that he was motivated for some reason to hurt her. "They can be pretty hard to talk to," I offered. "Women."

"You know, I never had steady girlfriends," he said. "All through high school. I couldn't ever figure out what to say. Nobody taught me. My old man used to polish valves at the dinner table. Carburetors, shit everywhere. I got on the school bus smelling like gas. Nick-oline, they called me. I knew car talk, but there's a lot better talk."

"So start now," I said, meaning talk to Mary Ann, but then meaning—no, find someone else. Start over.

"Yeah," he said, far away. "Yeah."

I reached for the second window crank El Caminos have, the one that opened the triangle vent. "Mary Ann saw the babies," I said, watching the little window open. "In the maternity. That's part of why she's upset."

When Nick turned to me, I wasn't ready to see such a look of concern, and after a long indecipherable moment he opened his door and got out.

He had the hood up by the time I came around the front. Using the fender as a pillow, he reached over the engine—only a 327 (Bobby had likened it to Hendrix playing acoustic) but a perfectly tuned four-bolt 327. The fan pushed back his hair, and closing his eyes he turned the mixture screw until the idle imbalance, so minuscule you didn't notice it until he fixed it, had smoothed. Afterward, he clung on to the air cleaner as if it was giving him something necessary to his life and he couldn't unplug himself from it yet.

I was so used to seeing him in this exact pose, listening for the soft personal voice of an engine, that it surprised me when he opened his eyes and turned, not looking at my face but looking to see that I was there. And if he was going to kill himself he would do it by lunging into a radiator fan, throwing himself into the very machine that called to him. It was like Russian roulette, his face so close to the fan blades—I went around and shut the engine off.

"I can feel him cold," Nick said. He was on his knees with his chin on the fender, as if in prayer to the tremendous achievement of the engine, and crouching over him I tried to absorb every sound he made. What I managed to understand was that he had been plagued by bad dreams the night Joey died. Something compelled him upstairs, and in the still light of dawn he leaned over the crib rail.

"But babies in China never get it," he said.

"Never get what?"

"Hardly ever, compared to here. It's in a magazine I didn't read until after. They sleep on their backs in China. They don't die in their sleep. Here, they think they'll choke on spit up, but no. They turn their heads. It's instinct. I never put him on his back." His voice made a tinny echo against the underside of the hood and the firewall.

"Nick, my little sister slept on her stomach. That's not why. Doctors don't even know why." I put my hand over his hand. There was no bone or knuckle, only the relaxed padding of muscle under skin as rough as cinder block. If he felt my touch there was no sign.

"In *Scientific American*. Right next to the couch. Two weeks it sat there waiting to get read." He pulled his hand from under mine and reached over now, as if the magazine were on the fender, and I was terrified.

He sniffed, and then he shifted his legs, swinging around and off the fender, and his knees clicked. He stood on the pavement, his thick hair parting in the warm night breeze, and he lifted his face a little into it, looking up at the night sky behind me, sky that must've been as low and starless as the sky I could see.

18.

I MIXED MYSELF A TANQUERAY AND TONIC, A STRONG ONE, AND turned on Nickelodeon for April. Then I joined Mom outside on a gift of an August evening, seventy-eight degrees by the ladybug thermometer, with a dry gentle easterly breeze. Mom was stretched out on a strap vinyl lounge chair, soaking up the late sun in a faded Tigger shirt from one of our old Christmas vacations to Orlando.

Allowing me to drink at home was in accordance with an unspoken agreement that I wouldn't add to her stress with my problems, and she wouldn't add to my insecurities by trying to be a father to me. She first let me mix her a drink when I was sixteen, and eventually I was tasting them to make sure the blend was right. A month before my high school graduation I asked if I could mix myself a weak one. By then she was trying to extract herself from Lou Costa, and her resistance was low. "Promise me you won't drive," she said, "and I mean promise."

Our relationship had since chilled to one centered on respect and the right to privacy, but sometimes on these gin-softened afternoons, we talked like old friends. April couldn't work the safety knob on the kitchen door, and on the back deck we'd drink and smoke cigarettes, trading confessions, and sometimes in the morning, a little hung over, we'd be shy with each other after the things we'd said.

"I go in the ladies' room in the Sunday school building," she'd told me. "They have AA out there, and you can hear right through the wall. 'I'm so-and-so, and it's been fifty-two days.' They all sound older. Drinking for twenty-five years, thirty years. And I'm thinking how late I got started. In my thirties, my *late* thirties. But how many times have I quit? I mean, which reset is going to be the real one? I know I'm getting pretty sick of it."

Then I'd said something like, "Junior year, this guy in homeroom wanted to kick my ass. I had to wait by the flagpole until Mrs. Bannister pulled in, and then talk to her about watercolors because she was a painter. I had to pretend I painted just so we could walk into homeroom together."

On this mild August evening, she told me that Costa had come by in his cruiser, and she had hidden with April in the basement. "He went around back and looked in the windows, can you believe that?" she said. "I tried to make it a game with April, but I know she had to be terrified. I just wasn't in the mood for him today. He's like something—sticky. Did you ever lead a girl on? I'm kidding. You wouldn't do that. I know I get what I deserve."

I was more embarrassed than I should have been to hear her belittle herself, but I waited to see that she was done before I changed the subject.

"So Don wants to start having lunch with me."

"He told me that. Are you?"

"I don't know. Maybe just phone calls. I don't want him coming to Waterbury."

After a moment she sighed and looked uninterested, though there was a hint of effort, a tightening in her jaw. "I know he hopes you'll forget what he put you through the last five years. He thinks he's smart and the world's stupid. Same old Don."

As I watched her drink, I remembered growing up, seeing Don many times with a drink in his hand—at publishing parties or the

Milford Yacht Club, where we had dinner most Saturday nights— and seeing him walk away from a half-full glass, something that didn't seem strange until I started drinking myself. I had never seen him drunk. I often wondered if Mom was only trying to be like him in the beginning, before the Tanqueray in half gallons.

She was only forty-one and still pretty with her feathered hair-style and turquoise earrings a shade lighter than her eyes. Her skin was shiny and red from the sun. Tonight she reminded me of when I was twelve and all the guys at school had a crush on her.

"What if we had someone come over to help out with April?" I said. The idea had been taking shape ever since I saw Mary Ann watching the babies, and now with the gin and the coppery light, it all came together as a plan.

"Honey, I can't even pay you to watch her."

"Somebody I know might do it for free. She's a friend."

"She?"

I felt my cheeks warm. Kimberly had never wanted to come to my house, and I never pushed her to—I imagined her uneasy and guarded while Mom made small talk. Mom always did me the fa-vor of never asking why I didn't have girlfriends.

"A friend of ours?"

"Just mine," I said, and then I should've kept talking. She was three or four drinks in and mistrustful. After watching me for some time she said, "Do people think I'm unfit to watch her? Is that it?"

"Nobody thinks that, Mom. It's just if you needed a break."

"Are they starting a charity?"

"It would help her, too," I said. "My friend." I hadn't planned to, but I told her Mary Ann had lost her baby and her husband was leaving her. And I didn't say more but let the implication stand that friend was a euphemism for lover.

"That poor woman," Mom said. "Does she drink?"

"Not really."

"That poor woman," she said again. She looked at the glass in her hand and set it down. "God knows I could use some time."

I went in to check on April, who was dancing around she had to go potty so bad. She didn't want to miss her show. "Go," I said in a booming voice I hated to use on her.

When I came back out, Mom was leaning forward watching hummingbirds needle into her hanging fuchsias. She looked at me for a few moments in such a way that I expected her to say she loved me, but instead she said, "Don't be a drunk, Justin."

"You're not a drunk," I said, and it was hard not to look away, because I was starting to feel above her, my own mother. When she was still married to Don and happy, she would talk me down from my hormonal rages with patience and reason. Now I didn't want her to think I was better than she was, and I sure as hell didn't want to *be* better than she was. Yet I couldn't say that Mary Ann and I were . . . I didn't even have a word to use in my mind. Dating? Involved? It wasn't that Mom cared what people might say about seeing me in the yard with an older woman. She was too busy working and watching April and trying to replace Don to ever care what anyone said. It wasn't her, it was me. I wanted to feel proud, but I didn't know how.

"You get a few afternoons like these," she said, "with the sky and the honeysuckle, and you think it'll be this way every time. But mostly it's just getting dizzy, and then sick and ashamed, and suddenly you have the whole morning to get through. That's the worst part. You remember how much I used to love mornings?"

I did remember. She'd run seven miles of beaches, Oyster River to Fort Trumbull and back, before I sat down to breakfast. Alternating weeks teaching aerobics at dawn. The Milford Marathon.

Suddenly she went to the railing and threw the glass over the fence into the clumpy wetlands. "I don't know if that's it," she said, "but I hope that's it."

"It's a good start," I said.

She smiled and went in the house, coming back out in a minute with the quarter-bottle of gin, some vodka, two wine coolers from the fridge, even the sherry she used for cooking. They all went over the fence. The airplane bottles from her purse I side-armed for distance, little spinning blurs, and when I brought out the big unopened bottle of Tanqueray from the pantry she said, "Hey, I can return that. Let's not get crazy."

19.

AT THE END OF THE WEEK A NEW SIGN HUNG IN THE LOBBY.
NO CUSTOMERS ALLOWED IN BAYS WITHOUT A TECHNICIAN. I went
out to share the good news with Bobby, who was depressed over a
dumb thing he'd done to keep his ex-girlfriend from taking him
to court. Expecting a pay raise in Miami, he'd promised in writing to increase his child support by three hundred dollars, starting
in October.

I told him to go out and read the sign, but when he came back,
holding a fresh coffee and smoking a fresh cigarette, I had to stop
him from just walking right past me.

"They can't come out in bays anymore," I said. "Fucking righteous."

He turned and leered at me. "So all of a sudden we're technicians," he said.

Mechanics from all over the state and into Massachusetts applied
for Ray's old job, and Nick interviewed the gearheads one at a
time back in his office. Bobby and I were swamped. Over fender
mats we held sandwiches in black fingers (I missed the mind-

balancing spell of a good hot hand washing). What I saw of Mary Ann was only in glimpses when I dashed to the lobby for coffee. She'd be standing behind the counter cashing out a customer or explaining a line on a job application.

The gearheads' boycott of Out of the Hole began with conversations like this: "How many guys named Rod you ever heard of that wasn't queer?"

"I guess he went to car school."

"Nick can fuck himself if that's who he's going to hire."

And in the space of a week all of Nick's disciples abandoned him.

Rod Thibodeaux was an APEX tech school graduate with experience in computer engine controls. He was between Bobby and me in age and taller than the six-foot booms of the oscilloscopes, but he couldn't have weighed more than a hundred and fifty, his long forearms flat and square as two-by-fours. He had a twangy drawl that was sort of southern hippie. "*Jew*-ly," he said for July, "*Mun*-roe," the Louisiana town he was from. Instead of "hi" he said "hey now."

The first job he pulled in was a late-model Pontiac Fiero, a low two-seater he had to unfold himself out of. I strolled over behind Bobby.

"I dig them tats," Rod said to him.

Bobby turned his arm to show the full sleeve. The central character was a biker riding through a desert between cow skulls and rattlesnakes, and a cougar that seemed to be racing the chopper into the sun.

I read over the work order for the Fiero. "It's only an eighty-four. Why doesn't he go back to the dealer?"

"Over on mileage," Rod said.

Bobby looked at the complaint. "Intermittent stall," he said. He turned his face down to the engine and flattened his lips.

"Bobby," I said, thinking he might spit on it. I must've sounded urgent, and he watched me for a second after I told him never mind. "Has to be some kind of computer fuckup, right?" he said to Rod.

"That'd be my guess," Rod said.

"I mean, before computers, I never even heard of 'intermittent.'"

That was almost true. Occasionally we'd get a muscle car in with, say, a cracked distributor that only misfired when it rained or a wire that contacted a ground over bumps, but, in general, mechanical systems either worked or they didn't.

"Once in a while you get a guy," Bobby said, speaking to the engine it seemed, "milking the warranty, trying to make shit up. 'It's not doing it now, but every couple days . . .' Them cars I don't even bother pulling in. 'Come back when it's happening.' But now, with computers, who the hell knows?"

If he hadn't been staring hatefully at the engine, Bobby would have seen how indifferent Rod looked, his arms loosely folded, his attention half on Bobby and half on traffic at the intersection. It didn't seem right that upon meeting senior employees, whose house he was in, Rod wouldn't be a little more obliging and eager to make friends. I thought of how wildly earnest I had been in my first weeks here. My first months.

Rod turned to me unexpectedly and said, "Give that mass air flow sensor a knock for me, would you?" I looked at the idling engine and adjusted the fender mat where the corner had folded over, anything to buy time, glancing sideways at Rod, who I knew was testing me. Bobby cut in, "I can give you a little ass air flow," and Rod chuckled and pointed to where the sensor was on the intake hose. I gave it a hard rap with my knuckles, and the car stalled.

"Bing-o was his name-o," Rod said. "They short out right around fifty thousand. I just made ten bucks commish for five minutes' work. That's two a minute, if my math's any good."

"He got you on commission already?" Bobby said.

"I don't take a job without it." Rod started the car again and went up to the scope, where he looked at the emissions readings and started a cylinder balance.

With my brows up, I looked at Bobby—see? computer jobs make money—and he frowned. "Swapping pieces of plastic." He looked at what Rod was doing. "It's the wave of the future, I guess," he said. "Computers telling motors what to do."

"Engines," Rod said. "Motors are electric." He pushed the KV button and looked at one of the hanging leads. "I like Sun Scopes better," he said. "These here, you can't even interface."

There was a big uncertain moment before Bobby sighed, finally, and said, "Just came over to say hey."

"Right on," Rod said. Bobby held out his pack of cigarettes, but Rod shook his head. "Long story," he said. "I'm an alcoholic. Trying not to be, I mean."

"It's a cigarette," Bobby said.

"I light that, next thing I'll be on a packy run. No thanks, friend. You can keep it."

Two days later I was ditching behind oscilloscopes to avoid him. Not only was he overbearing, but there were tendencies toward exaggeration and self-promotion that went against my idea of mechanics or men, but his skill under the hood gave me an opportunity. When I had asked Mary Ann if she could babysit April, I told her I could help cover the counter, since Rod was turning over jobs at least twice as fast as Ray, and there were more breaks for me. I found myself speaking rapidly, nervously, and when I was finished she seemed not to have heard, looking up from a stack of checks and smiling as you do when you're pretending to understand a foreigner.

"Thank you," she said. "I have to think about it."

But the next morning she called me at home and said she would love to watch April. I fell into a kitchen chair and started to laugh, and then she asked what I was doing today, what my plans were, if we could meet somewhere in the country.

"Great," I said. "It's supposed to be hot."

"Then maybe we could swim."

There were two popular lakes in Levi, with beaches and rope swings and fire pits, that I'd explored in the early spring when kids from school weren't around. Most of my swimming I did from a blow-up mattress on a mile float down the Pomperaug. Occasionally there were trout fishermen running spoons through the nervous water on the upper stretch, but farther down, between wooded banks that bordered soybean and alfalfa fields, I was certain enough of my privacy to jump naked into the pools. I could live in my fantasies in that slow-winding isolation, the still water amplifying sound so that even my foot splashes would surprise me. In places where the river got wide it smelled like a sweating body and drying mud and even like the little rainbow trout they stocked every spring. The deeper water had its own cool mineral smell, and I'd pass through bands of honeysuckle that sent me into spinning dreams of love and sex.

At the end of the float was a bedrock shelf hanging ten feet over the water. Two years ago, the summer before junior year, I spent a solid month under the shelf dredging leaves and muck and pea gravel, wrestling pillow-sized rocks off the bottom for a dam I made on the downstream rim. When I needed more rocks to fill in the spaces I took them from one of the mossy stone walls you find in the hardwood forests of northern Connecticut—two or three feet high, perhaps dating back to little Pilgrim neighborhoods. When my work was done I had a chest-deep pool, into which I could jump from the ledge and lightly tap the bottom with my heels.

I hadn't been there in more than a year, and that morning the path from Skunk Hollow Road was wider than I'd remembered. Knobby tire tracks had ripped through the carpet of plant life to the rocky dirt, and at the end of it the shelf was littered with hook wrappers, Styrofoam worm cups, webs of monofilament, cigarette boxes, candy wrappers, beer cans and tins of Copenhagen snuff, a little fire pit full of all matter of half-burned crap. I didn't have a trash bag with me, so I ran armloads into the woods and made a heap behind a rotting stump. It took more than an hour to get it like I wanted, and then I had to haul ass to the Levi Shopping Plaza, where Mary Ann was parked in front of Harrison's Hardware, having a cigarette in the shade of an ornamental tree.

"Are we calling this our first date?" she said, riding in the passenger seat of my Nova.

I was smiling and dumbstruck with such a wholesome idea as a first date, after what we'd done in her kitchen and up in Holy Land. But later, as I parked along the gravel shoulder, I thought, Why not? Why couldn't we fall in love in the right order like everyone else?

On the river path we walked by a patch of Queen Anne's lace where I'd missed two Coors cans. "So it's not spectacular or anything," I said. But she stopped to hum a few gratified notes where there was a break in the woods and you could see water. As she walked ahead of me, her thighs shook in the firm way muscle does, and her smooth calves tightened and loosened. Kimberly had been out of shape at sixteen, and here was a woman almost twice her age who looked better naked than clothed. Her breasts were soft from nursing, but from the stomach down she could have been in a centerfold.

Where the path widened, she waited for me to walk beside her. "It wasn't fair at the house the other night," she said. "I don't know what was wrong with me."

"I wasn't sure what to say."

"You're his friend. I remember what that feels like."

"He ought to talk to you more," I said, but it came out mumbled, like a fast lie, only this wasn't a lie. It was just my first time talking about him behind his back.

"You don't have to take sides," she said. "You're not in the middle of anything." She smiled with dreamy sad eyes, eyes that contained the knowledge of past sadness like wisdom.

Our clearing over the water was framed by a mossy boulder and three crooked shagbarks. I smelled heat in the little breeze coming up from the fields. We had maybe an hour before the full sun, when even the scissored shade wouldn't be comfortable, and I spread the checkered blanket over the dry crumbling earth.

Mary Ann had scooped up some pebbles and was pitching them into the water one at a time—I could just hear their tiny chirps—and studying the effect. From the blanket I could see the part of the tea-colored water where every few seconds, after the last ripples had vanished, she'd toss another pebble.

"It's clean water," I said. "I wouldn't drink it, but cleaner than Waterbury, anyway."

"Where I put Joey reminds me of here."

I gave her a few moments and said, "In Oregon."

"Where the fall salmon spawn, the Chinook. But the ashes didn't float like I thought they would. They tumbled in the current. They parted around these big red fish and washed over the eggs."

There was nothing to say, and I found the wine in her canvas bag. Pinot Noir from the Russian River Valley, the label said. I wasn't great with a corkscrew and took my time to not go in at an angle. When I looked back again she had stepped to the ledge. In one continuous motion she pulled off shorts and panties and tank top, and I was staring at the pink memory of waistband around her hips as she tossed her clothes into the fiddleheads of a cinnamon fern. I hopped up and threw off my T-shirt, and there came a torturous second, as in a dream where you need to run but can't, when I knew what would happen but couldn't produce an action or a sound to prevent it, when time in fact stretched out so that I felt the first blanketing weight of mourning her death, her subtraction from my life.

The soles of her feet were pale angel wings as she dove where it wasn't safe to dive.

I slid down a side path, and when I got in the water she was already up and pushing back her hair. Two heavy, slimed-over branches caught on my rock dam had brought the water up a few inches, but it was only inches. She'd gone in at an unrepeatable angle, not perpendicular but severe enough to curve off the bottom without crashing her head into the gravel ledge. Inches.

In the water I pulled and pulled her slick against me, as if she were a ghost briefly materialized, and her surprise was just another strong emotion in the boil. I found her mouth and banged and slid over it with mine, and she kissed me with my hair in her fist. Water crashed up around us. "Yes," she said, the word of her wanting me to be unapologetic, unwavering, not as I'd been with anyone before. We broke from the kiss and my shorts were gone—ripped off by one of us or both of us, and sinking away, and my rude wanting was her wanting. It drove me past her consent to a burning feral intent that couldn't have been stopped.

On the blanket later, we sipped the peppery red wine from plastic champagne flutes. Only then, dripping and cool enough to huddle, did my heart return to any kind of normal beat. "I can't believe you dove."

She rubbed my knee and laughed. "I'm sorry I scared you."

"If you asked what the chances were of not breaking your neck, I'd say about ten to one."

"Is that true?"

"Roughly."

The hills we stared at were wimpy and lush with bent little hardwoods, nothing like the sheer cliffs and sky-scraping forests of Oregon, I figured, but she seemed genuinely captivated, glancing from canopy to canopy as if they weren't exactly the same.

She took a plastic knife from her bag and spread Brie onto a cracker. "One time I brought some home and forgot to tell Nick what it was. In the morning there was a spit-out bite of a bagel in the sink and a note that said, 'I threw out the cream cheese.'"

I liked that Nick already had the association of a mutual friend, and that the difference in our relationship to him was only that she had known him longer. I kissed her bare shoulder, thinking of those summer floats I couldn't enjoy all the way for feeling ashamed— holding my polyester trunks in my fist should I need to roll into the water and slip them on. We were naked on public property, which counted as a crime in Connecticut, but Mary Ann knew the higher laws that were nature's laws, maybe everyone in Oregon did, and to feel the moving water between your legs, and now the sunlight and the air, was to feel that we are a beautiful species and it was the world that was obscene for making us hide.

Moments before, the water cool on our stomachs and cold on our feet, the sand tapping our shins in the light current, she angled her lower body so that I was inside her with a squeaky-clean kind of friction, and with the sweet water on our lips we kissed more slowly. She gripped me as her hand had gripped me and told me not to move. To close my eyes and picture her all around me. "It's going to make me come," she had said.

Now she watched a contrail make its Etch A Sketch line up the sky. She had strong, high cheeks that were the Indian in her, her Jones—she'd told me that her Klamath grandmother had been instructed by a government agent to pull her last name out of a hat.

"Will she like me?" she said.

"April? Of course she will."

"And you think I'm ready?"

It hadn't occurred to me that she might not be ready, and I paused with a brief and unexpected protectiveness of April, feeling at the same time the sudden shock of Joey's death.

"Actually," she said, "I don't think I really can."

"Mary Ann."

"As far as time. It's probably not—"

"You're ready. You're perfect."

She closed her eyes a moment and breathed. Then she looked at me with pink swimmer's eyes and rested her chin on her pulled-up knees. With her freckles and no hairstyle and colorless lips, she could have been my age. This was the face she saw in the mirror after a shower, when she was the woman and the girl together. "Okay," she said. "Okay," and for a second I thought she might say she loved me. I felt my face flush, as if I'd already heard it and was only waiting on my voice to say it back. But she didn't say it, not in words, and instead she stood and walked to the ledge again. I didn't know what this meant, and the earlier panic of her dive rose in me, but she held her hand open behind her, a few shimmering water beads running down her back, her beautiful ass pink and creased from sitting. "Come jump with me," she said.

20.

AT LEAST ONCE A WEEK, NICK AND I RACED THE ZL-1 AT WICKER-
sham's. We staged undramatic upsets against cars that had been
exalted like royalty over fish sticks in the school cafeteria.

I kept my promise not to tell Mary Ann about the races, and
having secrets infused me with a self-possession that I imagined
important men had—senators, generals, technology engineers. It
was a man's burden to keep secrets. Though of course there was
the other secret, the cowardly one I still couldn't dare myself to
tell Nick. But I kept the truth from Mary Ann because she would
worry, and that she would worry made the racing dangerous,
though that was never how it felt with Nick behind the wheel.

From the Corvette's passenger seat, I only saw how strategi-
cally he drove. He'd lurch up to the back fender and fall back, then
pull even just before the end, so that every time it seemed he'd
won by dumb luck more than anything—a bad shift or an ex-
tended burnout by the other car. He got nowhere near red-lining
the Corvette—he didn't need to, was smart not to, though inside
I begged him to, just once, just once. There was no sense of chance
and thus no fear I felt, no adrenalized clenching or loss of spit,
because Nick drove without surprise, feeling the perimeter of the

Corvette as if it were an extension of his body, reading the minds of anyone who put up money against him, and surging not a second sooner than was required to win.

This is what I mean when I say reading their minds: Most races are won or lost in the first two seconds, when a novice might dump the clutch at too high an rpm and break the tires loose. This happened with a big Fairlane Cobra, as Nick knew it would. Of course he wasn't reading minds. He was just aware of how the kid revved the engine to clean the exhaust before the flag came down. Nick said to me, "He's going to fishtail," and then he launched us faster than he had before, faster than I knew the car was capable of launching—the front tires came fully off the ground and slammed back down after breathless floating seconds, when I saw that the Fairlane was not beside us, that its headlights were swinging through the corn, and I turned back to see the car's rear end in our lane, pulling out of a fishtail that would have sideswiped us had Nick not gotten the fuck out of there.

I understand now that my complacency was irrational. Anything can happen at a hundred and fifteen miles per hour on a dark, unpainted road barely wide enough for two cars, and once we crossed the finish line he had only seconds to let off and start feathering the brakes so that by the time we stopped there was maybe fifty feet before the road turned to gravel and swung up through the big hardwood trees. But Nick was in his element. Watching him behind the wheel of the Corvette was even more exhilarating and holy than watching him work. Rather than driving the car, Nick plugged in to it, an infinite mind to an invincible body, and I had been naïve before, scheming in my clumsy way to rescue his marriage, to think that I could know what would make him happy again.

With a lesser driver behind the wheel, the Corvette would have been a suicide machine. A rush to half-throttle in any gear would send the rear end fishtailing. And who wouldn't lose his shit when the tire grab lifted the front end right off the ground? The car was flashy, thundering, triumphant. It complemented Nick, picked up where the man fell short, and Nick, among all men, had the skill and discipline to be its master.

He never socialized for very long after the races, and I know he wasn't racing for the money. Nick made my cut half, and he didn't look at it more than to divvy up before cramming fifties and hundreds down in his front pocket like tissue he'd wiped his nose with. No, it wasn't fame or riches, but every few nights it seemed he was calling me up to go back.

It was the intoxication of those thirteen seconds, and the stunning release that came next. When we stopped he would let off a sigh that was the end of his reserve, and then he was free and boy-like again. His eyes pulsing, he'd slap me five then pound the steering wheel screaming, "You beast!"

After the races, I made it a point to stay close to Nick while he consoled the loser. But on the night of our fourth race, somebody called my name—three or four guys were facing us with their backs to the bonfire—and if I didn't go over they'd think I was afraid.

As luck would have it, it was Dave Bowers, one of the few respected kids who never taunted me at school. That night he asked me about work, and I took a chance and really told him. A valve job on a 413 Wedge, a rebuild on a giant 830 cfm Holley mounted to a Tunnel Ram. He took it all in, interrupting only with a breathy "Damn," and "Jeeze," and I felt safe shifting from engine specs to mechanic philosophy. "You've got the guy over here who has a big block but can't work on it. So okay, he can drive, maybe he even races it. But then you've got the mechanic, who can make a car go, and knows *why* it goes. He can see the valves open and close in his head. The power stroke, the crank whipping through the oil. He knows when something's off. He hears the car tell him what's wrong. Which one of them you think gets more out of driving?"

"Sort of like if you play guitar, you probably get more out of the radio," Dave said.

"Exactly."

I was so caught up in his being caught up that it took a while to notice Ed Rawley watching me from the other side of the fire. As soon as I saw him, I looked away, then heard "Hey Bailey," and ignored it. He said it again and I had to look at him.

"Costa still banging your mom?" he said.

"Rawley," Dave said, answering him before I could get my voice. "I heard your old man got loaded and ran into Jack Zimmer's kid."

"Zimmer's full of shit."

"Go tell him he's full of shit."

"Why? Where is he?"

"Up at Wickersham's," Dave said, nodding toward a floodlit outbuilding on the edge of the cornfield.

Rawley smiled and the guys got quiet, and then a six-foot board fell out of the fire and Rawley hopped up and stomped it out, laughing and cussing. But it wasn't a big deal, the ground was only mud and two other guys were closer. Rawley could have ignored it and said something back if he had something to say.

At the shop Bobby was suffering. He and Nick were drifting apart, as they had a year ago, but then it was different, there were no bad feelings between them, it was just that Nick was otherwise involved, and I didn't mind it then because the person he was involved with was me. But now Nick's preoccupation was Rod— Rod and his know-how with computers—and for Bobby it wasn't just that Nick had a new favorite, but that the shop was evolving. Bobby was still under the illusion, as Ray had been, that we somehow wouldn't have to adapt to the technology of the times.

Rod was a demoralizing omen for me as well, though not because he understood computers. I worried about his personality becoming a new paradigm. Mechanics could be daring and high-spirited as Bobby, confrontational and heedless as Ray, but they should never be self-important with their talents. Beyond his arrogance, I saw in Rod a tendency to recognize his own feelings and needs, which spoke to another unmanly quality of his character. He was uncool; I knew because every day for me was a battle with uncoolness. When Nick hired Rod over the dozens of good men who had applied, it undermined my conviction that mechanics shared a mystique anchored on self-possession and laid-back reticence.

Once in a while I'd see Bobby give up on a computer car. He wasn't as dramatic as Ray had been. Usually Bobby would just go over to the boom box and slam his head to a song from *Master of Puppets*, which he played ten times a day. I'd look through the *Chilton's* manual he was using, and pretty soon he'd wander back.

Once he yanked a wiring harness apart so hard its plastic clips went flying.

I straightened from the *Chilton's* manual. "They're a pain in the ass. But if you get the tip of a screwdriver right there in the seam—"

He went over and turned off the music. "What do the directions say now?"

"I'm not trying to be a dick."

"Just say what now before I sledgehammer the fucking thing."

My plan had been to ask if he could recommend a good AA meeting for Mom, but now I didn't want to piss him off. I was pretty sure that the problem with the car he was working on—the idle racing and the bucking—was the TPS, the throttle position sensor, but I pretended to be no further along in my diagnosis than he was.

Rod came over after a while and said, "Where y'at?" which was some kind of Cajun greeting, to which we were supposed to answer, "Ah-rite" but never did. Rod was one of those guys who are hard to like because he thoroughly and erroneously believed himself to *be* well-liked, and so unless you put in the effort to be blatant with your contempt, he would go right on thinking he was your friend.

"*Quid Aere Perennius?*" he said. "Man, is that a strange-ass motto." He poured Skittles in his hand from one of the pound bags that he said helped with his sugar craving from not drinking. He offered them around, and I betrayed myself and ate some.

"That your motto?" I said.

"Naw, man, it's yours. Waterbury's. You got it right on the back of the building there. Don't y'all ever look up?"

Bobby straightened from the opposite fender and lit a cigarette.

"In English," Rod said, "it goes, 'What is more lasting than brass?' And where's all the brass factories now? Ironic, ain't it?"

"'Dickis in the rectumis,'" Bobby said. "Go carve that somewhere."

Rod laughed and skimmed the work order for Bobby's car. "Sounds like a bad TPS," he said.

21.

A CAR SLOWED IN THE STREET. THROUGH THE LIVING ROOM WIN-
dow I heard but didn't see it, and though it could have been the
Brockmeiers, who we shared a driveway with, or someone visiting
them, I knew it was Mary Ann, I sensed it was her.

She was standing by her Malibu when I came out, and I could
tell already that she was less sure of herself. "It's cute. It's charm-
ing," she said, taking in our house, which was only a vinyl-sided
split-level with a black eagle on the screen door, red window shut-
ters, and a well house in the front yard painted to match. "Like a
Christmas-card house," she said. She reached in the car window
for her purse, her foot lifting out of a cork-soled sandal, her lightly
tanned leg bare up to the hem of a whitish-bluish tie-dye dress.
She came to me brushing the hair out of her eyes and then for a
moment didn't seem to know where to put her hand, and I knew
that I loved her, and loved her achingly, though I was afraid to say
it so soon.

Her arms under mine, we hugged with an urgency just shy of
pain. I lifted her and turned her most of a circle. When she laughed,
I felt it in my own chest.

Mom was washing a plate when we came into the kitchen.

Earlier she had changed into capri pants and a sleeveless button blouse, and though she looked ready for company, I was nervous about this first meeting. I wondered if they'd be able to talk at all, if Mom would feel daunted knowing that Mary Ann had lost her baby, and if Mary Ann would feel daunted knowing that Mom was only one week sober.

I missed my cue on the introductions. Mom was drying her hands, and there was this sweet awkward moment when Mary Ann said, "Hi, Mrs. Bailey," and waved from five feet away. But as if Mary Ann were every pretty girlfriend I'd never brought home, Mom instantly became the warm hostess she had been in our years with Don, turning a handshake into a hug as she told Mary Ann, "Carol, honey. I'm Carol." In five minutes she had brought up her own miscarriage, the baby who should have come between me and April, and both of them teary, they hugged again. But the pleasure of witnessing their bonding ended for me when I thought of the lie I'd told about Mary Ann's husband leaving her.

"It's almost quarter of, Mom," I said, and she went out to have a quick cigarette before a three o'clock AA meeting at Prince of Peace Lutheran.

"We call it quiet time," I said as Mary Ann followed me up the stairs. "It's not really a nap anymore." In the hall I walked lightly to April's door and put my ear to it. "Because lions start with L and turtle starts with T," she was saying musically. She liked to line up her stuffed animals across the floor.

When I put my hand on the knob, Mary Ann touched my elbow. "Aren't you going to knock?"

"She's four."

She smirked and reached around me to knock. "It's me," I said through the door.

April said, "Oh."

"Can I come in?"

When I pushed open the door, April, naked, hollered, "Ah," and ran into her closet.

"Where are your clothes?" I said. I wasn't mad—she did this a lot—and in fact I liked the chance to quell some drama in front of Mary Ann. I went to her closet, where she'd half-closed the door.

"In the hamper," she said. "It was too hot."

"It's not that hot up here."

She wanted me to dress her in the closet. When we finished I said, "Come meet somebody," and she held up her arms.

"Hold me."

Mary Ann was sitting on the floor behind a row of stuffed animals that reached from wall to wall. She looked up as she might have if April were our own daughter.

"Are all these alphabetical?" Mary Ann said.

April nodded, still facing away. "Even I put fish before fox."

"I am so impressed," Mary Ann said, and though it wasn't April's most impressive effort—the raccoon was behind the peacock, et cetera—I could tell that Mary Ann meant it. I sat with April on the floor.

"April, do you ever notice how dirty Justin's hands are?" Mary Ann said.

April turned around, and I showed her my hand, dirty certainly for an accountant or a cook, but the only way to get the black out of your knuckles and cuticles is to stay away from engines for a month.

"Maybe we should draw his hands," Mary Ann said. "Do you have paper and crayons?"

I set April down, and she brought over the spiral notebook from her bookshelf. "I can't have crayons in my room," she told Mary Ann. "I drawed on the wall one time."

Mary Ann found an eyeliner pencil in her purse, and they went to work tracing my hand. They made three sketches, which Mary Ann turned into porcupines and dinosaurs.

"April is a very pretty name," Mary Ann said. "Is that when your birthday is?"

"April sixth."

"Eighth," I said.

"Sixth."

"She likes to draw sixes," I said.

"Is I'm your favorite month?" April asked Mary Ann.

"Positively," Mary Ann said. She started tracing my hand again. "April, do you know what they put in makeup to make it shiny? It's really gross. They use bat poop."

"Eww," April said, and I jerked back my hand, but Mary Ann caught it. "Like it matters," she said. "Anyway, I think it's only in mascara."

22.

"TAKE IT, IT'S A GOOD DEAL." BOBBY AND ROD AT THE PEG HOOKS. "You work on new cars, give me the old ones."

"Plus you do all my oil changes," Rod said.

"Fuck you."

"You'll have to wine me and dine me first." Rod chewed a toothpick and seemed not to see the cold murder in Bobby's eyes. I would've offered to take on Bobby's computer jobs myself if they didn't hurt my daily commission, they took me so long to fix.

Later that morning Bobby knocked over a trash can backing a computer car into the oil-change bay.

I found Nick diagnosing a convertible and leaned over the fender opposite him.

"I think Rod could start showing Bobby some, I don't know, some compassion," I said.

Nick pressed his fingers against the valve cover, studying the vibration. "I never asked if he went to charm school."

I stood there a few more seconds, though that was all he had to say. Later I wondered if there was some resentment toward me in that answer. Maybe he thought I'd coerced him into telling me about Joey, and now he didn't like my having that secret.

I wandered over to the oil-change bay. Turning his cap back, Bobby brought his face up to the coil spring of the Grand National on the lift. He reached around the scorching manifold and flinched with the claustrophobia of plunging your arm to the hilt in a blind labyrinth of rusty metal, the scrape and the prickling coming right up through your spine. He swore as he contorted his body for leverage, twisting until a drizzle of black oil ran down from the loosened filter, and he jerked back his arm with two dull bumps of muscle and bone. I could see the red creases all the way down his forearm.

"Just don't open your face," he said to me.

"You shouldn't be doing his oil changes."

"I don't mess with microwaves or TV sets, either," he said. "You maybe got a brain that can handle invisible little pulses and flashes. I need to see it move."

"The needle on an ohmmeter moves."

"We did old school in here for three years. People clapping for us when the dyno goes up. Tipping us. We could retire on that if Nick gets right in his mind again."

"Bobby, how many hot rods are still going to be on the road in ten years?"

"Go on back wherever the fuck you were." He shoved his hand back up around the A-frame and spring. After a few seconds he yanked his arm back down, white where the scrapes were starting to bleed, holding a Fram filter that he turned in his fingers like a quarterback looking for the laces. Then he looked at me and side-armed the filter through the back window.

For the rest of the day, whenever I noticed the broken glass I looked over at Bobby and tried to think of a way to approach him. This is how I happened to catch him wiring a car.

We called it zapping, and what you did was cram some fourteen-gauge wire into the boot of an unhooked spark plug wire. You needed a spool long enough to run down under the engine so that your victim couldn't see the wire. Carefully you snaked it in through the passenger door and between the driver's seatback and seat with enough poking out for them to sit on. You cut off a few inches of insulation and splayed the wire threads until they were invisible on the seat.

Ray used to zap customers he didn't like. "Hop in and crank it for me, would you?" he'd say. Those eight thousand volts closed a loop between your ass and your fingers on the ignition key—I'd seen guys jump up and bash their skulls on the headliner. Whether getting zapped would be enough to cure Rod of his blindness, I couldn't say. By blindness I mean the way some people can't see who their enemies are. If you were to ask Rod what he thought of Bobby, I could hear him say, "Ah, he's all right. He gives me a little shit, and I give it right back."

At least Bobby might get something out of his system, I thought, as I got us a couple of coffees from the lobby and came out to watch. When I handed Bobby the coffee he said, "I need to check amps at the starter. Do me a favor and crank it over."

Hearing that was like a jump into ice water, but if he saw the color drain out of my face, Bobby gave no sign. I went around to the driver's door without feeling my feet touch the ground and sat on the wires. I owe him this, I thought, and I turned the key.

23.

IT WAS DURING UNEVENTFUL EVENINGS AT HOME THAT I FELL IN love the rest of the way. Mary Ann was coming over three days a week and staying through dinner. She cooked for me and came into my room, where no girlfriend had been before, with her smell and her soft voice, and looked at my posters and took down my books and beat me at Space Invaders on my little black-and-white TV.

"Where is he?" she said one evening, looking at a photo album page of me and Don.

"In New Haven. He's gay, now. He turned gay."

And oh, that it didn't matter. She had gay friends in Oregon, and of course it was there, in permissive Oregon, that someone like Mary Ann could ever happen.

She ordered a book from there and read it to April on the living room floor. "But why is he Bigfoot?" April said when she finished.

"Because he has great big ears like Dumbo."

"No," April barked.

"Because he has a nose like a beach ball?"

April begged her to read it again.

"Can Justin help?" Mary Ann said.

I lowered myself off the couch to the floor with them.

"Did I ever tell you that Nick used to hunt Bigfoot?" Mary Ann said.

"Nick?" I said. I nearly said, "*Our* Nick?"

"Not gun hunting," she said to April. "Picture hunting, like Toby in the book. He would hike way up into the Cascade Mountains."

"But who *is* Nick?" April said.

"He's my friend from Oregon, of course. And one day he asked me to go with him. How do you think that made me feel? I mean, should I be scared?"

"It wouldn't scare me," April said.

Mary Ann smiled. "I was excited."

I was, too, and not only because she'd called Nick just a friend. I liked to hear about her past. I wanted to go back with her, to the time before Waterbury and her short tragic motherhood, so I could fall in love with that Mary Ann, too.

"But then I thought of a really good prank," she continued.

"What's—"

"A little joke you play on someone," I said.

"I borrowed a tape player and made a recording of hitting logs together. Knock. Knock-knock. That sound."

April started to bang her feet against the coffee table. "I have a tape player!"

"Shh," I said. "Listen to the story."

"It's sort of the way Bigfeet use the telephone. Knock-knock-knock. So I recorded ten minutes of that. But I started after twenty minutes of blank tape so I could hide it in the woods and get away."

"Very smart," I said.

"Thank you. Then we hiked almost to the snowline and put up our tent. We found this little pond and sat there dressed up in camo waiting for a Bigfoot to come get a drink. But I guess he didn't want to be famous. He never showed up."

"But maybe they don't like ponds," April said.

Mary Ann took April's hand and kissed it on top. "So we got in our tent at night, and in our sleeping bags, and then I sat up and told him I had to go pee—"

"You pee-peed outside?" April looked shocked.

"Like you never have," I said.

"In the woods all there is is outside, but I didn't really have to pee. I started the tape recorder, and then—run, run, run—I got back in my sleeping bag. Pretty soon here it comes, knock-knock-knock. Nick jumps up but can't find his shoes. He had one of those giant Maglites that takes a hundred batteries, and it got left on, so he's trying to change the batteries in the pitch black. Meanwhile the tape recorder stops, and I mean you can't tell him it's just a joke, he's so excited now. He can't even cuss, he's so excited. He's saying, 'Oh come on, come on. Man, oh man,' dropping batteries everywhere."

"Why couldn't he cuss?" I said.

She looked at me. "Haven't you ever been like that? Something incredible happens and all you have are little-kid words again? I couldn't cuss at the end of my labor, and that was pain there isn't words for, and then you see this little cap of hair, and it's true. He's coming. Here he comes into the world."

April sat forward. "Who's coming?"

But Mary Ann was no longer with us. "Man, oh man," she said, gazing at a memory up on the ceiling.

24.

COMING BACK ONE EVENING FROM THE LAKE ON TRANSYLVANIA
Road (our one outing that failed—a skin of yellow pollen kept us
out of the water; Mary Ann got stung; April picked up a condom),
I stopped for gas at Arco, and as a consolation for a lame trip Mary
Ann took April inside for a Drumstick cone.

The lock on the pump handle didn't work, and I was bent over
the back bumper when a guy who'd once locked me in a corn silo
swung his monster GMC off Route 6 and skidded to a stop at the
pump opposite mine. "Bailey," he yelled down from his window.
He said a big-block Chevelle was coming out to Wickersham's
Saturday. "You guys could make some bank. He went for half a
grand with Kimball's old man."

I looked at the numbers on the pump and let go right at $9.98.
I had just a ten in my wallet. "Did he win?" I said, twitching in
the last two cents.

"Barely. And Kimball's old man drives like I fucking spit."

Eight or nine cars were on the edge of the strip, a few more lined
up in the field. We were waved to and I heard my name called like

a stadium chant, "Bail*ee*." In a few weeks, Nick and I had gone from being nobodies to being the home team.

Fireflies pulsed in the corn and Hank Williams Jr. sang about getting whiskey bent and hell bound. It was the first night there were girls, and the rich exhaust and cooked-tire smells were interrupted by the occasional perfume of tanned bodies passing by with cigarettes.

The Chevelle was a '70 with black SS stripes, five-spoke alloys, and a Cowl Induction hood. I couldn't believe the owner was sitting on the lacquer fender, a tall redhead standing between his legs. He was talking with a guy who wasn't very selective, who had even hung out with me a few times in the smoking area at school. When we got out of the Corvette the owner of the Chevelle bounded over to us with his hand out—Duane Pabst, from Torrington. He had a big handshake and sculpted arms that had to be the product of workout rooms with forty-five-pound plates and wall mirrors. He wore carpenter pants and a flannel shirt with the sleeves cut off, but he smelled like he was fresh out of the shower.

"Wrap your ass in fiberglass," he said, walking around the Corvette. "You got a big rat motor in that beast? No, don't tell me, don't tell me, keep it like poker. Maybe it's just a tuned-up mouse. I don't need to know."

I couldn't tell if the guy was on something. His bright teeth kept flashing, and he had these long dimples pleating his cheeks. "I can do a grand," he said to Nick. "You feel like doing a grand?"

I started over to conference with Nick, as we'd done before, to compare our vibes on the guy in private, but before I'd taken a full step toward him, Nick said, "Sure," and Pabst grinned and clapped his hands. "This shit is *on*."

It was agreed that Pabst and Nick would race alone, and when they walked over to the start line to give Motts their money, the redhead stood there by herself. The other girls didn't talk to her. She looked like a city girl, smoking her designer cigarette with one arm wrapped in front of her short biker jacket. I said hi and could tell she appreciated it.

But then I was called over to the keg, where I was handed a cup of foamy beer and someone asked if I'd had in any decent Mopars lately, and when I was going to try a run in my Nova, and somebody yelled my name, and I forgot all about keeping the redhead company.

It was like these guys had been my friends all along but I'd just misunderstood them. It was my own fault, all the surrendering—who could respect that? They wanted to see Pabst lose. What the fuck did he need a grand for? It turned out his family were the ones who brewed the Blue Ribbon beer.

And in a few minutes I was with Valerie Wilson, who I'd pined for more fanatically than any of the other top-tier girls in my class. Valerie had once written our names in a heart on a chalkboard in one of the Ag buildings, and for two days I tried to be where she was in the halls. Before I found out that the Justin she meant was a twenty-three-year-old house framer, I approached her in the cafeteria line, where she stood with two of her friends, big-haired untouchable girls like herself, and I chickened out so that all that happened thank God was a moment of awkward silence before I turned and heard behind me, "Ok*ay*," in a girl's heartless sarcasm.

"How's Waterbury?" Valerie said now. "I never go there, unfortunately."

I pulled out a piece of straw from the bale we were sitting on and dropped the names of a few bars I said I knew. Skinny's. The Shanghai. Hog Wild.

"God, I need an ID. Where do you even get one?"

I told her that Richie at Hog Wild would serve her, but I did have to warn her that it was a biker bar. "It can get kind of rough."

"It sounds like heaven compared to here." She gave a bleak glance at the fields, and in the same grim spirit she took my cigarette and brought it to that mouth that had never smiled at me before, leaving a lipstick print and giving it back, so that when I smoked it I was almost kissing her, and I had the impulse to put the filter in my pocket to keep, as I certainly would've done in high school.

"You know what I'm so sick of?" she said. "Everything all wet with dew. Stinking like bonfire and either sweating or freezing your ass off. Like in twenty years I'm going to wake up in this same freaking shithole. The only bar I've even ever been in is the Fireside." She reached down to slap a mosquito on her calf. "That's just like being here but without getting eaten alive."

Minutes later she was writing on a slip of paper, bent forward so that I could look straight in to where her breast lay in the formed pocket of her bra, I mean the whole thing I was looking at, its small spongy nipple the color of her lips (it would only occur to me later that she'd wanted me to see it, she spent so long writing her name and number), and I found my fingers cupping into the shape of her bra.

"Showtime," Pabst called from the road, and he and Nick got in their cars.

"You think Nick can beat him?" she said. She handed me, as if I'd asked for it, the folded slip of paper.

"We'll see," I said. "I don't know what he's running."

"A four fifty-four. My sister used to be friends with his sister."

I nodded. "It'll be close."

"L6 or something," she said.

I looked at her. "LS6?"

"Yeah, that's it," she said.

"Jesus." I started to get up to go tell Nick that he needed to race hard, but then he started the engine, and I hesitated. Maybe it was too late to run over there. Maybe Nick would hear, when Pabst did a hole shot to clean the tires, how little rpm was needed to break them loose, and he'd know. Or maybe I just wanted to see Nick finally lose, I can't say. I sat back down.

But after the race, when Pabst got out of his car at the far end of the strip, and the guys who'd called the finish came up around him, and I could hear yelling but not what was yelled, I was on my feet and running all-out, regretting that I'd let him race alone.

A quarter mile is a hell of a run when you're fired up, and by the time I got there I could only manage a fast panting walk, my lungs on fire.

"Son of a bitch is running nitrous," Pabst was saying. "What's out there can beat an LS6?"

"He don't have to show it, he don't want to," Burke said.

"Why can't he just open the hood? Make me a liar."

The guys around him—more had come over from where they'd watched the race halfway down—were shaking their heads and looking away, as if they'd already made their points.

Pabst looked at Nick. "The fuck you hiding, man?"

Nick could have looked around and seen that he had friends, but instead he stared at the pavement for a few seconds, and then he said, "Hell with it," and went back to the Corvette. When he opened the door, I thought he was getting in, and I started for the passenger side, but as the thought occurred to me that we hadn't been paid yet, he bent in and unlatched the hood.

Pabst came around the other side of the car as Nick lifted the hood from under the windshield—"Opens backwards," someone said—and Pabst ran to his Chevelle and came back with a flashlight. He searched the fuel and coolant lines, looking for a nitrous hose, and then he rested the beam on the open-element air cleaner. "The fuck is that?" he said. "What kind of race car engine you got in here?" He touched the screen over the carburetor throat.

"No blowers and no nitrous is the only rules," Burke said.

Motts came over finally with the money, and Pabst went up to him and said, "Here, gimme it back, just mine," instigating a shoving match. Three guys flew on Pabst, and more ran over. There was a shotgun suddenly, held by a guy I didn't know. He pumped it and a live shell flew out of the ejection port and hit me in the knee.

But that was the height of everything. In a few minutes Pabst got in his car and ran a hole shot that lasted almost the entire quarter mile, and he skidded to a sideways stop near the woman, who ran to the passenger door as if wolves were chasing her. Everyone was laughing and calling out, and the guy with the gun blasted orange thunder at the sky once before they told him to cut the shit, asshole, he was going to piss off Wickersham.

I could still smell the shotgun blast as Nick eased out onto 62, and I didn't trust myself to swallow, certain that even my own saliva could make me puke.

"He's either a cokehead trying to be a redneck, or the other way around," Nick said. "If he knew how to handle an LS6, it could have been interesting."

Nick was either simple or impossibly complex, I couldn't decide, dismissing Pabst like that, no concern that he might try to find us, tear us in half with all that muscle, no acknowledging the nightmare scenarios possible with a shotgun on the scene. But when I asked myself why I couldn't tell him about Mary Ann, Nick became complicated. I remembered running to save him—there were needles still in my lungs from having run so hard. Shouldn't we at least have full honesty between us? If only I could have predicted his reaction a little more. If only I knew him the way I wanted to.

With six or seven country miles to go, and riding with a man for whom the rumble of exhaust was more satisfying than any radio station, I breathed and tried to empty my mind. I put my hand on my stomach and focused on making the air come from the diaphragm instead of the chest.

"She's a good-looking gal," he said.

"Who?"

"The one you were talking to."

"I just knew her from school," I said, and the small loosening I'd been able to accomplish now tightened back.

"When I was your age, it was all hippie girls. In Oregon, anyway. They won't let you ever be quiet. They want to know where you're coming from. All the dope going around was supposed to open up everybody's mind, I guess."

I'd lived for moments like these, when something about my company allowed Nick to talk freely, but now I couldn't fully listen for thinking about Valerie. Without her here, without her fire-lit sandy hair and her Poison and her interest in me, I wondered what the hell I'd been doing. Given the opportunity, could I have betrayed Mary Ann?

"But man, you should have been around back then," he said. "It was the pinnacle of everything, right? That's the word. I'm thirteen when GTOs kick off the whole era. Then the Mustangs, Camaros, Chevelles. Super Cobra Jets are rolling off the lot when I'm your age. Hemis. LS6s. If the EPA never cracked down, we'd be living in a different world right now."

"How did you meet Mary Ann?"

He closed his mouth and laughed to himself. "She was broke down. She had this meat-grinder Bel Aire, three forty-eight with a Rochester. I mean, it had to be all the way gone through. I offered to. Free labor, just the cost of parts. But she wanted me to teach her so she could do it. She used to be into motors. Long time ago." He dropped his hand to the bottom of the wheel. "Long time ago," he said again.

"She wants kids," I said.

"She deserves kids, but I can't. I got the operation."

My pulse started to race. I wasn't going to act surprised. "Then why don't you get divorced?"

I braced for him to slam the brakes, but instead he began to nod. "Is she ready to?"

"How should I know?" It was a reflex answer, but after a second it was the only question I had for him. You know about us, Nick. Cut me loose. Tell me you know.

But his face stayed calm as he turned to look at me. "You two are friends," he said, following the road without watching. I looked ahead as headlights approached fast.

"Are you asking if you should get divorced? Watch the road."

The car passed with the sound of a small explosion. "She should," he said, and I leaned over. We were doing seventy. "She should want to," he said.

"It's thirty, coming up," I said. A station wagon appeared, and Nick passed it with a swerve out and back over the solid line, so fast the guy might've thought he'd imagined us. Then on a dotted-line straightaway he took on two cars with about thirty feet between them and a towering four-wheel-drive in the oncoming lane. I had no voice. Even the cars we were passing held down their horns, and the pickup we were about to hit head-on whaled what sounded like a semi horn, and I was suddenly not a part of this, removed by some kind of merciful disengagement I guess you're allowed right before you die.

I saw the tread pattern of the big truck's left tire as we veered back. The pain was in my fingers, both my hands buried under the seat into the springs, and then a big pulse of nothing when I let go before a different pain, a reversal of some kind in the nerves. I squashed my hands between my thighs as two miles flecked past, and then he let off the gas at the same second he cut the wheel all the way.

Another car would've rolled, but like a freefalling cat its belly stayed down, and we turned a screaming one-eighty in the shoulderless road, all the fluids in my body letting go of gravity as he slammed second gear, baking the tires to cushion the momentum swing. The car could've done it forever, fishtailing across the lanes until the gas was gone or the rubber melted off, but we didn't have forever because for all his flawless instinct of steering and acceleration, Nick couldn't see into the future, couldn't save us if a car appeared on the next rise.

I yelled his name, but only after it was too late to do anything— we rocketed over that rise in the wrong lane—did he let off the gas and shift.

For the next few miles he drove only twenty or so over the limit, and I took stock of my body, all the pounding happening inside it, trying to ease, ease, ease, and keep the breath going in and out and not cry. Nick finally turned on to a dead end shaped like a thermometer. Raised ranches were being built on either side, and there was a set-back farmhouse at the end, where he parked in front of a falling-down outbuilding of some kind. We were still three or four miles from the Arco station on Route 6, where the Nova was waiting.

He killed the engine and unwedged his cigarettes from under the emergency brake handle.

The minute that followed comes in strobe flashes. My feet are touching ground and the knowledge I am still alive and will keep living chills my lungs, I'm crawling on road sand, picking a rusted sheet metal screw from my palm, on my feet again. I can feel the howl in my throat. I'm at the outbuilding kicking a plank wall until my foot goes through, wrenching back the broken plank, the bent nails crying like small creatures until the plank breaks free.

A dog barks. At the glassless windows I'm knocking out wooden sashes with my bare hands.

"They're probably calling the cops," he says. I kick until something heavy falls over inside. The Corvette starts. I walk behind a construction site, cut across a back lawn.

On the long walk I tried to sift out fear from anger. Was it only the panic of a child whose father throws him into the air? Had I been safe all along—was Nick really that good? The great insect pulse of the fields at night helped me start to breathe all the way. I could feel the isolated soreness in my ankles and wrists, a stabbing in my right shoulder, as if I were waking from some violent episode of split personality, and I picked out splinters from my palm. In my mind I was asking Mary Ann to forgive me. If my love for her was stronger than Nick or Mom or Mary Ann herself had ever known—if it was real it should have made me resistant to temptation. I said the words, they hurt, but I said, Yes, I would've kissed

Valerie. I would've fucked her, and you deserve better. I'm so sorry.

The giant Arco sign was unlit when I crossed Route 6. Twenty feet from my car I saw the Corvette backed in on the other side of it, the driver's doors even, and Nick was watching me through his open window. I looked away instinctively, though for a moment I had to remember why I was mad at him.

It was strange that my door was locked. I'd been waiting a long time to be somebody whose car you didn't fuck with, and I had left my door unlocked on purpose. When I went in the glove box for my emergency cigarettes—I'd smoked my pack on the walk—I found folded in half on top of my registration papers a stack of hundred-dollar bills. Nick had locked my doors.

I sat back and opened the bills in my lap, five of them, half the money we had won.

I put down my window, either to tell him that I didn't want it or to thank him, I wasn't sure. Drab yellow in the cone of street-light, he smoked sedately, as if things were no different than when we'd gone to Wickersham's.

"You left her by herself on Joey's birthday," I said.

The cigarette dropped out of his fingers, and from where I was I could smell the carpet burn. I ran around and hopped in the other side, broke the orange head to ash on the passenger floor. Nick faced me with the steering wheel as his pillow, staring not at the gray mess on the carpet, which he seemed unaware of, or at me, but out through my window.

His eyes were wide, his mouth open. It was a look of fear and it made me uneasy. "I thought the rule was no smoking in here," I said. His eyes only shifted to me as if he'd forgotten I was there. "This was after," he said, his head never moving, as if someone were holding it like that against the steering wheel. "A couple days after."

He stopped, and I didn't give him more than a glance to say I was listening; in the body language of dropping my shoulders and sinking back into the seat I said, Take as long as you need.

"We didn't leave the house. It was . . . we couldn't even change clothes. Her sister was coming the next day. There was a bottle of wine in the pantry we opened. We sat at the table, and it all let up. It was like he was just upstairs again. How he used to make this one sound. You'd think, here comes his first word, he'd pull in all his breath and then, 'pwhat.' Just that 'pwhat,' every time."

A low hum rose in his throat, and twice, without heat, he beat his head against the top of the steering wheel. "We get in the shower together. We need one bad, it's been days. We wash our hair, get each other washed. And the water . . . I'm holding her. And I know what can fix us. It won't be so bad forever. Another baby. We can take care of him and be happy and live, a new baby, he can sleep with us always, I don't care, just keep him in the bed. Keep him safe.

"I take her in the bedroom. We're hugging, we're on the bed. Then she's . . . she stops kissing me. But we have to. We have to. She says, 'Stop.' She says, 'Don't.' But I do. I don't stop when she says." With a soft choking sound, Nick closed his eyes. "She's like she's dead under me. We have to, Mary Ann. We have to. Don't cry. Please." He sniffed deeply and swallowed. "And then she's laying there, not moving. She won't say if she's okay. She's staring at the door. What did I do? Jesus God. I pull the blanket over her. I go out in the garage and stay there all night. In the morning I hear her calling for me. She comes in the garage and calls me. She has to get her sister at the airport. She can't see me behind the boxes."

That was all he said, and I looked away when I was sure he was finished. I felt sore and tingling. I entered a brief fantasy of being there that night so I could pull him off of her. He slumped in the seat, his hands turned over on his thighs, a finger twitching in toward his palm. He stared through the windshield, though the thing he was seeing, that was making him look afraid, wasn't out-side—he was still in their bedroom with what he'd done. When I realized I could have forgiven him, I pushed myself out of the car.

I walked away with the sensation of emptying out and then refilling with hot, electric life. I started to run across the lot and then on the sidewalk. I was free of him, free of caring about him, and the shaking inside from before came back, and with it the cold-steel conviction that I never wanted to die or change.

25.

MOM WANTED TO DO SOBRIETY RIGHT, WITH TWELVE-STEP MEET-
ings and therapy, and some days she'd just drive up 91 to Massachusetts and southern Vermont, coming home with saltwater
taffy and maple syrup, a full roll of film and, I hoped, some
peace of mind. In the living room I'd look up from where April
and Mary Ann were doing puzzles or playing with resurrected
games that were interesting with a second person, and sometimes
I'd catch Mom brooding at the doorway. Her new freedom
seemed to have brought with it a sense of guilt, unfair regret
that she was more a guardian than a mother, making April dinner, folding her laundry, taking her places always with time as a
factor.

One night Lou Costa called again. "I hear you're turning
wrenches for Nick Campbell," he said. "What would he soak me
for a rebuild on the prowler, you think? Some of these soup jobs I
can't catch up to anymore."

"Depends," I said. I turned in the kitchen and Mary Ann was
watching me. After I rolled my eyes she took April out to the living room. "It ranges. I can ask."

"I'd be obliged," he said, and there was a short pause before he asked how I'd been. "One minute you're in high school, and next thing I'll be buying you a beer."

We had a few minutes of small talk, and then abruptly he said, "Listen, when she gets in have her holler at me. I'm just farting around over here tonight. Be up late."

The only thing I wanted less than to leave Mom the message was for Costa to find out that I hadn't. And a few nights later she called me from the church where her meeting had gotten over and asked if she could go on a date.

That night after bathtime, I went downstairs and arranged three candles on my bed stand while Mary Ann brushed April's teeth. On my way back I stopped near the door and listened to Mary Ann reading, her voice lowering and rising in pitch to accent the danger and triumph. I stayed there for a full minute. When I read to April I never paused, my mind always on whatever TV show I was missing downstairs. But Mary Ann had different voices for different characters, and she played the calm, discerning narrator in between.

The Gingerbread Man was in his annoying "Run, run, as fast as you can . . ." and Mary Ann couldn't stop or look up but acknowledged my presence with a smile as she read. I sat on the lid of April's toy box and watched them together, Mary Ann scratching April's back and finger-combing her hair as she read.

Call it karma. If I hadn't left Mom the message from Costa, and I was tempted not to, she would have been home by nine and Mary Ann and I would not have been able to lie together in the candlelight.

Beside her on the bed, I smelled lavender in her hair and hoped it would stay in the pillow. I wished I'd had the foresight to open the window, so that she might get under the sheet and leave even more of herself here. I held her hand, rubbing with my fingertips. Conversation was a little strained now that we knew we wouldn't be interrupted, or possibly because of what Nick had told me. She turned into glass, she was breakable, and I couldn't assemble my words because I was trying to radiate the words "You're safe."

And then April was screaming upstairs. It wasn't nightmares but what the pediatrician had called night terrors. The trick was to get up there fast, turn on her lights, and carry her around showing her the room until she remembered where she was. Mom had mixed up a concoction we called "scared spray," which was water with a few drips of red food coloring, and I'd hit all the corners and the closet and spray twice under the bed.

But this was a bad one. I pulled her tight against me as she convulsed and like a harmonica screamed on the inhale and exhale both. Our chests mashed together, I could only tell her where she was and who she was with and tell her she was safe, until her hands came to rest on my shoulders and I felt them begin to un-fist and soften. Her face was burning on my neck, the wet sticky and not sticky, and I held the back of her head and drew air long and smoothly against her still choppy, misfiring breath, whispering, "You're okay," with my eyes closed, searching for that telepathic wave we sometimes found.

Finally she settled. She started to yawn.

There was a creak, and I opened my eyes in time to see a shadow slide away from the door.

When I came back, Mary Ann was lying under the sheet, and slung over the director's chair was her dress, her panties and bra on the top of the dresser. I closed the door, trembling. When I turned back she threw the sheet off, suddenly urgent and bold, and said, "Here I am," and after that we didn't speak.

My room was right under April's, so we made our sounds softly into each other's mouths while we kissed, and after I was inside her we went entire seconds without moving. It was our first time taking our time. Our jumping, candlelit shadows exaggerated our stillness. I let go into her as she let go staring into my eyes. I lowered my face to hers like a bee coming down on a blossom.

"I wish I could sleep here," she said.

26.

I WATCHED NICK AS I MIGHT WATCH A WILD ANIMAL, FROM UNDER open hoods, in rearview mirrors, through the parts room window, trying to decipher his thoughts by his movements. He hadn't gotten a recheck in almost a month, which I'd attributed at least in part to what must've been reduced tension at home now that Mary Ann was happy, and he was taking in more jobs, and more complicated jobs, than he had before. But he was less excited about his work, sulking from fender to toolbox to scope screen with his head down, barely talking. Mary Ann had told me about his childhood, his alcoholic father, the school nights out in the garage while his parents fought. I'd started to see him as the product of a lonely childhood, which I knew about, but I held back, afraid that if I talked to him I'd risk understanding him. And I blinded myself to his wizardry until he was only the thing he had done to Mary Ann.

More than once in this dark time I thought about quitting, but I still saw the job as the right path to manhood, still was in love with the idea of myself a mechanic, and with less than a year's experience I'd be lucky to get hired on as an oil changer anywhere else. But there was also another reason that was strangely more pressing. I felt Mary Ann falling in love with me by slow degrees, and my quitting would eliminate our last reason for not telling Nick. I needed to hear her say she loved me before doing anything that might disrupt the balance and force her to decide.

And I wondered why she was still with him. What she was afraid of. There were days when I sent cars away with only half the spark plugs changed, and rechecks of my own were starting to rack up.

For two days Nick worked on a limited-edition Z-28, and the rest of us picked up the tune-ups and diagnosis jobs. Rod didn't seem to mind working behind the counter, coming out only to diagnose a computer car I had hooked up, like a dentist looking in a mouth and telling the hygienist what to do. I'd replace what he told me to, and we'd split the commission.

Waiting on a new crankshaft for the Z-28, Nick came out to the bays with the owner of a Galaxy Bobby had been working on. Bobby had left for lunch more than two hours ago and never came back. "Where is he?" Nick asked me.

I looked around. "He was just here," I said, and Nick flattened his mouth as though he'd expected me to lie and I hadn't surprised him. He asked the customer for another fifteen minutes and of-fered him ten percent off the bill.

In the lobby Rod was talking to Mary Ann while she changed the receipt tape on the cash register. Pouring coffee I was able to piece together that Rod thought Bobby was drinking again. "Watch how much he eats for lunch," he said. "He got that chicken cordon bleu yesterday and threw out half of it. He's starting to pull his pants up—pretty soon he'll be wearing a belt. He's smoking more, too."

"You're sure?" Mary Ann said.

"I'm the closest we got to an expert. Yeah, he's wet again. Maybe a little crank to boot."

"What're you spying on him for?" I said.

Rod looked at me, nodding. "I could of shut up when you came out, but you ought to hear it. You're his friend. Being blind is the last thing you want to do."

I followed Rod through the bays to a late-model IROC I'd hooked up. Rod sat in the driver's seat and plugged a paper clip into the diagnostic connector to check the codes.

"Thirty-five. Idle air control." He pulled out the paper clip and went around to sign off on the work order.

"I could have done that," I said.

"Then you should have." He grinned to say I had no choice but to defer to his logic.

"He was happy before you started working here," I said.

"Hey, cool. I've been the scapegoat before." But he didn't leave or get excited, or call me on my childishness, and my temper let up. "What would you do?" I said. "I want to help, but I'm pretty sure he won't let me."

"What about a sponsor you could call?"

From the locker room there came a loud retch, and I followed Rod to the source. "Sounds like he's back," he said. "Sounds like lunch was barley sandwiches." The bathroom door was closed and the violent noise was followed by a quiet splash, a little more than a dry heave.

He groaned when he coughed, and we knew by the voice it wasn't Bobby in there but Nick.

Rod knocked on the door. "You all right, boss?"

He retched again, coughed again, and then made a low whimpering noise. Water ran. Rod backed away from the door, and we waited for him to come out.

Nick's voice came through the door. "Can you go get Mary Ann?"

After Nick went home, I drove to Hog Wild and parked two spaces away from Bobby's car. Across the parking lot I strode with urgency and purpose, but then I yanked on the door too hard—the long handle bumped the adjacent brick façade—and inside I made my way through the bodies and smoke with affected heedlessness I hoped no one would see through.

Bobby was leaning back in the corner of a booth. He had a bandanna tied over his hair and a black tank top, his shoulders like rocks under the tight straps, a guy you'd trample people to get away from. Across from him a brunette with a pageboy was talking, and Bobby listened casually. They had a pitcher just about finished on the table between them.

I watched Bobby, my friend who had fought it for more than four years, drain the last inch of beer from a pint. In the car I'd engaged in a short fantasy of making it in time to stop him.

I ducked in between a couple of women at the bar. When Richie came over, I dug out a twenty and asked for a pitcher of what Bobby had.

In the booth he was staring at his clasped hands on the table. "No insulation is the one hitch," he was telling the woman. "But it's a couple thousand square feet. For the money, you can't beat it." When I set the pitcher between them, the woman pulled back in exaggerated surprise, and Bobby looked up at me without alarm, only curiosity.

"Look who's here," he said. "Computer-man. Mr. Joystick."

"Screw you, Bobby," I said, and he stared at me deadpan for a perilous second before he grinned and clapped me on the shoulder.

"Pam, meet my man Justin." He slid down for me to join them.

I wanted tonight to be our only night drinking together, our first and our last, when we would get drunk with comedy and candor before I dragged him back to his sobriety. In that spirit, I filled our glasses and held mine up: "To the people of Bolivia," I said, which had been Don's toast after Reagan said it to the president of Brazil. "This guy's insane," Bobby said, and I was ushered in.

Pam, his friend, was dressed in a way that made overweight

look buxom and seductive—you could look right down her blouse into a mile of sunburned cleavage—and her green eyes distracted your attention from the acne scars that the bad light filled with shadow. She started talking, tilting her head after every other sentence when she said "right?" as if you and she were the only sane ones left. Less than halfway into my first beer, I knew that her boss at the Ford dealership was a cokehead, that the salesmen got extra commissions for selling rust treatments that didn't work, that dried semen had been found on the mirror in the women's restroom. Twice.

She said "semen" without embarrassment, and I wondered if she and Bobby were lovers.

"Tell him your idea for a new club," Pam said, and she put her hand over mine and squeezed—I felt the warm metal of her rings on my knuckles before she moved her hand to the ashtray, where a cigarette the size of a mixer-straw was burning.

"See, you make it a singles bar," Bobby said. "Only the deal is at the door you got a guy with one of those finger prickers. You want to get in, you give him ten bucks and he gets your blood on a slide."

Pam turned to me. "Barf me out, right? But it gets better."

"In the back room, a scientist guy checks it for AIDS. If you're clean, come on in. If you're not, hasta baby. You make the blacklist. Call the place 'Free Love,' whatever. You're picking up chicks you know don't have the bug. Pam here thinks it's a million-dollar idea."

"Ten million," she said. "I said ten." She expanded the idea to include hotels and public swimming pools.

When she poured herself a glass of beer, Bobby looked at me. "Nick think I quit?"

"He's wondering where you went."

He grinned. "Let him keep wondering, he wants to hire dickheads."

"He went home sick," I said.

"Nick did? Jesus. One time I seen him zipped up in a wool coat with pneumonia changing plugs."

"He was throwing up blood."

Bobby stared at me a moment and then looked down and shook his head at the table.

I sat back and had a long drink. Across from us a guy at the pool table was pointing to the place on a low ball that he wanted his girlfriend to hit, but she kept giggling and missed the cue ball altogether. An older woman, upon finding the door to the women's room locked, went in the men's room and I heard her yell, "Too goddamn bad."

"Nah, I'm done," Bobby said. "I'll come get my tools, but that's it."

"Every shop has a punk, hon," Pam said to him. "You should see this new *spigotti* at Maxwell's. He wears cologne in the bays and all this hair gel, muscles out to here. Plays that shitty rap on the radio—bom, pitta-pitta—right? And everybody's scared to change the station. *I* have to go out there and put the radio back on PLR."

"That's just part of it," Bobby said. "I heard Cadillac's got a motor that runs on eight cylinders on the highway and four in city. All computer controls. What do you do with that? But it's fuck or die. Pretty soon, you don't know computers, you better sign up for welfare." Bobby sipped his beer and smiled mysteriously at Pam. Then he looked at me again. "I paid four bills for my GTX. You know what I could get for it now? Seven, eight thou. Even after what I put into it, I'm still clearing close to five. Say it takes me a month to do a car, and that's bottom-up. Sixty grand a year. Not too fucking bad for doing what you want."

"Restoring muscle cars?" I said.

He sat a little straighter. "You find a hot rod in the paper. You get the body straight and painted, beef up the motor. I got a place I could rent for three-fifty a month. One bay, toilet, air compressor, woodstove. I could set up a cot and quit paying rent." Bobby refilled our glasses from the pitcher and laid out the plan, which was fairly straightforward. A convenience store on Baldwin sold the big newspapers from every state in the country. He'd go up and down the East Coast buying used muscle cars.

"Right now there's a Boss four twenty-nine Mustang in *Hemmings,* needs a tranny and a rear-end, for seven thou. You know what you could turn that over restored? A Boss with a three fifty-one Cleveland just went for twenty-four. After the first seven or so, it's just reinvesting."

"Hon," Pam interrupted, "exactly how much are we telling here?"

"I trust this guy more than that brother-in-law of yours. He told me it was the Russians that took out the space shuttle."

"Go scratch, Bobby. He's sweet."

"Lot of sweet guys in D block."

"So you need start-up money," I said.

"Bingo."

Pam clapped her hands and sang, " 'I–N–G–O.' Oh, come on." She got up and I watched her leave, her thighs almost rubbing, but sexy, strutting like a runway model toward the women's room.

Bobby watched then looked down at his beer and sighed. "Yeah, well. I'd rather have a bottle in front of me than a frontal lobotomy," he said. He took a long drag from his cigarette, which seemed to perk him back up. "Listen. She can get me addresses of repo cars before the repo man gets them. My brother, she can even get a copy of the keys."

"Your capital is going to be stolen cars?"

"No, not stolen, no. Not really, not technically. Even if it was legal it couldn't be a whole lot safer." He took a sip and glanced around the bar. "She gets me the key and the address where the car's at—they ain't made the payments, it's just sitting there waiting on the paperwork. See? Repo man's coming day after tomorrow. But there's no car when he gets there because I go out the night before and"—he made the sound of ignition—"drive it away."

"Yeah?" I said.

"Think about it. Dude gets up the next morning, what's he think? His car got repo'd. Then the repo guy shows up, and what's he think? The dude must've unloaded it for parts. It's a great big cluster fuck."

I watched him skeptically. "What if the guy calls the cops when you're taking it?"

"I got the key in my hand, bro. Dude comes out, I say, 'Legal repossession, talk to the dealer. You need your sunglasses and Trojans out of the glove box, get 'em.' Then I shag ass."

"What if they figure out it's an inside job?"

"All right, yeah, I thought about that. So her cokehead boss also had some gambling shit up until last year. And Pammy's clean, not even a speeding ticket. Who would you think the bad guy was? And if it ever happened to get that far, which it won't, well, we're done. We're out, no more. They got nothing on her or me. Or you. That's what I want to talk to you about."

The evening turned into night, and then into my first time closing a bar. When the lights came on Bobby and I were playing pool and Pam was dancing alone next to the jukebox.

Bobby wanted me to be his ride and his lookout. I would drop him off and then watch the street while he got in the car. Any trouble and I'd cause a distraction—do a smoke show or something—until he pulled away.

He didn't need an answer tonight, he said, but as we were putting up our pool cues I gave him one. If I didn't, I knew I would lose Bobby. First Ray, now Bobby—pretty soon the shop would be lost to me altogether, and I dreaded that in the same way Bobby dreaded the inevitable birth of new technology. And besides, it was hard to believe the scenario he'd described could ever actually happen, though that should have told me something—much of what I'd done and witnessed these past two months I never would have believed.

"I'll do it if you come back to work," I said. And it was brilliant. All I had to figure out was how to make the job more bearable, and he'd see that the risk wasn't worth taking.

He didn't agree until we were in the parking lot, when he said, "Just keep fuck-stick away from me. I'd hate to have to go back inside for murder."

27.

FRIDAY AT THE SHOP WE TURNED AWAY HALF A DOZEN TUNE-UPS
before lunch. Nick didn't show up—ulcers, Rod said, after he'd
called Mary Ann. "I know that tune," he added. "Feels like you
got run over by a Peterbilt." And Bobby was hung over, rubbing
his temple with one hand while he opened a throttle with the
other. "Keep out of the shitter if you like to breathe," he told me.
He managed a couple of oil changes and a carb overhaul. I bought
him an egg-and-cheese bagel off the roach coach, but he barely
touched it. He ran on a liquid diet of coffee and Dr Pepper until he
had some KFC mashed potatoes at lunch, and I gave him the last
three Bayer I had in my toolbox.

That evening I came home to find an empty driveway. "She
called to say she wasn't feeling well," Mom said, grabbing her purse
to make a six o'clock meeting. She turned and blew April a fast
kiss on her way out to the garage.

"It's Nick," Mary Ann said when I called. She'd taken him to
Mercy that afternoon, where he was prescribed medication, bland
food, and rest. She wouldn't be able to watch April for the next few
days at least.

"We only did about ten cars today," I said.

"I'll come in tomorrow to work the counter."

"Can you talk?"

"Not really," she said. "Not now."

For the next three days, I couldn't get her alone. After work she made the bank deposit next door and then went straight home to Nick. My own drive back to Levi, which I'd been making in record time the last few weeks, became a torturous slog in which I was only dimly aware of other drivers blaring their horns or flipping me off.

One day Bobby invited me to Hog Wild after work, but I was afraid he'd want to talk about stealing our first car, and so I told him I had plans and then felt shitty for lying. At home, Mom had grown used to having her evenings free. She went out on dates with Costa, to movies and to restaurants in Southbury, and they did the circuit of late-summer carnivals, the ones guys from school used to get drunk at and then brag about in the fall.

I tried spending more time with April, but my need for company seemed to drive her away. To my questions she gave short, testy answers, and it was hard to get her to look at me. If withstanding loneliness was a form of conditioning, then my high school years should have made me a marathon champion of being alone. But I hated not having her in the room. I sat with her through hours of lame cartoons, and at bedtime all she'd talk about was Mary Ann. Then the grief came flooding back, and I'd realize that on the outside I was acting, trying to live a rock ballad where dignity overcomes the heartache.

"Is she coming back the next day after today?"

"Tomorrow. I'm not sure."

"Because she's supposed to," she said. "And I really really really miss her."

The Z-28's owner wouldn't let anyone one but Nick wrap up the job. In the lobby Mary Ann explained that Nick was home with a peptic ulcer, but the guy kept pressing. "Okay, fine," she said and grabbed the phone receiver. "Let me just call and see if he'll come in with his bleeding stomach and set your fucking idle."

The other customers looked up with alarm and curiosity, but Mary Ann stayed committed and unapologetic even as the poor slob backed away saying he'd call.

One evening after the customers were gone I came out to the lobby as she was batching up the last work orders. She glanced at me, and her smile was really just a loosening of her lips from their taut line of concentration. My plan had been to tickle her, but instead I leaned on the wall behind her and watched her reflection in the bay window. She pulled apart the yellow sheets from the pink ones, and faintly I smelled her oils, pine and citrus, until the silence became corrosive. I imagined the many possible ways she could take anything I said.

She looked at my reflection. "I feel confused," she said. I knew she wasn't crying but I hoped for a second that she might be. "It's hard to take all these fucking changes, you know?"

"Let's go somewhere after work," I said. "Just to talk."

"I can't. We've got friends coming by tonight."

I nodded and stayed calm, but Jesus Christ, friends coming by? Wouldn't Nick and Mary Ann pretend they were still happy in front of their friends? Couldn't pretending lead to the real thing?

I felt helpless. With Mary Ann, I had been more charitable and impulsive and funny than I'd been with anyone else in my life, but when she was away from me, I saw that my best wasn't enough. Nick offered her something better that I didn't understand. On a scrap of cardboard I'd started a list of everything he was and wasn't. Not anxious, never hysterical. They say anxious people live in the future and depressed people live in the past, and it seemed that Nick's quiet suffering was more deserving of sympathy, at least of Mary Ann's, than my lingering unease. He was brooding and silent and uncynical, and all of these, especially not allowing himself the release of criticizing people who deserved it, were the very aspects of his personality that were probably eating away his stomach. He didn't take care of himself, which I used to think was a plus in my column, but I didn't work out for my health or for any noble reasons. I did it to impress or intimidate people. Nick, on the other hand, was exactly what he appeared to be.

I wondered how he could see his life as being livable if a woman as good-looking and tragic and brave and thrilling and misunderstood as Mary Ann was subtracted from it. He didn't fear what seemed, to me, looming—the regret of having not seen what his marriage was worth—and I had no idea why. But it was hard for me to keep pretending that Mary Ann didn't find some or all of this irresistible.

Now she stood staring at the floor, and her eyes seemed to soften. "Monday," she said. "We can talk after work."

28.

ON MY LUNCH BREAK MONDAY I WENT TO THE PACKAGE STORE
and paid twenty-six dollars for a Pinot Noir from California; at
Caldor I bought champagne flutes, a corkscrew, and a Jefferson
Starship cassette that had "Miracles" on it, the most romantic song
I knew. After work Bobby was lounging in one of the customer
chairs with a Heineken resting on his thigh when Rod and I came
out to the lobby. Bobby handed me a beer that I would've declined
if he hadn't opened it already. "Hey Nimrod," he said, "bust some
suds?" He held up what was left of the six-pack to Rod.

"You're cold, my brother," Rod said. And I drank my beer
against feeling bothered by this new tolerance, if not the first impulses of a friendship forged, between them.

Mary Ann put together the night's deposit with an amused
awareness of us, like a mother doing dishes while her children run
rampant in the kitchen.

After work I pulled onto the shattered concrete lot at Holy
Land. There were a few other cars and some guys standing around
a low crackling fire. I parked facing where the sun would set on a
pair of sugar maples already turning color. I decided to wait on the
Starship song, which was after all a lovemaking song, and plugged

in "Bell Bottom Blues." Like "Layla," Clapton had written it for Patty Boyd, who wasn't as good-looking by a long shot as Mary Ann. I rewound the song and sat with the key off as long as I could before I had to get out and smoke a cigarette.

The nights were cooler now, and over my street clothes I had on my brown shop jacket, which I hoped would have the same effect on the Latin Kings as my uniform. None of the parked cars was the Celica from the last time. The music was rap, which Ray used to call jungle boogie, and now I tried to decipher the rhythm so that I might nod a little with the bass beat. I brought out the wine and champagne flutes, hoping that anyone watching would see I was only waiting on a girl.

When she turned into the lot I got back in my car. She parked beside me, and I leaned over to open the passenger door as she came around, clutching her purse.

As I showed her the wine, I explained how coastal vineyards give the grape a long, cool growing season (I'd read it on the label—the guy at Liquor Mart barely knew red from white), and I couldn't tell if she was impressed or just being polite when she said it sounded yummy. As I was pouring her glass she said, "That's enough," and I didn't like the way she said that, so I pulled the bottle back with some drama.

"Too much is going to put me to sleep," she said. "But thank you."

We didn't have a lot of time before the sun set. I was hoping the view would spark something for us, but Mary Ann yawned twice without apologizing, and I worried that each break in conversation would become her cue to say goodnight. She asked about April, so in return, and since it felt so goddamned formal between us, I asked about Nick. He was getting better, eating more, sleeping through the night.

"I heard you won't let him go out to the garage," I said.

She watched the sun, which was just getting liquid near the big cross, and sipped her wine. "A few days ago he went out to invent some kind of new distributor tool," she said. "I heard him throwing up in the driveway."

"Well, he's lucky he's got you," I said, intending next to say that he didn't deserve her, but Mary Ann shrugged and said, "For better, for worse."

The only thing that kept breath in me was that I couldn't tell if she was being sarcastic. "It seems like all you get is the worse," I said.

She stared for a few moments at a long frayed cloud soaking up the color before she looked at me. "Meaning I'm not supposed to have compassion?"

"Does he?"

She smiled bitterly, right at the peak of the sunset, and put her champagne flute on the dashboard. "Thank you," she said. "This was fun."

"The answer's no, Mary Ann."

"You're pushing me, Justin. I know you're nineteen. I know you think everything is your business."

And here it was all at once, the crossness, the implied giving up, that I thought she would never—even on those nights I dreamed of our marriage and children and hand-in-hand passage into old age—use on me.

"You know the times you thought he was staying late at the shop? He was racing the Corvette for money. He didn't want you to know. He lied and said I had to lie." I stopped myself as the venom of having betrayed Nick yet again spread through me, but I didn't take my eyes off her. She stared ahead, the sunset flattering her face almost more than I could bear.

I'd stunned her, and now I wanted to keep stunning her with the truth. Showing patience hadn't worked, and if I was going to lose her I was going to tell the whole truth first.

"He used to race in Oregon," she said. "I'd go with him, sometimes." And she seemed almost relieved. Perhaps she'd thought I was going to say that he'd been out with another woman.

I took a moment to breathe, to swallow. "He told me what happened that night. Before your sister came."

She turned and watched me. "We had dinner. I took a bath . . . what? You tell me, if you know everything."

"He told me, Mary Ann. In bed, when you didn't want to. He told me."

She closed her eyes and breathed. Nothing happened for a second or two, and then she reached for the door handle. "Goodnight, Justin."

I started out my door, but then I looked back in the car because she was frozen there holding the handle, her door still closed. A tiny choking sound came from her throat, and she lunged forward. When I leaned back in and touched her she jerked away, mashing herself up against the door before she found the handle and got out.

She didn't close the door. The music outside seemed to be louder now. She walked around the Nova, hugging herself in the last of the sunlight. I didn't know what was happening, and when I got out she went to the front of the Malibu and started kicking at the grille.

"Don't go back to him, Mary Ann," I said. "You can stay with us."

She kicked out a headlight that burst with a firework pop just as I was getting to her. "I'm so sick of these fucking cars," she said, kicking wildly. She stomped her heel through the grille, and plastic pierced the radiator, hot antifreeze spraying onto her pant leg. She swatted at the liquid as if it were a swarm of bees. I pulled her away, and when she was clear of the car she turned and pushed me off. "Who do you think you are? My God," she yelled. She charged into the park.

I caught up with her, but she was holding her head and didn't know I was there.

"Aw, shit," called a silhouette moving near the fire. "She fucked that shit *up*."

I looked back at the cars. My passenger door was still open, and I jogged back, got the keys, shut the door, and then saw that her keys were still in the ignition. I got them and locked the Malibu, and when I turned back she was gone.

I called her name, and the voice from before called back, "Watching you, home." The light was draining, and a few of them might have been coming toward me. I took out the two ten-dollar bills I had in my wallet and jogged over to them. "Could you keep an eye on her car? I'll be right back."

In the Nova I zigzagged along every narrow street around the park. They were neighborhoods of tar-shingled cape houses with rusted-out beaters at the curb. Dusk hung like silt in the air, so I had to pull up close to people—one shirtless psycho in camo pants hollered, "I got what you want!" and chased me off the street. Down at the river where she jogged, I scanned every foot of sidewalk my headlights touched, and then I turned around and started the route again, but she was nowhere.

It was full dark when I pulled in to the Cumberland Farms on Cooke Street, two blocks from Nick and Mary Ann's house. I parked away from where the cashier could see and cut through the park so that it was just a climb over chain-link into their side yard. I crept around Nick's El Camino on the edge of lamplight thrown from the living room window. I darted in behind a half-dead rhododendron with my back against the house and caught my breath.

I was standing under the window that looked out at the park. I inched up toward the glass, my stubble raking the aluminum siding with the sound of a wire brush on a cymbal, and I rested at the bottom corner to close my eyes and listen.

A woman on TV said, "Calgon, take me away," and I crept higher until I had an eye barely over the sill. Nick was crammed back into the corner of the futon, with his hand over his mouth, staring at the TV. He could have been engrossed in the commercial or he could have been deranged. I wondered if Mary Ann had let him know that she'd be late tonight. If he was capable of regret,

I would say he was suffering from it profusely. I had an impulse to go around to the door and just tell him what had happened. Be ready, Nick. You shouldn't have let this go.

And then incredibly Mary Ann came out of the bedroom. She was dressed in a T-shirt and pajama pants. She must've jogged part of the way to have been there long enough to change clothes. She carried a pillow and the comforter from the bed.

Nick didn't look up as she walked by him, but just as she was at the stairs he said, "You don't have to tell me, okay? I just can't figure out if you're hurt. Are you hurt?"

She paused, looking up the staircase at Joey's door, and I could see only her back, but I saw the shudder, and against it she hugged the pillow. When I thought she was over it, that she would go up without a word, was exactly when she dropped everything on the stairs and swung around—I dropped out of sight.

"This is your world! You did this. Your bullshit silent world. Live in it!"

I don't know how it would've felt to have seen her face. It was terrifying, of course, but also thrilling to think of her yelling like that at me—to be hated and loved enough to inspire that kind of outrage.

I stayed at the window for a long while after she went upstairs. I watched Nick go in the kitchen and come back with an ashtray and a glass of milk. He stared at the TV as he lit a cigarette. I prepared myself to jump back should he come to open the window, but he seemed too distracted to notice the room filling with cigarette smoke.

He took out a card from his wallet, picked up the phone receiver from the end table, and dialed. "Is Justin there?" he said, and then he dropped his forehead into his open hand. "Can you ask him to give Nick a call?" He gave Mom his number and thanked her.

Later he disappeared through the door to their room and brought out a pillow and a sleeping bag. I kept spying on him, feeling low about it at first, then rationalizing that I didn't deserve any more surprises.

It was after ten when I got back up to Holy Land. There were no cars anywhere and only a wide swath of pebbled safety glass shimmering in my headlights where, instead of jimmying the lock to the Malibu, they must've smashed a window and brushed out the glass.

29.

DON WAS MAKING AN EFFORT TO BE MY FATHER AGAIN. HE CALLED once a week, and if I didn't feel like talking he'd catch on after a lull or two and say he had to let me go.

"What was it like telling people?" I asked one night, sitting on my bed with the door closed.

"Remember the time you and Alan Tate stole the newspapers?"

"It was like sneaking around?"

"No, I mean after. When Mom made you go house to house to apologize. It was like I'd misbehaved, but they were going to be generous and forgive me. It was relying on the kindness of strangers, except they weren't supposed to be strangers."

"Mr. Percy?"

"Sure, the Percys, the Vanns. All the dinners and parties and house-sitting for eight years. Did you know that Tom told me to stay away from his kids?"

"I never liked that guy," I said. "They act like they're such great Christians."

"But they're grown-ups. They can understand nuances like you or I can. If a book turns you into a zombie, close the goddamn book."

Zombie, I thought. That's just what I'd been at Northwest. There was a transfer kid with a lisp who got called Fag Bag, and he didn't last a month. No way could I let it get out that my father was gay.

"But do you ever feel like you're acting?" I said.

"How do you mean?"

"Like when you talk to somebody, all you're thinking about is how they might take it. If they're still going to like you."

"Isn't that the definition of in the closet?" he said. "Sure, I've done that. I still go out of my way not to mention my personal life. Once in a while I'll pretend I'm straight."

"You do that?"

There was a short silence. "I was in a cab in the upper eighties, and the driver saw a young lady in the crosswalk. He said he'd donate his right one to science after a night with her. He said . . ." He laughed voicelessly. "He told me he'd eat twenty yards of her shit just to see where it came from."

"Classy. What'd you say?"

"I said, 'Me too.'"

"Come on."

"I mean, what could I say?"

I laughed and could see his smiling face in the quiet afterward. Before I could stop myself, I was telling him about Mary Ann. Everything, more or less, came out, except the word "rape," which I described as a bad situation. "But it's like she doesn't remember."

"It's possible she doesn't," Don said. "Repression, you've read about it. Sometimes it's called motivated forgetting. Psychogenic amnesia. It's a defense mechanism."

"I don't think that's it. More like she taught herself how to forget."

"Would you want to say what kind of situation it was?"

"Something right after she lost her baby," I said.

"That's terrible," he said. "That poor woman." He sighed and then said my name in a sober voice. "I'm not sure how to ask this."

The phone beeped.

"You mean is she okay to watch April?" I said.

"Well, her frame of mind. I can't imagine losing a baby."

The phone beeped again. "Hang on."

I pushed the switch hook and was caught off guard by Nick's voice on the other end. "Feel like taking the car out?"

"Not tonight," I said. "You go if you want. They know you now."

"Not without you," he said. "Wickersham's is your place."

"Would Mary Ann even let you go?"

"Maybe. I don't know." He sounded weak, distant. "She's out getting some kind of herbs for my stomach. It smells like the Far East over here. Listen, don't ever get an ulcer. You lay there trying to sleep, but it feels like you drank hot coffee too fast."

It was strange hearing him talk about his problems. I thought of how suddenly and resolutely life changes—how grateful I would've been only weeks ago to have him confide in me.

I listened to his quiet as he must've been listening to mine. I still couldn't predict Mary Ann's reaction if I finally told Nick about us. The odds that she would love me seemed about even with the odds that she would hate me, now that he was sick.

"I feel like I'm keeping some kind of secret," he said after a moment.

"Then tell her the truth."

"I don't know what that is anymore."

"What happened to Joey wasn't your fault," I said. "What you did was."

I could hear him breathing. "Keep talking," he said. "Please."

"She's the one you should talk to. She's your wife."

"I can't."

"What do you want from me, Nick?"

"I don't know who my friends are."

"Everybody's your friend."

"Because they don't know," he said. "You're the only one who knows."

My pulse was suddenly throbbing in my temples, my chest tight, and before I could speak again I hung up the phone. When it started to ring with Don on the other line I yanked the cord out of the wall.

30.

"THE GUY SHOULDN'T OF QUIT THE PAYMENTS," BOBBY SAID. He was driving my Nova through the Hopeville neighborhood at night. "That's on him, not me. And not like I give a rat's ass about a bunch of executive fucks, but they get more off the insurance than repoing it and selling it used. Pam told me that." He glanced around at the dim triple-decker houses in lamplight. "Listen, all we're doing is stepping in when the car's between owners. Same as finding a buck on the sidewalk. It's nobody's until we find it, and then it belongs to us."

Mary Ann was supposed to come over to babysit that night. She couldn't, she'd said on the phone, and in her voice I heard that she couldn't forever. Now I was trying to take comfort in asking what the hell I had to lose. But my legs were shaking so bad I had to hold my thighs together with my hands. It's safe, I tried to think. It's worth it. I'd been wanting an apartment in Waterbury, and this car alone would be first month's rent.

With his thumb hooked on the bottom of the wheel, Bobby glanced at me and said, "Adrenaline. Just means you're alert." He was driving my car this first time. He'd visited the scene a few nights before and knew where the Taurus would be parked. Instead of following Baldwin the whole way, we took the parallel street and then cut over toward the eight-hundred block. He eased us down to the intersection.

Baldwin was one of the streets that enforced alternate-day parking, and cars were bumper-to-bumper on the north curb. He shifted to neutral and killed the engine, and then he coasted through the intersection, coming to rest gently against the curb under the stop sign. "Better than being the only car on that side," he said as he shut off the headlights. The day before he'd installed a toggle switch under my dashboard that turned off everything in back—taillights, brake lights, license plate light—and now he reached under and flipped it. "Don't forget to turn that back on later," he said. "After we're a few blocks away." A click at a time he pushed down the emergency brake pedal, then let out a long breath.

Looking around, I felt a little easier. The block of Baldwin was lamplit on each corner, and only two people were on the sidewalk. It was just after nine at night. Bobby thought it was a good idea to operate during TV prime time rather than later; people tend to look out the window when a car starts at midnight.

We watched the window where Bobby had determined the car's owner lived. There was blue flickering TV light. I kept thinking I saw someone, but then the light would brighten and the window would be empty.

"Want to call it off?" he said.

"Seriously?" We hadn't done anything yet except park under a stop sign, and the trembling moved up into my jaw. It suddenly took everything I had not to giggle.

Bobby shook his head, grinning. "Jesus," he said. "I can't believe it's you I got out here doing this."

Typically I would have defended myself against the implication that I was just some innocent kid, but out here now, fifty yards from being an accomplice in a felony, I groped for my innocence. I wanted to hide in it.

I could hear Bobby digging under his thumbnail. "What happened to her Malibu?" he said.

I looked at him, and after a long second he shook his head.

"Man, you think I ever would of brought you out here? I mean, there's not a whole lot of corrupting you anymore." It was Tom Carter who saw us. He used to deliver parts for NAPA but now worked at Harrison Hardware, where Mary Ann had parked the day we went swimming and where I had kissed her in between our cars.

"He'll keep his mouth shut," Bobby said. He didn't say more, and the truth was just there without my having to confess to it.

"I love her, Bobby," I said. I felt myself rocking in the seat.

"Nobody's saying you don't, Romeo."

"Nick did something to her," I said. "Right after they lost Joey. He wanted another baby. You get it? He wanted to and she didn't."

Bobby sighed and swore quietly as he opened and closed his hands on the steering wheel. "It's what he got cut for?"

"So he wouldn't try to get her pregnant again."

The sound of his breathing filled the car as he glanced now and then at the window. I felt sick. It was this nobody-ever-say-a-fucking-thing bullshit macho ethic of holding it in. "He's not God," I whispered. "Everybody acts like he's God."

"He's a friend, is what he is."

I thought about that. Bobby had told me stories about prison, stories that just seemed entertaining at the time. Like they'd bet who could go the longest without jerking off, money bets that relied on each man's honesty. How a prison thief was the lowest scum, because what a man owned in jail was all he had left of his life. Bobby followed a kind of honor code, I realized, but I didn't fully understand until now that he expected me to follow it, too.

"Watch your dick," he said. "I know a guy doing a life sentence over his dick, and I knew the guy he shot up."

I breathed to calm myself, and after a moment I said, "Her Malibu's gone."

"Nick told me. Stolen?"

I nodded, and I had to sit on my hands. Just minutes ago, I'd been trying to communicate with him telepathically to change his mind about stealing the car, and now there were all these hot, defensive impulses crowding out everything else. "I love her, Bobby," I said again.

"Keep your voice down." He stared out the windshield for a while, and without requiring more explanation from me he slowly began to nod. "This is just how we get there," he said. "Next time I get on the wagon, it's for good. I'm doing this right. I get this shop going, and then no more. No stealing, no dope, no drink. No fucking around with married gals."

"What if she's divorced by then?"

"Then I guess maybe I'll have to grandfather you in."

Finally now I could laugh, it just fell out of me. I was still shaking.

"All right," he said. "Shh."

And then the thought of working for Bobby felt pure and wholesome, even in its first inception in my mind, though we didn't mention it again that night. My stomach unclenched for the first time since I saw him waiting for me in front of his apartment that night, and I had to take a leak. Suddenly all I wanted was to be done with this so I could go piss behind a Dumpster somewhere. "Let's do it, if we're going to do it," I said.

Bobby clapped a hand on my knee without taking his eyes off the window. He got out and eased the door closed. On the sidewalk, he stuffed his hands in his pockets and became just another insomniac out for a stroll. He looked at his wrist where the cuff of his jean jacket ended, and then he brought his wrist up to his ear, as if he had nothing on his mind except why his watch had stopped working. I slid across into the driver's seat. Bobby cut between the Taurus and the car behind it, taking careful sidesteps in the tight gap, and he had the keys out (he'd even thought to put them on his keychain) when he reached the door.

I stared at him intently for any false gesture, but he was all the way—there could be no doubt to any passerby but that the car Bobby slid the key into belonged to him.

And then he was inside, closing the door silently at the same moment he started the engine. Three back and forths to get out of the tight parallel spot, and then lights on and he was rolling down the hill. A full two-second stop at the sign—my cue to leave the scene. But I waited a little longer than I should have. The street was silent again, and it felt like there was supposed to be something more.

Bobby planned to meet the chop-shop guy alone, in case there was any trouble, and I'd see him at work in the morning. On Wolcott Avenue, which after two miles intersected I-84, I drove exactly the speed limit and intended to do so all the way to Levi. The light at the intersection in front of the shop was blinking red at this hour, and though I typically coasted through blinking reds I stopped for this one, still wired with the residue of a felony still on me.

In the dim security light I spotted movement. I eased past the shop and then cut fast into the People's Bank next door. Up through the side alley I saw that the door was partially opened. I reached for the handle but stopped myself, imagining some crackhead thief caving in my head with a pry bar. Or was it an associate of Eve's looking for the Corvette? I climbed on one of the junk engine blocks and looked in through the chicken-wired glass of a casement window.

There was nothing for a few seconds, and then she walked over from the drill press. In the bay under the window she opened the hood of the Z-28 Nick had just finished that afternoon.

Sabotaging a car is something few people know how to do without getting caught. Any decent mechanic can spot sugar in the carburetor bowl, or a line cut with a blade, or every drop of oil drained without bad seals or gaskets. Then it's just a matter of fig-uring out who your enemies are. But with metal shavings, you can wreak your havoc anonymously. When the owner takes the car, knocking and smoking, to the garage, perhaps suspecting his enemy of sabotage, the mechanic will diagnose a plugged oil port or a spun bearing from a high-rpm rev. The final insult comes when the mechanic assumes that the damage was caused by owner neglect.

Mary Ann had what looked to be half a cup of shavings she'd collected under the drill press. I watched her remove the fill cap from the valve cover of the Z-28 and dump the tiny shrapnel into its virgin oil. When the cup was empty she wrapped it in a paper towel then dug through a trash can to bury it deep.

I dropped onto the foul gravel of the alley, sitting and lurching and falling back, wavering between pardoning her and catching her in the act. I imagined saying, "It was you all along?"—but no, I'd let her have this revenge. One act of sabotage for every heartbreak he'd dealt her, was that the cost? And this one, so catastrophic—a full rebuild on a collector's engine—in retaliation for the night he could never take back?

I imagined one day she'd confess it to me. And I'd tell her I understood.

When I looked again she was checking around the engine with a droplight. She wiped a shop rag over the valve cover, and then abruptly she turned and marched away from the car. Her impetu-ousness made my heart race. Unexpectedly I was angry and couldn't let her get away with it. As fast as the impulse came to me, I pulled open the side door at the same moment there came a crash inside. I dropped behind the fender of a black Cyclone in Bobby's bay. An-other crash and I slid under the car, stomach-down on soggy cat litter, and knocked my head on the driveshaft as I inched forward to see into the locker room.

One of the louvered metal doors was still shivering as it flapped itself closed. Mary Ann was leaning against the bathroom door, her arms folded severely, as if she were forcing herself not to wipe away or touch the tears on her face. She stared into the sink mirror. I thought she was about to say something hateful to herself, and I waited a long time to hear what it would be.

But in fact she spoke only once, when she sniffed sharply and said, "Okay." It wasn't with relief or reassurance, but more of a cold announcement to no one and to everyone that it was over now.

When she came out to the bays I mashed my face on the backs of my hands, holding my breath as she walked past. I considered changing the oil in the Z-28—if that would even matter; you couldn't get out every crumb without taking the engine back apart—but then she slammed the side door behind her, and in that resolute burst of wood and metal I heard the sound of her leaving Nick for good.

31.

NICK CAME IN ON WEDNESDAY, AND WHENEVER I SENSED HIM
approaching—keenly receptive, as I'd become, to the reward of his
attention—I shied away, and finally in the locker room he threw me
a casual "Hey" as I washed my hands.

The loathing I tried to feel was, as soon as I felt it, hollow and
manufactured loathing. I looked within myself for Mom's outrage
when she'd been wronged, but then I could only nod with the
usual craving that he like me and say "Hey" right back.

He leaned against a locker and hung his thumbs in his front belt
loops, his forearms hard and everything else gone fleshy.

"Do you know what happened to her car?" he said. "She's not
saying."

I shook my head and stared at the grimy wall over the sink,
Jackson Pollocked by years of dissolved grease—all shades of black
and gray—flung on it. After a while I turned off the water and
ripped two feet of paper towel from the dispenser.

Nick brought his hands to his hips and looked like he wanted
to exhale but didn't know how. I dried my hands, balled up the
paper towel, and lobbed it into the trash. As I started by him, he
said, "You got a couple minutes?"

I followed him toward the side door to the alley, my mind racing with sudden crazy thoughts—that he'd have seen my cigarette butt and ass-print in the gravel and ask why I'd been sitting there—but no, he turned the other way outside and we went down toward the parking lot.

Just then Rod came up and handed Nick a coffee. "Blonde and sweet," he said, and then he turned to me. "Lucky son of a gun."

Nick tore the tab off his coffee lid. "I was just about to tell him."

Rod led us down to the gravel parking lot, where his Duster was backed in next to a gorgeous vinyl-top 1970 'Cuda.

"We won it last night," Rod said.

"You took him to Wickersham's?" I said to Nick, my voice close to breaking.

Nick shook his head.

"Behind the airport in Oxford," Rod said.

"You don't even have the title," I said, and it was pathetic—it only gave Rod the opportunity to say, like some Hollywood badass, "Don't matter, long as they think you do."

"It's quick," Nick said. "It's a Hemi."

A Hemi. I wanted to say "Good for you" and be unbothered and sincere, but it was impossible. I should have been in the passenger seat when he beat his first Hemi.

"You can have it if you want it," Nick said to me, and I lost my breath. A Hemi? If I want it? The engine NASCAR moguls banned from racing for a season because nothing could touch it? I can *have* it if I want it? I heard his voice again, as if it were coming out of the intercom upstairs. "Give Mary Ann your Nova, you take this. We'll call it even."

Rod patted me on the shoulder, and I tripped over my boot and sprawled out in the weeds. He helped me back up. "You feel that earthquake?" he said. "That had to be like a nine on the sphincter scale, no?"

It took half the morning to finish a tune-up. I had trouble following one thought to the next, and all of a sudden my leg would start shaking. When I saw Mary Ann in the lobby, I spun in the rest of my spark plugs with an air ratchet so that I could bring her the work order and stare at the side of her face as she punched numbers on the calculator.

I'd planned to tell her about the 'Cuda, that would be my opening, but when she saw me her eyes fluttered closed and she pressed her temple. We were back in Holy Land again. The same ice dread filled my chest.

"I thought you'd want to know that he told me," I said.

She glanced around and then stared at the paper in front of her. "Lower your voice."

"I thought you'd want to talk about it. That's all. Or I wouldn't have said anything."

"You're nineteen," she said. "You couldn't wait."

"We need to talk, Mary Ann."

"See?" she said. "You just can't wait." She took a work order off the counter and walked around me and out to the bays to hang it on the peg hooks. I went to the window that faced the bays and leaned my face up on the glass. I liked it when she didn't know I was watching her, when I didn't have to think about how I looked or what I was going to say, and all of my energy was in my eyes. She was the one I knew I'd always compare other women to. I had the strange regret of never having carried her in my arms. If I had done that, it somehow seemed that she would still want me.

Through the window glass I could hear the roar of a car on the chassis dyno, that outlandish scream of engine and high-pitched whine of tires that should never be heard indoors, and I thought at first it was this sound that had frozen Mary Ann. She had put up the work order too long ago to still be standing there. Then I looked where she was looking, and of course it was Nick, who had just opened the hood on the Z-28 she had sabotaged and was walking around to the driver's door. When I looked back at Mary Ann, she had a hand pressed over her mouth.

Had the car behind him not been racing on the dyno, I wonder how long it would have taken Nick to hear the metal shavings scuff and gouge and destroy the engine he'd spent three days rebuilding. He put a sniffer in one of the tailpipes, and then came back and kicked down the fast idle with a snap of the throttle. He went up to the oscilloscope to do a final emissions check, and that was when the racing stopped and the bays were quiet again.

I couldn't hear the knocking where I was, but instantly Nick lunged away from the scope to save the engine. His foot kicked out, and he was on his side on the floor by the time Mary Ann got to him. "Shut it off," he screamed, and she ran around and killed it. Nick got off the floor limping a little as he went over to the car, where he stared down at the engine—the crankshaft scored, the bearings and maybe the cylinder walls ruined—and then dropped onto his knees and lowered his head to the grille.

Mary Ann stood behind him, and for a moment I imagined her smiling, celebrating another act of retribution. But without hesitating she held him by the shoulders. I don't know if he even felt it; he seemed less than human in his detachment from her touch. As he shook his head at the Z-28, like a captain watching the final mast go down, she stayed beside him, closing her eyes as if to infuse him with the sedative of her understanding.

And all at once it was clear that he wasn't the object of her malice. Maybe he had once been, when the hurt, the indifference, still stung. But not now. Mary Ann wanted the jobs to stop coming. She wanted the shop to close.

PART
THREE

32.

THE 'CUDA HAD A SMOOTH WOOD-GRAIN STEERING WHEEL WITH a matching pistol-grip shifter, and I mean it was scary fast. On empty roads I broke loose the tires with a bump of the throttle, the rear end swinging as if on a frozen pond, the backseat filling with burning white air, and I studied the counter slide. I tried to own its power and measured my advances in rpm, daring myself to bring the Stewart Warner tach close to redline, hammer down for just another second, like holding your hand over a flame.

I played in my mind the movie of Nick finessing the wheel of the ZL1, never overreacting, even as the front tires began to float before the car's gravity evened out. And then it was about the shifting. You could hit second too hard and send the ass end into another slide; you wanted to chirp the tires, not bake them. I pushed the car to maybe half capacity and was terrified.

Mary Ann didn't come in on the day, a week later, when Nick and I signed titles over. I'd planned to take her for a test drive and show how the steering shook a little over sixty, how the transmission shifted funny from second to third. An hour left before closing, I went down and stashed a few mementos in the Nova in a way that looked accidental: a tube of ChapStick, half a pack of Certs, a socket, two Allen wrenches, a matchbook from Hog Wild. They say smell is our strongest memory trigger, and I brought down the stick of deodorant I kept in my toolbox and rubbed it over the carpets and headliner.

The next evening my Nova, now Mary Ann's, was parked in the driveway when I arrived home. I hurried in through the garage. On the back deck she was grilling burgers while April dunked nylon straps in a bucket of soapy water in the backyard, and though I'd about leapt out of my car, I decided at the last second not to show my excitement.

The old Char-Broil grill shot up flames a foot long where the burners had rusted out, and I grinned vaguely at Mary Ann standing over it as I bounded down the wooden steps to give April a hug. "Look," April said, pushing me away to dip her straps into a bucket of foam and water. When she ran across the lawn a tube of oily bubble followed her and left a rope of slime when it popped.

Mary Ann and I were cordial that evening, by which I mean we had pointless, reflexive conversation. I thought she was only tolerating me for April's sake. In the bathroom I rehearsed unimpeachable monologues, after which I told my reflection to just let it go, to be forgiving and love unconditionally. But when I came back down Mary Ann eyed me evasively before returning to a jigsaw puzzle they had going, and I wanted to tell her exactly what I deserved. That is the thing—entitlement, not love—that conquers all. I saw glimpses of the path to insanity as I suffocated on my feelings.

"So now you hate me?" I said, in the kitchen one night while April was watching TV.

Mary Ann looked up from chopping black olives. "Is that what you think?"

"I wouldn't have said anything. I mean it, Mary Ann."

She set down the knife and sighed.

"It's not your fault," I said. "If you're embarrassed, I mean. He's the bad guy. He's the one to blame."

She brushed hair out of her eyes with the back of her hand. "Tell you what. I can let it go right now, if I can just say something first."

"Of course you can."

"You wanted to remind me so I'd hate Nick. Is that true?"

I shrugged. After a moment I said, "Yeah."

"Then you shouldn't have said it, Justin. Not to any woman. Your heart told you that, didn't it? That's what you should be asking me to forgive."

"Okay. You're right. Would you?"

"I think so."

"What can I do?" I said. "I mean to help with that?"

"Why does April have bad dreams?"

"We don't know."

"Is it because people pull away from her? Your father. Your mother, now."

I nodded, though the doctor had said that there didn't have to be a reason at all.

"She needs to be sure you won't leave her," she said. "You have to tell her that. You have to let her know."

That night we read *Come Back, Amelia Bedelia* together. I was a fearsome Mrs. Rogers telling poor Amelia, "Now go!", and I was the other angry bosses that couldn't excuse her blundering. Mary Ann as Amelia, so misunderstood and dejected, melted me with her quiet lines and her sad, blinking eyes.

After we finished the book April sat up suddenly from the pillow. "I am a very important person," she said and looked stunned.

"That's right, you are, sweetie," Mary Ann said, and before she looked at me I said to April, "You sure are."

"Do you dream about all the fun you're going to have in the world?" Mary Ann said. "You're going to see everything. Everyone's going to love you."

"And you love me, too?" April said.

"Of course I do. Of course, of course. You knew that, crazy."

"And you love Justin?"

I should have seen this coming, but my heart was racing, everything suddenly at stake. Mary Ann was right, I couldn't wait, and when she smiled at April it wasn't a real smile, but a lobotomized smile that provoked me more than any answer she might give, and I lurched over the bed to tickle April and call her Ms. Nosy and explode the moment into unsalvageable shards.

Downstairs I followed Mary Ann into the kitchen where she finished a glass of water from dinner. I struggled for something to say, but she wasn't far from her purse, and its presence on the counter was the only evidence I had that she wasn't about to leave.

"I'd like to take her somewhere on a day trip," she said.

"Just you two?"

She sighed and set down the glass. Then she turned resolutely, as if she were about to say one thing, but she seemed to change her mind. And whatever she was seeing on my face was the truth. I couldn't pretend to be okay. I was empty.

She would have said no. She didn't love me. I was sure of it by her expression, her eyes as deep and sad as they'd been that day in the parts room, after hearing my phone call with Kimberly.

"You can come with us, Justin," she said. "You're invited."

I took her hand lightly, as a friend, and led her away from her purse into the living room. We sat on the couch together. It felt like a last chance, and I was careful not to say anything ambiguous or emotional. After a minute she picked up April's Cabbage Patch doll and set it on the coffee table. "I understand why he did it," she said. "He wanted another baby."

"He told me that."

"But did he tell you he went crazy? Did you know that part?" She was urgent, and I braced a little for what she might say next.

"He was holding Joey and shouting at me. He said to fill the bathtub with warm water and put salt in it. I mean, it was too late.

He was holding Joey and you could see it was too late. I was supposed to get the batteries, all the nine-volts, and put them in the bathtub with the saltwater. I was opening the smoke detector when the paramedics came. If they saw Joey in the bathtub with the batteries, can you imagine? He'd still be locked up."

She stopped talking and looked at her lap, where one thumb rubbed the other as if sharpening a knife. She wasn't going to break down, though. She shook her head, and like that the door to the memory seemed to close. Whatever had gone on at their house, the past few weeks had brought her to some kind of resolve. And it made me uneasy that she seemed so assured, that I couldn't somehow fix things for her.

"He's going crazy now," I said. "He wants to build a time machine. He thinks you can redo the past over and over."

"He told you that?"

"Mary Ann, he needs to get help. One of these days he's going to drop a car on himself or fall into an engine. Maybe run somebody over, I don't know." But none of my melodrama evoked a reaction. The idea of the time machine seemed to hang in her mind, softening her mouth and putting her into a daydream that made me invisible.

Headlights through the window ran over the fireplace, and the garage door opened. I jumped to my feet. "Let's go out and have a cigarette."

"I don't want one," she said. And as I watched her stand and walk around the coffee table, these were the things I couldn't say without yelling: Would it kill you to have a cigarette with me? Aren't I worth five minutes?

As Mary Ann was getting her purse, Mom came in with two bags of groceries. "I stopped at Grand Union," she said to me. "Can you get the rest of it?"

Mary Ann took a bag from Mom's arms and set it on the counter. "I can't come by until next week. I'll call when I know my schedule."

Mom looked from her to me, and I looked away. "She'll miss you," Mom said.

I followed Mary Ann out to the garage, intending to ask in the driveway what exactly she meant by her schedule, but at the side door she turned and gave me a sudden kiss on the mouth. I was too stunned to speak. "Help your mom," she said and went out to her car.

I carried all four bags at once, thinking only about a cigarette, hoping it could be everything I needed it to be.

"Is she not feeling well?" Mom said when I set down the bags on the counter.

"What do you mean?"

"She looks tired," she said, lifting two Wonder Breads out of a bag. "Or like she's getting over something."

That night I drove out to Waterbury and turned on Cooke Street. Like before, I parked at the convenience store, hiked in through the park, and hunkered under the window.

Mary Ann was sitting not with him on the couch but in the easy chair against the wall, where she was reading a magazine by lamplight. The TV was on, and Nick was either watching it intently or was distracted reading and marking up his books.

I felt depressed watching them. There was nothing. She would look up from her magazine and be thinking, what? I'm ready to not want anymore. Let me be old. She was at peace with her surrender, and I wanted to throw a rock through the window of their tranquility.

I planned to wait and see what the sleeping arrangements were, but a breeze picked up and after a while I was really shivering. With the money from the stolen car—my cut from Bobby—I'd bought a lined Vanson biker jacket that I'd left at home. I stayed as long as I could stand it before I ducked and walked miserably back to the 'Cuda.

33.

LATE ONE AFTERNOON, ROD CALLED ME OVER THE INTERCOM TO
take line one. Mary Ann hadn't come to work, and I was suddenly
electric with the certainty it was her calling me. On my way to the
parts room, I convinced myself that she'd had a change of heart.
She knew what Nick was capable of and though she'd tried, she
could never forgive him.

I closed the door to the parts room and then stared at the flashing light on the phone. "Be loving," I said three times before I
picked it up.

"Justin, where is she?"

"Mom?"

"Tell me where she is right now."

"Where's who?" I said, though I knew immediately.

"She called this morning. She asked if April could stay home
from preschool. I came home for lunch at one and they're not
here. I came back at three and they're not here. No note,
nothing."

"Mom, slow down. What time is it?"

She didn't answer, and I thought Mary Ann might be pulling
in, that the danger was over, but I heard her whimper. "Why

aren't they here, Justin?" I turned around the radio clock on the desk. It was almost five.

Mom was standing in the driveway smoking and holding the phone. There were no words to say because she had only one question and I had only one question. She'd been crying and I saw on her face that my saying sorry wouldn't help. She was near a point of detonation, and I didn't know what form it would take. Somehow it was right that I just take the phone out of her hand rather than asking for it, and when I did she folded her arms and sighed, as if she'd been waiting for something like this all along.

I called Mary Ann's, as I had done before I left the shop, let it ring until the machine picked up. "They're in town somewhere," I said, giving her back the phone. "They have to be. Stay here."

I didn't find them at the park or downtown or at the river or at the ice-cream shop on Route 6. I drove frantically, speeding, blowing stop signs, chirping my tires everywhere, racing home when the sun went down because I thought they must be back. They had to be.

The front light was on, and sitting on the concrete steps under the front door was Mom, who stood as I was pulling in, then sat and hugged her knees.

She'd been through a stronger fit of crying, and her nose and eyes were red when I stopped in front of her. "What did she do?" she said. Every time there were headlights on the street she stood. "What is she capable of, Justin?. Tell me that now. I need to know." Her voice was softer than I'd expected, pleading. "This is April, honey. This is our little April."

A car slowed, we heard it before we saw it, and we both stood, but it was only Joanne Brockmeier, our neighbor we shared the driveway with, who slowed and looked at us. I thought she was going to stop, but then she waved briefly and rolled past.

"I knew better," Mom said. "I knew . . . was I out of my mind? When did she lose her baby?"

"Mom."

"*When?*"

"I don't know. A year ago."

"Oh, what did I do?" She began to speak with long intervals in between. She said things I didn't want to respond to, that I had no response to. She'd trusted April with a crazy person. Even five years wasn't enough time.

I could only listen. I had nothing factual to disprove what she said, and I didn't want to lie to her, to make up evidence. And what had I been ignoring myself?

It was getting colder. I went in the house, turned on the lights and brought her a sweater. As I helped her into it she turned and hugged me fiercely. "What's going to happen?" she said. "What did we do?"

"She's okay," I said.

"God, let her be."

We had Levi's version of rush-hour traffic for ten minutes, head-lights passing one or two a minute, and we stood on the lawn watching. Afterward Mom walked back to the front porch and started dialing the phone.

Lou Costa arrived in his dark LTD cruiser without the police lights on. The center cap on the passenger front wheel was missing, and I had an automatic adverse reaction whenever I recognized the car. After Mom broke up with him the first time, and he parked in the driveway opposite ours and took radar, I'd see that wheel as I pulled in and feel sick as he gave me a very slow two-finger wave that seemed fraught with calculations.

Tonight he was cold toward us. She'd broken up with him again—or tried to: I'd heard her on the phone blaming it on her sponsor's advice not to pursue a relationship so early in her recovery.

"I'm not going to tell you his name," she'd said. "He's sixty years old, Lou. God, you sound like a jealous kid."

Now, after she told him what had happened, Costa said, "Oh, no. Juney?" I'd all but forgotten the dumb nickname he'd given her, as if he couldn't remember the month her name was. "Could she be around town somewhere?" he said.

"She isn't. Justin checked. No."

He wrote on his little notepad. "Where else could she go?"

Mom shook her head impatiently.

"Waterbury, maybe," I said.

"Do you want me to call it in as a kidnapping?"

"That's fine," she said.

"Wait. Come on," I said. "Maybe they're at a restaurant or somewhere."

"Call it whatever would get her back," Mom said.

"She'd never hurt April," I said.

Mom turned fiercely and said, "You shut up. Don't say things you don't know." Her eyes seemed to pulse for a moment before she looked at Costa again. "Think the worst thing," she said. "I'll apologize later if I have to."

"I can get it out on the radio," Costa said.

"Can't you just do a 'be on the lookout'?" I said. "Do you have to say why?"

Mom let out a sound that must have stripped the skin of her throat raw. She stabbed the phone at me—"Here"—and when I took it she walked around the side of the house into the backyard.

Costa and I watched where she had gone, but she came right back and asked him for his flashlight. "What are you looking for?" he said.

"Forget it. I'll get my own." She started for the stairs, but Costa handed out his long black Maglite. "Take it," he said. "I just meant could I help."

"I'm fine," she said, and with the flashlight she started again toward the backyard.

"She's still bitter," he said when she was gone. I recalled what his attention used to mean to me. Around town he had a rapport with the badasses at Northwest: "Uh-oh, here comes trouble. How come they let you off your leash?" There was also talk that you could bribe your way out of a ticket with a case of Black Label beer, a rumor that persisted regardless of its unlikelihood—fifteen dollars' worth of beer he could've bought for himself. But the stories gave him stature, and what I tried to remember now was how it felt when he'd swing into Arco with a squeal of his tires and park his cruiser at the pump opposite mine to talk to me through his open window.

But now he grinned as if the whole situation was suspect. "Where'd you get the new wheels?" he said.

"In the paper."

"No shit," he said. "I need to get me a subscription to that paper."

I focused on having no expression at all.

"She know you been going out to Wickersham's?" he said.

I assumed he'd told her about the races out there, or that he was willing to tell her. "Yeah, she does."

"Are you going to feel like telling me the truth anytime tonight?" he said. "I guess I can find out."

"Don't, okay? She doesn't know."

"Well all right, then. Wise-ass. Next time answer me straight."

She didn't have the bottle with her when she came back, but the cigarette she was smoking didn't cover the smell of it on her breath.

"What kind of car am I looking for?" he said.

"It's my old car," I said. "Seventy-four black Nova." I gave him the plate number.

His mouth hung open as he wrote on his pad. "So, you ended up selling this gal your car?"

"They're dating," Mom said.

"Well, hell. That kind of puts a spin on it." He looked at me. "You two have a spat?"

"Can you just call it in now?" Mom said. "She might be driving by a policeman somewhere."

"I will, Carol, if you just calm down."

"We didn't have a fight," I said. "It's probably she ran out of gas, or they're having dinner."

Costa pushed the light on his digital watch. "Late dinner for Juney, ain't it?"

"Just don't talk, Justin," Mom said, her arms wrapped around herself as if trying to still the jerky twisting of her waist, and she looked at Costa. "Her baby died and she's still grieving. She's . . . disturbed. That's too much to deal with."

"Well, goddamn, Carol. This thing keeps taking twists and turns—"

"She's not disturbed," I said.

Mom glared at me. "How do you know, Justin? How the hell do you know? You have no idea what she needs. You think you can date somebody like that?"

"She's been through more than you ever have," I said. "And she's still trying. She's not getting lit all the time."

"Hang on, boy," Costa said. "You just turn down the volume. Everybody calm the hell down." With his hands on his waist, his chest bulged out, he looked back and forth between Mom and me until he was satisfied. "Now Justin, I understand you got no father to teach you, I get it. But you show your own mother some respect. Be a man."

Of course I didn't see it then, in the moment's red flash, that he was doing the right thing, putting me back in line. My only thought was that he would be the one now. He was going to make me a man in his own image. It hadn't fully sunk in until that moment that he was back in our lives again.

I'd never been in a real fight before, and it was here, it was just throw the punch, any of the thousands I'd thrown at the Everlast bag downstairs, throw it, do it, and I did. When I swung he stepped to the side and with a lightning undercut laid me right out. Part of it was my own mistake, I'd decide later, breathing in instead of out when I threw the punch, so that my stomach was soft when his fist shoved up and in between the ribs. Then I was on the grass suffocating, gasping at a plum-colored sky full of sweet air I couldn't have.

Mom screamed. Then her cool hand on my forehead, pushing the hair back. It seemed from very far away that I heard his voice: "You saw. I ought to put the cuffs on him right now, goddamn it."

I sat on the front stoop feeling strangely invigorated, a tenderness in my stomach reminding me of each life-giving breath I pulled. I looked up to see Mom standing in the grass covering her mouth, Costa slouched beside her with his arms folded, looking misunderstood, both watching the road, where a yellow blinking light was reflected in the wild bushes in front of the Madden place, and Mary Ann turned into the driveway.

"Oh, thank you," Mom said. "Thank you." I joined her on the edge of the pavement as Mary Ann parked, already apologizing through her opened window. "We lost track of time. I wanted to call, but I didn't have change."

Mom went around to the passenger door, which Mary Ann leaned over to and unlocked. April was asleep in her car seat and Mom lifted her out. I walked with her as she came around the hood, trying to get a look at April in the dim light. Mary Ann had gotten out of the car and was standing by the fender. "It's late, I know," she said. "I'm so sorry. We missed our train."

"Train?" Mom said. She looked down at April in her arms and started to cry.

"I took her to New York. I'd been promising her." Mary Ann looked at me. "It was a special trip."

"Oh, my God," Mom said. She pulled April closer and April began to move with a breath. "Do you know what you did to me? Do you know what kind of things—what awful things. For eight hours? You don't know what you did to us."

"What do you want me to do?" Costa said.

April stretched her arm out. "Mom?" she said. Mom kissed her forehead. "Did you eat, honey? Are you hungry?"

April shook her head and rubbed an eye furiously as Mom walked toward the house.

"Wait," Mary Ann said. She started toward them with plastic shopping bags, but she stopped on the sidewalk when it was clear that Mom wanted nothing to do with her.

To Costa, Mom said, "If she comes onto this property again, I'll say it was kidnapping."

"Carol," Mary Ann said, and then, pleading, "Really?"

"Can I come in?" Costa said.

"No, you can't."

"He came at me. You saw it."

Mom wrenched opened the screen door, went in, and kicked the front door closed behind her in what seemed to be one unbroken movement.

Costa pushed his hand through his hair. He tore off the notebook pages and threw them on the lawn. He didn't look at me or Mary Ann as he went to the cruiser. I saw him talking on the radio for a few moments before he started the car and swung it back to within a few inches of Mary Ann's bumper. Then he pulled out of the driveway with a chirp of his tires.

In the silence that followed, Mary Ann and I looked around at the too-still darkness as if a spaceship had just taken off.

"We went to FAO Schwarz," Mary Ann said softly. "I meant for us to be back before dinner. I took her to the bathroom. We missed the train, and the next one wasn't express. I didn't have enough change to call long-distance."

I breathed to settle myself, to become acclimated to the end of the danger. I lit a cigarette and smoked the whole thing without moving more than my arm and hand. Mary Ann was still there when I flicked the butt away and looked at her, and through my rising anger I was distantly aware of the promises I'd made to God that I'd forgive her everything if only April came back safe. It bothered me that Mary Ann didn't seem more damaged. I realized that since she'd turned in the driveway, I'd been half inside a daydream in which she was driven crazy by her suffering, by distortion, seeing her little Joey in our April, and it would all be clear, palpable, and I would be there for her at the bottom.

"Do you think you can give her these?" Mary Ann said, holding the bags out to me.

"It's probably not a good time."

"She was safe, Justin."

"You could have asked my mom first."

"I thought she'd say no." She went to the Nova and put the bags in the backseat, and thinking she would leave I came around and got in the passenger side. We both sat on the bench seat and closed our doors, looking at the house. After a minute or two Mom crossed in front of the living room windows, stopping to look out with the phone to her ear. It wouldn't have been Costa she was talking to so soon. He was probably still on duty, parked somewhere with his radar gun, cursing us all. No, it wasn't him. I hoped that it might be her AA sponsor talking her out of going out behind the fence again.

"I guess I thought you'd have more to say," I said to Mary Ann. "It's nine o'clock."

"And then at the parking lot I spent twenty minutes looking for my old car. I just forgot what I was driving. It was dark. I guess I thought you'd trust me."

I cracked my window and took out my cigarettes.

"Don't smoke in here," she said.

"Why not?"

"I quit."

"Since when?"

She watched me for a moment, then sighed and looked back at the house.

"You called the police on me?"

"She did."

"What did you think happened?"

I stuffed the cigarette pack in my jacket pocket.

"Justin," she said, "was there ever a single time . . . why would you think she wasn't safe with me?"

"It happened. It's over."

"I told you I wanted to take her on a trip. It was important to me."

"Why? So you could say good-bye?" I couldn't look at her now, because I didn't want her to just nod and have it easy. She was going to have to say it. And then I couldn't stand to hear it, and I said, "I know what you did to the Z-28. You didn't know I was there. I saw you."

Mary Ann started the car. "Get out," she said. "Oh, my God."

"It's not that hard to imagine you could take her. I mean, if you'd do that to Nick."

"Get out of this car, Justin."

"You want the shop to close so he'll take you back to Oregon, right? I'm right."

She was gripping the steering wheel, my old steering wheel, with white fists.

"I get it. Life was good out there and you hate it out here, I get it. But how am I supposed to know what to think? You smash up your car. You disappear with April. And now you love the guy that raped you?"

"It wasn't that. Fuck you, Justin. Were you there? How do you know what it was?"

"Then what was it?"

I don't know if it was accidental, but she mashed the throttle—the tach needle shot up to redline before she let off. "Get out of this car," she said. "I'm crazy, I'm psycho. Get out before I fucking hit you."

I thought I could do something with this. She'd made her point, and I was ready to apologize a little, but then she turned the key, and with the engine already running the starter pinion ground against the flywheel teeth with a horrific sound. "Okay," I said, and she did it again. I opened my door and got out.

As Mary Ann pulled out of the driveway I thought about following her, but my keys weren't in my pocket, and at that moment I had no idea where they were. I went in through the garage, and Mom was on the deck smoking under the spotlight that shone over the yard.

I came up beside her on the rail. "I don't think I'm going to sleep tonight," I said.

She didn't turn when she said, "Why are you talking to me now?"

I was thrown for a moment, clutching at the time before my fight with Mary Ann. I couldn't remember what had happened with my mother.

"What do you want to hear?" she said. "I know I'm a bad person. I know I put her in danger."

"I'm sorry, Mom. Can we just let it be over?"

"I'm sorry, too," she said. "I'm sorry my life isn't shitty enough for you. I'm sorry getting abandoned with a four-year-old doesn't meet your criteria for having a drink."

I breathed and picked my words carefully. "Do you know everything that happened tonight—standing around outside and Costa—if we just did nothing, it would have ended exactly the same? Do you realize that? April would still be asleep in her bed right now."

"I wish I was a strong person," she said.

"I can help her," I said. "Why can't I help her? You don't know. Why can't she be happy with me?" I was yelling at this point, and it seemed to stun her only for a moment. She turned and shot her cigarette into the yard. "I'm sorry I'm weak," she said. "And you couldn't have a normal family." She picked up her pack of cigarettes and swept away from me, and I said, "Mom," just as she yanked open the door. But there was no hesitation at all as she heaved herself through the garage landing and into the white light of the kitchen.

I turned back to the yard, and behind me the kitchen light went off—two window squares on the back lawn vanished to black. Above me a cloud glowed like a ghost with the moon behind it, and I had a few blinking stars and nothing for sound except the tiny static of my smoking and the creak of the deck rail when I leaned on it. I punished myself, trying to imagine the worst that could've happened, but even in insanity there is some sanity that remembers our essential selves, and I couldn't see Mary Ann ever hurting April. But she could have taken April from us in the hopes of giving them both a better life. When I thought of this, I saw them in a motel room, Mary Ann braiding April's hair with such trembling enthusiasm it made April cry.

I went inside, and at the foot of the stairs I waited a long time until the line of light under Mom's door went out. Softly as I could I crept up the steps. In her bedroom, in the fanned-out cast of her nightlight, April looked as if she had been frozen by a spell, her arms over her head and her chin high, her mouth open slightly, her breath making a tiny whistle on the inhale.

I sat on the floor beside her bed and tried to open my senses to the surreal idea that I could tell what she'd been through by watching her sleep. What was happening in her dreams? I realized for the first time that she had a smell that was more than No More Tears and fabric softener, her smell, April smell, that was the smell of her hugging me goodnight and her sitting on my lap at breakfast, and I explored the coldness in my chest of letting myself imagine her gone from my life. I laid my head on her pillow so that her hair was in my eyes and whispered that she was a good girl. Not until the tears were running off my jaw did I realize I was crying. I almost never cried, and when I did it was for many reasons at once. It was for the hours she was unsafe. For my not being able to find or help her. And when I said that she was a good girl, it was that she hadn't thought there might be danger—that, in her goodness, she couldn't imagine danger—that was so unspeakably sad.

Gradually I found peace in her deep steady breathing. It gave me confirmation that there had been no trauma today. Mary Ann hadn't lost her mind, but she was sensitive enough to possibly lose her mind, and wasn't that very quality something about her I loved? When she told lies, as she had to the nurse about Joey, it wasn't for the usual reasons—to save face or to take an advantage. She lied like a child does, to make the world friendlier. To pretend. Isn't that the idea behind prayer and chants and meditation, say it enough and it is? Say it until you believe it?

I didn't go to bed that night. After I left April I went in the basement and made a fire in the woodstove. I curled and bench-pressed and threw darts. I didn't even yawn.

I saw myself in my old life, without Mary Ann or Out of the Hole, and my stomach wrenched and burned. Around dawn the plan came to me and quickly took shape, and when I went out to smoke in the damp grass I was on the top rail of a ferry (Point Judith? Block Island?) with Mary Ann after she'd stopped missing Nick and had realized the long life she still had to live. We'd tell each other everything we'd once felt for Nick and then be free of him.

34.

WHILE BOBBY WAS TAKING APART AN ALTERNATOR, I WENT OUT
the side door and tore ass down to the Dungeon. By the light of
a match, I searched along the flagstone foundation for the loose
mortar behind which Bobby had hidden the key, along with the
model and address of the car.

He and Pam had a system worked out. The first time, giving us
the key for the Taurus, she came in for a tune-up on her Cavalier.
With this second car and with all cars thereafter, she'd come in
complaining of a rough idle or bad mileage. It was Bobby's idea, to
keep them from being seen together. From her glove box he'd get
the key and address, and rather than take them home he'd stash
them downstairs in case she got busted and turned on him, which
had suddenly become a possibility.

Bobby was paranoid. At times I thought he might be on something like crank. He'd lost some weight—his arms were harder
and veinier, his cheeks thinner, his eyes glassy—though that didn't
have to mean anything between the hydrocarbons in the air and
the changing seasons, which had been gusting wood smoke through
the bays.

I took a Mercury for a test drive to Kmart, where they copied the key while I waited. This was the nerve-wracking part, playing the odds that Bobby wouldn't go down to check the key while I was gone. The odds were well in my favor—we weren't supposed to take the car until Wednesday night—but I started getting diarrhea cramps right in the store. Bobby was where I'd left him when I got back, on a stool at the bench nearest the radio, and I went downstairs, copied the address, and stuffed everything back into the wall.

I couldn't focus that day. I needed more caffeine, but I didn't want to go out to the lobby and face Mary Ann, who had come in so that Nick and Rod could meet with a salesman about a new Sun Scope that interfaced with onboard computers.

I did a lot of staring from a distance, mostly at Bobby. He would take out tools and lay them on a fender mat, light a cigarette, and then go back to his tool drawer and say things like, "Where'd you go, you little cocksucker" for a minute or two, and then find that he'd already set the thing he wanted on the fender mat. Once, he dug his grimy fingers in his mouth, retrieved a wad of Bit-O-Honey and said to it, "You sure are a chewy motherfucker." He was always moving except when he was looking at the scope, and then it seemed to take a long time to interpret what he was seeing.

My head was killing me that morning. I couldn't quit yawning. I thought maybe I could take about a quarter of whatever Bobby was taking and see what it did.

I never would've asked, but I figured the shop was going to close down soon because Nick would be in jail. I couldn't say for sure if I'd ever see Bobby again. Fuck it, I went up to him and said, "You got anything I can stay awake with?"

"Get the fuck out of here."

"No, really, Bobby. Just give me one. I'll pay you."

He stepped closer and slapped me. "How's that?" He did it again, and I fell back against the air filter shelving, out of his reach. "There's your fucking wake-up," he said. "Quit being a punk."

"Asshole," I said.

"All right. I'm an asshole then."

I ended up running across the street for some NoDoz and a large Brazilian Bold from 7-Eleven.

I took a Firebird out to the address Pam had written down. By chance the three hundreds were only a few blocks from the west entrance to Fulton Park. Chase was a big double-lined street, residential on one side, commercial on the other—Dunkin' Donuts, a repair shop, a locksmith. The houses on the west side were all little capes with low stone walls and tiny elevated yards. Their cracked driveways carved into the rises of yellow lawns, and the single-car garages were pushed in like drawers under the front windows. I found the house, and there was the hunter green LX Mustang parked in front of it. My throat closed.

I only meant to scope the car, but all at once it became clear that now was the time if I was going to steal it.

My plan had been to come at night and then stash it in a parking lot, hoping no one found it before I came back the next morning, when Nick and Mary Ann were working. But wasn't that too risky? What if the car was found? What if Mary Ann stayed home tomorrow?

I swung into the lot of a Food Mart and parked out of sight of the register. It had to happen now. I heard my breathing, and it had to happen now. Go. Take the keys. Leave the Firebird here and come back across the park for it. Three o'clock. Plenty of time.

I left the car and then I left my body. This is the way it happens. I saw how people committed the highest and lowest acts of humanity—the most virtuous and wicked and vile and noble acts—by imagining the extreme, by staring at it in your mind and finally dragging it out of the abstract. Then it is simply a matter of obeying, of keeping it going. I had never been this far inside a moment—even making love to Mary Ann hadn't put me in this far.

Trombones in my ears. I had a hundred minds. My feet had minds, my legs, arms, eyes. React. Keep it going. I saw myself from above.

Last night in the basement I'd made a fire and with the stove door half opened, so I could exhale my cigarettes inside, I came to understand, the way you understand the truth of everything staring into fire, that Mary Ann would spend the last of herself on Nick, not knowing that he wasn't even able to accept, much less return, her love. She would try too hard with him and afterward be too broken. She'd be gone beyond my ability to help her. I saw her eyes charred and dim with Mom's evening stare, not knowing how to make herself happy again. With that image, all other thoughts fell away.

I would give Mary Ann a different afterward. When Nick was in custody, I'd tell her that he'd wanted me to lie and say he was working late at the shop if she'd asked. I assumed he'd been racing the Corvette, Mary Ann, but my God. This is what he'd really been up to. The rechecks had been costing him too much business, and even the racing money wasn't enough . . . My God.

And who knows? Maybe he'd believe he'd really done it. Maybe it would finally be the escape I was certain he'd been longing for.

To not be seen from the house, I went south to the deli and crossed the street there. A paper Frankenstein, three weeks early for Halloween, hung on the front door of the house. I blocked out the idea that these were good people who decorated, who brought some festivity to the dismal neighborhood. I wasn't hurting them, not really. If it wasn't me now, the real repo guy would come soon. This was just speeding up the inevitable. The blinds were down on the windows directly over the garage, and the Mustang was parked there a few feet from the cinder-block retaining wall.

I got in the car but didn't want to close the door in case it didn't start and someone came out and I had to run. But it was only a year old, and of course it started on the first crank. The seat was so far back I was barely on it as I dropped the floor shift into reverse. I backed up and the open door scraped along the retaining wall, bending back with a sickening creak, and in the seconds it took to realize the door would come off if I didn't pull forward, I saw him come out of the house, and I pulled my cap over my eyes, jumped it forward until I could pull the door closed, but it wouldn't close all the way—something was bent—and I slammed it into reverse again and swung around in the street as the big, bearded man came down the steps, his arms swinging wildly. I held down the horn, which jolted him, and he fell on his ass on the sidewalk, and in the road an oncoming car swerved around me, blaring its own horn. I saw the big man in my rearview mirror cutting over the grass and then finally stopping at the end of his little yard and watching bent over with his hands on his hips, heaving for air.

I turned down different streets in case I was being watched or followed. I needed to get off the road before I passed a cop, who would be able to see that I was only holding the door closed with my hand.

I eased off Cooke into Nick's driveway, where I pulled right up to the garage and shut it off. One second became another second, and then I was out and running full speed over the cement to the side door. I found the key under the brick, opened the door, ran around shoving toolboxes against the walls, heaving milk crates and chains and a folding chair out of the way, then looped around back to the garage door, twisted the handle to unlock it. The door was heavy with disuse, the rollers squealing and scraping until I had it as high as my chin, which was plenty, and I ran under, got in the car, fired it up, and pulled it in. I yanked the door back down, and then I was able to breathe.

I found a rag and started wiping down everything I had touched. I was amazed by how fierce and streamlined my thoughts were, how acute my senses. As I was coming around to shut off the light, I saw two of Nick's wrenches covered in black fingerprints, and the idea came to me fully mature, as if someone else had spoken it. With electric tape I lifted prints off a wrench and stuck them on the door handle, around the steering wheel and shifter. I couldn't tell if they had transferred, but why wouldn't they? And what else would the cops need? How could Nick talk his way out of it now? And how could Mary Ann believe any scenario other than the obvious one?

From Nick's I ran across the park and back to the Firebird. I unplugged the mass air flow sensor to set a trouble code, and I was back at the shop less than an hour after I'd left. Rod came up to me as soon as I stepped into the bays.

"What'd you do, go take a nap?"

"It kept cutting out," I said. "I had to let it cool off."

"Any codes?"

"Fifteen."

"Mass air flow," he said. "Tell him he needs a tune-up on top, and you got yourself a pretty righteous ticket."

35.

"THERE'S A STOLEN MUSTANG, LICENSE NUMBER 7-1-5-G-L-E, at 161 Cooke. Look in the garage." In the parking lot of Burger King, I said it in a deep voice with a rural drawl, and then like a New Yorker, and then like a Brit. Burning in my front pocket was the number for the Waterbury police department, and since I didn't know if they traced incoming calls (my research had yielded only that grand theft auto landed you one to five in real jail time) I planned to make the call from the pay phone on the sidewalk when I finished eating.

I forced down one French fry at a time and was still partially outside my body, catching myself staring curiously at what my fingers were doing.

Bobby would hate me; that was a fact I needed to live with. I'd say I must've mentioned it all to Nick, even where the key was. Bobby would either think I was a jackass or he'd think I was much worse. But what was he going to do? He couldn't save Nick without incriminating himself. I tried not to care as my intestines kinked and cramped, and then I was across the lot and inside the restaurant men's room, landing on the seat just in time.

I was in there for fifteen minutes. I felt weak, the way even mild sickness can seem like a punishment, can make you wonder what kind of person you are at heart. What you deserve and don't deserve, the karma you create. I remembered the look of puzzlement when Nick had a car come back, as if he didn't recognize where he was. That was the expression I saw when they led him in handcuffs down an echoing hallway, that was his face—not even suspecting me, not bearing hatred for anyone except himself—as he sat on his bunk locked away somewhere. When he got out and Mary Ann was gone and his shop was gone, he'd be the disheveled, unshaven bum on the sidewalk, sitting in the park, standing at the rail of the bridge, old and mute at forty, nothing running through his mind but the constant-loop movie of what went wrong.

I couldn't do it. He deserved whatever he deserved, but it wasn't this.

Tomorrow morning early, before work, I'd come to the house and tell him. I'd say I was jealous of him and Rod, which was half true, and leave Mary Ann out of it. We'd get rid of the car somewhere. Wipe it down. I'd make sure to wipe it all down.

But Christ, I couldn't wait. What if tonight was the night Mary Ann let him go in the garage again? Why wouldn't he call the cops, who would then find his prints on the wheel and shifter and wonder why he was lying about not having driven the car?

It was full dark when I left Burger King. Daylight savings time was next weekend, after which night would come on before five. I looked at the dim blue clock numbers on the radio. They'd be done with dinner. Maybe I could signal to Nick in the window, and Mary Ann would never have to know.

I parked in the street so they wouldn't see my headlights. The light was off in the kitchen and I went around to the window I'd looked in before, its buttery light casting a long rectangle on the driveway. Nick was alone on the futon, and I glanced back to make sure the Nova was there beside his car. It was. She was somewhere in the house.

I could see Nick pretty well from my angle. In the soft light of the overhead fixture his face was sunken and loose as he leaned over a legal pad on the coffee table, working something out with a pencil. I saw a flash of the picture when he held it up, some kind of a Venn diagram it looked like. Suddenly and in one deft motion he leaned forward and pushed the legal pad under the couch. He must've heard something I couldn't, with the street sounds and, farther off, the highway sounds. And then he stood up and looked directly at me. I ducked down. I'd lost my focus watching him and wasn't ready to speak. I closed my eyes for a few moments, and then whispered what I was going to say.

The familiar blue flickering appeared on the side of the garage, and I could hear TV voices. I don't know how long I waited, but my toes were starting to tingle. I straightened, and at the exact second I looked in the window, Mary Ann appeared in the hallway parallel to the futon.

Her hair was wet and combed straight back, and she wore only a towel wrapped around it, which she held with her hands crossed over her chest. She stopped at the threshold, looked at Nick, at the TV, at Nick again. He hadn't seen her yet, and her look, as she watched him, seemed uneasy, brooding. She blinked slowly, her eyes made up with liner and shadow, and then she swallowed and drew a long breath. "Here I am," she said, the exact words she'd said to me from my bed, and she smiled what seemed a brave smile. When Nick turned to her she let go of the towel and stepped toward him.

And, oh, her body, pink from the heat of the shower. The twin moles, the deep navel, the curveless, girlish hips and thighs. Around her neck she wore a silver chain from which a small blue stone, a sapphire, hung over the valley between her breasts, where I'd never seen jewelry before, and she had trimmed her pubic hair to almost nothing for him, a stripe down the center. The glass between us and the distance made her seem like a version of herself, a lookalike whom I could touch no more than I could a woman in a photograph.

Nick had fallen back against the futon, and she took the remote control from his thigh and turned off the TV. She tossed the remote to the side and straddled his legs as she reached down—it all happened in one continuous motion—to hold his face on either side with her open hands, forcing him to look into her eyes as she had never had to force me, and kissing him. His arms thrown back, one hand compressed the corner of the futon mattress as if it were only a towel, but she was determined and he went limp in the kiss, letting go of the mattress corner, which sprang back to shape, and finally lifting his hand to her waist.

I watched without a specific emotion but with all emotions, frozen and pulsing, consumed. She was holding his face and kissing him from one angle and then another; his big rough hand on her waist was softening, patting, caressing. His legs unbent and slid forward. She drew back and began to speak words I couldn't hear but that I knew were about the love I'd tried to make myself believe no longer existed, never existed.

Then he turned his head and started pushing her away, lightly at first, but his eyes became wide, the way they do when you sense danger in the dark and are trying to see it. She brought her face to his ear and spoke to him, and I saw her hand reach down between her legs, between his, and Nick tried to stand. He pushed against the back of the futon, which tipped a few inches into the wall, and Mary Ann yelled, "No!" and wrapped her arms around his neck.

Nick stood despite her weight and was only handicapped from a normal stride by her legs holding around his waist and her feet pushing into the backs of his thighs. He took a few steps toward me before he swung around and folded forward over the futon, holding himself by the back frame. But she wouldn't let go. Her face was buried in his collarbone. With one hand he pried her arms off, and as she was falling she tore out his hair and he jumped back.

He stumbled, rubbing his head, and at the bookshelf he grabbed a little car, a metal model of the 1905 Olds Runabout, the first

American production car, and he threw it at the framed picture of Cape Blanco Lighthouse, where they had been married. The little car splintered the glass, but somehow the picture didn't fall.

"Look at me," Mary Ann was saying. She got off the futon staring at him, and then stepping toward him as in a crime drama. *Please just hand me the gun.*

"You don't get to hate me, Nick. Look at me. What did I do wrong?"

Before she could reach him, Nick grabbed a ceramic bowl from the shelf and hurled it at the opposite wall. And she kept coming. He pulled the shelf over so that it fell between them, so that it crashed and exploded and shook the house—I felt it with my face against the siding.

She backed away, shaking her head. "What did I do?" She collapsed on the futon. Nick left the room. "What did I do?" Mary Ann called, rocking side to side, knees balled up to her chest. Had he hit her? Had I somehow missed that?

The kitchen door pulled open ten yards away and I fell back into a rhododendron bush. Nick came out, trying to light a cigarette with matches. He ripped off three or four and cupped the small torch, walking the whole time toward his car. I watched him from my cover. I was a coward, nothing compelled me from the heart. He dropped into the driver's seat, and the outline of his dark head nodded and shook. Then the high whirr of the starter on a strong battery, the rumble from the tailpipes, and I started ripping out the sausage leaves of the rhododendron and kicking at the gravel. I came out as he was backing up. In the street he didn't pull away— he'd seen my car and wasn't moving. I ran down the driveway.

When I was in his passenger seat he rolled the car forward and banged into the curb. He slapped the shifter back and forth in neutral. All he could say was, "What? What?" He rolled down his window and threw out the cigarette. "Sometimes . . . you're here. I don't know if I'm awake sometimes."

"You're awake. Trust me."

He looked back at the house, then at the park, where there was no sound, as if he were on some drug that heightened or distorted his senses. He was holding his stomach. "She wants a baby again," he said. "I can't. I should have told her I can't. But you're here now. I don't know why you're here." He didn't look at me as he spoke. I could see that he was nearing a place where the possible becomes unlimited, where the laws of nature don't hold. I tried to steer him back.

"You could've broken her foot with that bookshelf," I said.

He leaned forward and the gauges cast his face in a red glow. He didn't ask how I knew, how I'd seen it. He was breathing hard, and he leaned back against the seat. A car started somewhere on the street behind us. He closed his eyes for a moment, and then glanced quickly over as if he expected me to have vanished.

"Can you go see how she is?" he said.

I stared at him. "Me?"

As if the sound of the idling engine was more than he could bear, he lurched and shut it off. "She never wanted to come out here," he said. "She said it's not our kind of people. I said don't worry about the people. But that was wrong. We should have. She should be with people."

"But you didn't tell her that," I said, looking for my courage. Everything was going to come out tonight. "You can tell me, but not her."

"Every day I think she's going to ask why. How I could do that. That night she got rid of her car, I thought maybe you two talked about it. I thought she was going to leave me."

"She gave up on you," I said, looking down at the floorboards. "She should."

"She loves me," I said. "We're in love." The words gave me a hot jolt of legitimacy. White noise came from inside my head in a finale of flashing neurons, any emotion possible from the great stew, until I looked up and found him watching me. His mouth hung open. "You mean you were together?" he said.

Before I said yes I began to say again that we were in love, but Nick looked as if he had turned off every thought in his mind waiting for my response. He had to have known. That's what I realized I believed. It was impossible for him not to know, and yet he didn't. "Yes," I said.

I thought he might say my name, certain that if he did I would start to cry. But he gave only a weak, mechanical nod. After a moment he covered his mouth with the back of his hand.

"But she's happy?" he said.

"Yes."

"That's good," he said. "You two. I don't . . . How long?"

"Since July."

"This whole time." He leaned against his window, looking up at the dim city sky. He was sanctified by his inability to imagine such a betrayal, and I had to look away from him again. A hundred yards ahead of us the narrowing street ended in sodium arc light over a chain-link fence. Under the dark silhouettes of trees there was movement in the shadows, this park in the disguise of country, but it wasn't country. It was dangerous with people. I stared at a pair of sneakers hanging from the phone lines.

"She should be in love," Nick said. He was grinning when I looked back at him. "I'm glad she is," he said. Amazingly he started to laugh, uneven spits of laughter at first, like the sputter of a cold engine, but then warming into the easy laugh of last summer when we'd run our cars into each other at the lights. More than a year ago. Only a year ago. "She seemed happy again," he said. "Does she laugh?"

"All the time, Nick."

"And April," he said. "She brings home the crayon pictures. She has you and April now." He smiled and breathed as he leaned back again in his seat. About tonight, her seducing him, I thought to explain that she must've been a little out of her mind. Thinking it was a different time. Understandable with all the changes. But I only got as far as telling it to myself, trying to believe it myself, because Nick didn't seem bothered by the inconsistency. Suddenly he reached over and grabbed me around the shoulder. He pulled me into him and kissed me on top of the head. Then he hugged me and let me go.

"Let's go talk to her," I said.

"You go. I'll leave you two alone. No, okay. Yeah. Tell her I'm happy about it. I'm happy for both of you."

We sat there quietly for a few minutes. Just before I opened my door he said, "You know what I'd think sometimes? What made me feel better? I'd think what if Joey had turned out like you."

The house was warm inside (it occurred to me later that she'd arranged their lovemaking right down to setting the thermostat), and I heard it as soon as the kitchen door clicked shut. One low droning pitch from the back of the house, a high stutter when she gasped for breath and then the enduring moan.

In the living room I stepped over the toppled books and mementos, already smelling her blends, cinnamon, lavender, frankincense, her potions. I picked up the towel where it had fallen off her body and put it to my face.

I took a few light steps into the hallway and listened to her moan that same note, broken only by her stuffed inhales; I began to hear a stretched-out word—"no," or "don't"—and it took some daring to walk farther down the hall.

The bedroom door was open. Mary Ann was on her side and curled, fetal, humming and sniffing, and, closing my eyes, I breathed her in. I saw her coming to Nick as she had never come to me, her eyes filled with yearning and fear, so determined, hungry, and insistent, so sexy. I could smell the clove now. The cypress and rose.

I got on the bed behind her, and she grabbed back for my hand and pulled it to her chest. For a few seconds neither of us moved.

"It's me," I said.

She let go of my hand and drew away from it but didn't sit up.

"How are you here?" she said, her voice wet and breaking, and with the hand that had only a second ago seized mine she wiped her nose. She turned over on her back. I could see only the outlines of her face, which was turned not to me but to the ceiling.

"He knows about us," I said. "It's okay now. He knows."

There was no sound, no breathing from either of us, and then she shuddered. Her crying came in voiceless spasms, and her tears ran into her hair. I brought my arms around her and kissed the side of her face as she cried—I could feel her cheeks tighten as her eyes pinched closed, and the tears, the salt trickle, the sloppy wet. She started hitting me on the spine with the sides of her fists, the blows just enough to shorten my breath. I knew it wouldn't last and it didn't, and she was hitting me with unfisted hands that rested finally on the tops of my shoulders. I lifted my head, and she pulled my face down to hers and kissed me hard. I undid my pants and slid them off just enough, and her hand was on my tailbone pressing down as I entered her.

I told her I loved her through the frantic kissing. She started whispering, and I couldn't stop myself from interrupting: "April needs you," I said. "Mom forgives you. We're okay, Mary Ann. Finally. We're okay."

Her lips kept moving, and I pulled up from her. In the dim light of the open door she drew her hands over her navel but didn't look at me even as I was staring down, even as our lovemaking had stopped, even as I said her name. Her lips were moving. She was talking to the ceiling. "The baby," she said. "The baby, Nick."

I was spinning, weightless. When I clicked on the ceramic lamp she rolled into a tight ball and was quiet. After a moment she reached back for the comforter and threw it over herself.

The silver chain was gone from around her neck—had he torn it off? Had I? I touched her shoulder, and she recoiled right up to the edge of the bed. I backed away on my knees. I saw my erection and was disgusted by it. I pulled up my pants and got off the bed.

In the kitchen with my eyes closed I relived the summer, I looked down on myself making love to Mary Ann, I eavesdropped on our deepest conversations. Could she have been only wanting a baby? It couldn't be, the evidence just wasn't there, but the question already had a steel edge of truth.

I was slumped over the table when Mary Ann came out in her bathrobe and put the teapot on the stove. I was afraid, not of her but for her, that she'd lost her mind. But after a minute or so she spoke without looking at me. "You saw him?" she said. "Outside?"

I told her I had, and after I was sure that she was done asking questions I said, "You're pregnant." I wasn't asking or telling, but just putting the tremendous fact into existence by saying it. The words weakened me, and right there I started to feel like I was getting a cold. My sinuses drained, and I was almost shivering. I pressed my hands between my thighs and crouched forward a little. When I closed my eyes the silence became massive and dizzying.

The teapot whistled, and as she poured the steaming water into a cup it all became clear. Her not smoking. Her good-bye to April.

"How long?" I said. "How far along?"

"It was that night in your room. I didn't have my diaphragm in."

I couldn't really digest this because I knew there was no hope, and yet the night I thought about constantly having been the night of conception gave me hope.

She held the cup under her nose and breathed the steam, still looking outside with her back to me. "I'm sorry, Mary Ann," I said. "I shouldn't have come in."

She was still for a moment, and then she turned without looking at me and went out of the room. I stared at the tabletop. How had it happened? I didn't recognize my hands. I couldn't make myself move. I couldn't do the right thing or do anything but stare at the flecks in the Formica.

I'd lost control of myself, I'd done what I never would have believed I could do, she'd trusted me and I was no one who could be trusted. What else would I watch myself do? I wasn't seeing the flecks anymore but seeing myself on her, and hoping it was only a short time, a time she could forget, please God let it erase itself for her.

I mashed a dish towel over my mouth and cried. It was half an hour later when I looked at the clock again. I got out of the chair, my ribs sore, and pulled on my jacket. I blew my nose in a napkin and looked around for a pen and something to write on. Passing the doorway to the living room I just happened to glance in, not expecting her to be there, but she was on the futon, lying on her side in the kitchen light, watching me. And that lie inside me came alive again that maybe if we talked. If only we talked.

I stood over the bookshelf, and she wouldn't look at me. I lifted it back against the wall—it was lighter than it looked—and put back on the shelves everything that hadn't broken.

Mary Ann pulled her legs up, and I sat on the end of the futon where her feet had been. I propped my head back on the flat edge of mattress, feeling drugged from the crying and all the bad sleep. "I'm going. I'll go," I said, fighting a helpless, empty sleep I was afraid of.

When she spoke, the source of her voice seemed to come from inside my head. "He could have believed the baby was his."

I nodded with my eyes still closed, and these were the last words of my consciousness: I'll get him back for you.

36.

IT WAS RAINING. I RUBBED THE HOT CABLES IN MY NECK, TRYING to remember, by the strength of my headache, how much I'd had to drink. She was dressed and standing by the window, the source of the dim grainy light in the room. Very slowly the night came to me, beginning with the awareness that I wasn't hungover.

"Can I use your bathroom?" I said.

She didn't turn around. "Where is he, Justin?"

"Did you call the shop?"

"All morning."

The numbers on the wall clock took a few seconds to come into focus. It was seven thirty. No one would be there yet unless Nick had slept on the couch in the office, which I assumed he had, and wasn't answering the phone, wasn't, perhaps, ready to participate in the circumstances of his life just yet.

"I'll see if he's there," I said. "I just need to pee quick. I'll have him call you."

But in the bathroom, mid-stream, the events of yesterday came flooding back with the sound of trumpets, and I couldn't finish fast enough. I surged out to the living room and told Mary Ann about the Mustang in the garage, and I told her the truth—when I said I had wanted Nick out of our lives, she squinted at me as if she didn't know who I was. I told her the plan I'd come up with just now. Mary Ann went past me into the kitchen and grabbed her purse. "Let's go."

I drove in front in the Mustang. The cold and the light rain came in where the door wouldn't close. I stopped at every stop sign, trying to replay in my head a few minutes before, when I told her to just keep going if a cop pulled me over, to see if there had been anything at all sympathetic in her look when she nodded.

I parked the Mustang not far from where her Malibu had been taken at Holy Land and wiped everything down with the arm of my jacket. There were no other cars, no people that I could see, and no sounds of people. But it was early, and the rain looked to be the last of a front, the sky already lighter in the west, and there was a chance that the day would dry out completely and people would come.

I got in the Nova, and she started away as I was closing the door. As we drove it occurred to me that this was the last time I'd be inside my old car, and I touched the dashboard over the glove box. I thought about the person I was when I owned the car and the person I suddenly was now.

She didn't speak until we were less than a minute from her house, when she said, "I didn't plan this," and looked at me. "Getting pregnant, any of it. This whole year, I didn't plan." She said this without intimacy or emotion, only to prevent me from misunderstanding. We weren't going to talk again, at least not how we once had, after this car ride.

"When I came in the house, I heard you crying," I said. "I knew you loved Nick. And I knew what was right, but I went in anyway. I'm sorry."

She turned into her driveway and stopped so that I would have less of a walk to my car in the street. But she shifted to park, which gave me a small hope, though she wouldn't look at me.

"Are you going to have it?" I said. If it came to an abortion, I'd go with her if Nick wouldn't. But she was only angry now, and when she shook her head, it wasn't in answer to my question but in disapproval of me. As I turned to open my door, she said, "Justin, what happened to you?"

I drove to the river. I wanted the sound of it, but as I sat with my window cracked in the spitting rain, wishing I had coffee, I heard only the wet rush of morning traffic on the Connecticut Avenue Bridge. I drifted off for a few minutes and woke with the sudden awareness that I had work today. I fell right into time, found myself pulling into the back lot only ten minutes late. Rod's Dodge was there, Bobby's AMC, and Nick's El Camino—as I had figured it would be. Where else did he have to go?

I was ready to bury my head under a hood. Nick was right about engines. They didn't change. Even the computer-controlled ones just became more efficient at what they did. Fuel and air and spark, for a hundred years. I wanted that mechanical simplicity to overrun my mind and wash out everything else.

But as I walked up the alley to the side door, I knew I was on my way to the back office, where I would tell Nick and tell him everything.

When he was done yelling at me or beating me he would go to her, while I packed my tools and silently eliminated myself from their life.

I fell against the greasy side of the waste oil tank, the strength suddenly gone from my legs. "My baby," I whispered. The shiver the words gave me was detached from any image of what my baby would look like—I only saw her holding it in a blanket. Let them be happy, I tried to pray. What if raising my child would be enough penance for Nick? Let them be happy. My penance would be never telling the secret. I saw the future and was terrified and satisfied and alive. The only thing that mattered from now until infinity was being a good person.

Bobby opened the side door and stepped out carrying a drain pan, a cigarette in his lips. He saw me, jutted his chin, and went to the waste tank.

"Hang on." I came around him to open the lid. As he started to pour it down, I apologized for the other day, and I wanted to keep apologizing—it felt cowardly to have so much relief. I was on the brink of telling him what I had done, this monstrous twenty-four hours, the Mustang, Mary Ann, all of it, when he brought down the drain pan and said, "Look, man, I'm not giving you a disease." I followed him into the bays. "That's all it is, a disease. The junk and the booze. Like one fag giving another fag AIDS. Go listen to 'Puppets.' It's all in that song."

Rod's voice came over the intercom telling me I had a phone call. In less time than seemed possible, just a second or two, I rocketed from the panic of the cops having found the Mustang and a fingerprint I'd missed, or that the guy, the fat man, had seen the logo on my hat when I was stealing the car, to the wavering relief that it was only Mom, wondering why I hadn't come home.

But then Rod, seeing through the lobby window all my pale bulging expressions, continued, "Al Wickersham. Second time he called."

37.

IT HAD NEVER OCCURRED TO ME TO LOOK IN THE DUNGEON, WHERE
I would have seen that the Corvette was gone. Wickersham said
he'd heard a car out there this morning when he was milking
cows. "Don't know how he rolled it," he said. "A car that low to
the ground. Wasn't even raining yet."

He was quiet, and it wasn't a quiet I could break, a moment of
silence it seemed. I hadn't said more than "Hello."

Then came another voice on the line, and it was Dave Bowers.
"I went by your place. Your car wasn't there."

"Did he die?" I said.

"What's that?"

My hand—I felt it clamped over my mouth. But I couldn't
bring it down any more than I could open my eyes. Dave cleared
his throat. "Me and Al were up in the stall barn. De-balling the
Guernseys. We hear this motor revving down at the track, so we
got on the quads. It's barely daylight. He's got the 'Vette, only he
put fat cheater slicks on the back. Fifteen-inch baldies. He's got
that car doing wheelies. Jesus Christ, that goddamn car." There
was the first of a number of pauses as he told his story. I heard him
exhaling hard through his nose. "He asks do we have a digital

watch. I got mine on. He wants me to time him. He says he's going to hit ten seconds." As he paused again, I was there in the weak light, rubber in the air, and I made no sound, afraid to influence the story from other than the exact truth of it.

"I can't tell if he's nuts or what," Dave said. "Ten seconds. Fuck. So I go down to the line and he takes off. But then I don't know. There's no brake lights. What the hell? He swings it, like he can one-eighty, but he's got the slicks on and they must've grabbed and then he's rolling. Side over side, rolling. Jesus Christ."

We were both panting, and tears ran over my hand. After I don't know how long I heard Wickersham in the background say, "Tell him what he did."

"What?"

"The time he ran."

"Aw, fuck you, Al," Dave said. "The guy's hurt, now. He's really hurt."

After I called her, I wandered outside. I wanted to be there at the hospital, but not if she didn't want me to be, and I certainly didn't want to be there first. I found myself in the damp coppery air of the Dungeon, the unlikely place where he had done his greatest work and, it turned out, could have done it without me. I don't know where he'd gotten the cheater slicks, but the rally wheels for the 'Vette were two to a stack in front of his toolbox. I picked one up and screamed. All my strength sent it only a few feet, smashing some buckets, and a rat shot out squealing.

At Mercy I parked in the row she was in and ran under the emergency room awning, following signs to the trauma center. They told me Nick was still in surgery, and in the third waiting room I found Mary Ann in a plastic chair, staring up at Joan Lunden on a ceiling-mounted TV.

When she saw me she got to her feet too fast and fell against me. I was ready and strong for her. "They don't know," she said. "They said I have to wait. They can't tell."

She was shaking like she might crumble apart, and my mouth opened wordlessly, breathing the words he would live, he would make it, a car could never kill him. This was a warning, but everything would restart. And now we'd know better. Now we'd have the truth.

The first blow came to my ribs with a dull burst. I closed my eyes and welcomed the pain. She held me with one arm and hit me with the other. She found a place on my spine that sent cold lightning to the base of my skull. She pounded me in the kidney. I opened my eyes just as an older man stopped in the hallway, looking at us, horrified, and I waved him past before I closed my eyes again. Each time she hit me a new color surged.

I wasn't ready for it to be over when she draped her arms around me weakly and cried. In a few minutes she was saying she was sorry.

I said, "Don't be. Don't be."

There were chairs and a cloth couch, and I walked her to the couch. We sat beside each other, leaned against each other. The sun came out in the hallway window, and I don't know how many times the TV shows changed. Twice a doctor came out and spoke to us.

I wouldn't have expected a doctor to be fat, but he was, he was enormous, and your mind does things—I had an impulse to ask for a different doctor, as if his big hands getting in there could . . . what if it went long and he couldn't keep standing . . .

Broken wrist, broken femur, radius, humerus, broken ribs, but no sign of organ injury. The real concern was the brain swelling. They had taken off a piece of his skull and would put it back when the swelling went down.

People came in and sat and cried softly and laughed barking laughs and left, and it didn't matter what anyone said. We were all suffering. Here, if nowhere else in the world, insanity was ignored, you could say anything without getting looks. These were some of the things Mary Ann said:

"One summer he caught a coho salmon on a valve spring. He stretched it out to spin in the current. He should have gone with fishing. Imagine if he fished.

"His father sold one of his rebuilds for three thousand dollars. He was twelve. This dad of his lied and said he sold it for four hundred and gave Nick half of that. He told me that the day he died, from the hospital bed, the son of a bitch.

"Don't ever tell him I told you, you promise? When he reads books he moves his finger down the page. It embarrasses him." She smiled, shaking her head, crying.

When a nurse came out to say she could see him now in ICU, Mary Ann started to follow her and then looked back at me and said I was Nick's brother.

He looked small in the mechanical bed, a good foot of empty mattress extending beyond him on both ends. His head was elevated and bandaged around like a Q-tip, and in front the bandage slanted down over one of his eyes. A yellow ventilator mask was strapped over his nose and mouth. His left leg and left arm were in casts, and the other arm looked swollen, his thick hand palm-up beside him. His face was lumpy, his cheek bruised almost black. His left leg they had put a stocking over, and behind its elastic fabric his leg hair curled up like pencil etchings.

The ventilator machine operated with the sound of a woman drawing a long breath and politely sneezing. Two hanging IV bags were plugged in to his forearms, and a tube from under his robe connected to a bag a quarter-way filled with urine.

Even in a coma they say a person can hear you, and in that strange way you experience volume when you're in temporary shock, I heard Mary Ann's voice faintly and then coming up. "Okay, honey," she was saying to Nick. "I'm here now. I'm not going anywhere. And here's your friend, Justin." She wiped her eyes, but you couldn't hear anything in her voice. She sounded happy.

Nick's hand, warm and dry, felt stiff and gave me a pang of dread that this was all for nothing, the artificial breathing and the monitors, because rigor mortis had already set in. "Hi, Nick. Hi, buddy," I said, bringing my other hand over his as well.

"Justin needs help with a car. Tell him," Mary Ann said to me.

It was too soon to try something like this, and I stood over him imagining only the most basic chemical reactions and electric pulses happening in his swollen head. His brain couldn't possibly be ready for abstract thought.

But for Mary Ann's sake I told him about a car with an intermittent stall, and I held his hand as if we were shaking hands. After a time of talking to him this way, I had fantasies of purging him of the poisonous thoughts and memories, only some of which he'd been able to tell me.

"We need you back," I said. I looked up at Mary Ann, hungry for her approval, but she had covered her mouth, her eyes narrowed and holding back, then bulging all at once in shock before she turned and left the room.

"She went for a Dr Pepper," I said. "You thirsty, Nick? Need one?" As soon as she left the room a sweet warm mist seemed to dissolve, and I saw in a harsher light that he was only his body now. He was just a man, and all of us were guilty of not letting him be just a man. I stared at his closed eye for a quiver, anything. I put my forehead down on his. I closed my eyes, smelling the Styrofoam smell of his bandages, and prayed for him. I sold myself to God to bring him back. "She forgives you, Nick," I said at the end. "She doesn't love me, she loves you. Trust her."

The next morning, I went to Dobson's, Firestone, Meineke, Maaco, Classic Coach, the dealerships along Route 8, and rounded up all the gearheads who'd once hung around the bays at Out of the Hole.

The hospital room was about the size of a shop bay, and at one point there were nine guys, half of them over two hundred pounds, standing around in that awkward, wrist-holding way of men not used to standing around. I was counting them the way I used to count friends at my birthday parties.

Mary Ann would leave the room graciously, and as soon as she did shoulders fell, sighs were released, giggles bubbled up. They dropped in the fabric chairs. They talked about old times, old engines Nick had built. They cussed and laughed, and I shut the door to the hallway when they got loud.

"You guys see Shorty Long down in Emergency? One time I seen that fucking guy cram four pool balls in his mouth."

"What happened? He swallow one?"

The only thing that mattered was that they weren't awkward talking to Nick—swollen and bandaged, his life being blown into him by a respirator. Coming here was some unexpected good in their lives. I imagined them lathering their arms at a tub sink, that communal place mechanics have at the end of the day. One saying, "They got fifty-cent Hamms at Brass Balls. We ought to partake."

Another one, "Can't. I'm going up to see Nicky."

They started the tradition of bringing him a Matchbox car from the gift shop. From a wing of the hospital under construction, they'd ripped off a windowsill six feet long. It was wide enough for a six-car Matchbox race. Tommy Burns went to work oiling it down with thirty-weight. He even rigged a starting gate that swung up on a pair of eyebolts.

"Are we ever going to use this thing, Tommy? You're not making fucking furniture."

"Before Nurse Ratched gets back."

They put down money on the races. Lyle Keaton found a Matchbox El Camino, and that was Nick's car. Naturally, it smoked all the rest. Nobody complained, even after it was revealed that Lyle had Superglued a couple of pennies to the undercarriage. They gave me Nick's money, and I passed it on to Mary Ann.

Ray came by one afternoon. He was pulling parts at NAPA now and looked ten years younger. I wasn't used to seeing him clean. His stubble was gone and his hair, parted over, gleamed with a Listerine-smelling pomade. He stood by the bed for a long while before he spoke quietly to the still, discolored face that only faintly resembled Nick. "How you doing, kid? I hear you got all the nurses fighting over . . ." He smiled severely then turned and left the room.

In the hallway I caught up to him, dropping quarters into the coffee machine. "Weird how it's computers keeping him going now," he said. I put a hand on his shoulder. We went and sat in chairs by the window. "How long since I was in here?" he said.

"A month. A month and a half."

"Seems longer."

"You were funny," I said. "You kept calling the nurse Dolly."

He wiped his eyes. "You see them milk cans? Dolly Double-D."

"Remember I went to get you your snuff?" I said. "Mary Ann stayed."

He nodded and looked at the cards on his coffee cup. The nub where his middle finger had been was still the glistening red of a scab fallen off.

"Did you guys talk?" I said.

"You mean about you?"

I thought I was ready for this, but suddenly I had ice in my stomach and the urge to look for a bathroom.

"Kid, I was so loopy on Vicodin I remember shaking hands with Terry Bradshaw on his TV show. That don't mean it ever happened."

I went to work because Nick and Mary Ann would need the money, and I made a surprisingly effective stand with Rod and Bobby that we weren't taking commissions anymore. I expected to have some resistance, especially from Rod, but they agreed.

One evening after Mary Ann went down to the cafeteria, something happened. I'm not certain if the squeeze was intentional, but when I told Mary Ann later I said it was in response to my asking if I should check a distributor cap for carbon tracking. Mary Ann didn't want me to leave that day. She went down and brought me back dinner, and while she was gone it happened again but in a lighter way, and when I wasn't talking to him, a kind of flinch.

I told him he and Mary Ann were going to have a baby.

On the tenth day they took out the ventilator and put a tube through a hole in his throat. This was a tipping point, the doctor had said. With a napkin I occasionally leaned over him to wipe away the gray mucus at the site of the hole. When Mary Ann would leave the room, unable to help my selfishness, I would confess to him. "I thought you were immune to everything. I'm sorry, Nick. I know you weren't. You didn't mean to hurt anybody, and I did. That was the real difference. Can you hear me? When you build the time machine, I want to get in now. You tell me what you need, and I'll get it. I'll bring it here. Forget everything, Nick. We just start over."

The day after the tracheotomy Mary Ann interrupted me as I was presenting him with a new engine scenario. "Justin can't do it without you. They'll have to refund his money. It's a shame. I don't know how long you plan on being here, Nick. Honey. They need you."

Her conversations with him now were just that, conversations, with answers anticipated in the silences. Should they go back to Oregon for Thanksgiving? Or should they eat at Across from the Horse again? Remember that sweet potato pie? Should they finally get HBO? She brought in a cable guide and told him about the movies and the new shows on MTV.

The doctors tested him on the Glasgow Scale, and he flexed his hand to pain. There was improvement. Then he opened his eyes one day when I was at work, and the tube was out of his throat that evening. A few days later he was looking at the pages of a glossy muscle car book. I'd forget myself and talk to him the way I first talked to April. Mary Ann scolded me out in the hall-way. "Don't insult him. It's better if he's a little confused than insulted."

"You were right," I told him when I came back. "We'll get it again. With computers and intercoolers."

Wickersham had the Corvette towed to the shop, where it was spatulaed off by a hydraulic flatbed. All four fenders, the passenger door, and the trunk lid had been torn off, and the windshield was blown out, a back and front wheel were missing, but remarkably the hood had only superficial scrapes and one of the T-tops was still in place.

And this was the very best we could do, our greatest effort at road travel, as near as we'd come to building a car from the future. I thought of what Mary Ann had once said about God looking down on Holy Land USA and holding Himself accountable for ex-pecting too much. Now I imagined God looking down and shak-ing His head at these remains.

Bobby came into work late one morning with a swollen eye and a bandage on his jaw. He didn't explain and I didn't ask, and after that day he stopped coming in at all. Rod helped me pull the engine and transmission from the ZL1, and he sold the body and frame to a scrap yard for almost exactly the cost of the tow from Wickersham's. A few nights a week after I left the hospital, I went back to the shop and worked on the engine, which had been mostly spared in the roll. It needed only external work—a fuel pump, a water pump, thermostat housing, the passenger-side exhaust header, and a carburetor overhaul.

I did the work in a back bay upstairs and covered the engine with a tarp during the day. It took me five nights.

I placed an ad in *Hemmings Motor News,* and a little after mid-night I started hooking up the engine to the dynamometer. By two I was ready to test it, something we hadn't done after the overhaul, thinking we didn't have time before Eve came to pick it up.

The 430-horsepower rating that Chevrolet had advertised was

at 5,200 rpm, but when I hit that mark the dynamometer read 512 horsepower. I kept going—6,500, 7,000. When fan belts began to drop from their peg hooks the dyno read 640 horsepower, and I was afraid to push it any more.

I left the engine hooked up to the dyno and two days later brought it up to 7,200 rpm once again for a man who had driven up from Georgia. He was the guy, the only other person in the world, who also owned a ZL1, the white one, and he paid me twenty-five grand in thousand-dollar bills for the engine (I threw in the tranny for free, what the hell), and I couldn't help telling him that he now owned the last remaining ZL1.

"Tell me what happened," he said. "Wait." He ran out to his big Chevy truck and returned with a pen and a notepad. "For the record." He wanted to know everything—the name of the driver, the cause of the wreck. I shook my head. He went into the envelope and held out another thousand-dollar bill.

"It matters," he said. "Otherwise, it's just a rumor."

"Forget it."

He left while I disconnected the engine and returned when I had it up on the lift, and he backed his truck carefully in underneath it. I lowered the engine to rest between two blocks of wood, and he cinched it with ratcheting tie-downs. We didn't shake hands. He got in the truck and put the window down. "I would have paid forty thousand for that engine," he said before he drove out of the bays.

The best times were the ten or fifteen minutes when Mary Ann was out of the hospital room. Nick would turn sluggishly to the sound of my voice and stare at me impersonally, as a healthy person might from twenty feet away. I told him that he and Mary Ann were more in love than anyone I knew, that soon they would have a baby, and that being a father was the best thing a man could be. I'd build to a culmination of happy circumstances, and in a way that had changed now, that was full of the best intentions, I said, "I wish I was you."

One evening Mary Ann came out into the hallway after I knocked. She closed the door behind her.

"Did something happen?" I said.

"Can you walk with me?" she said. "I could use a coffee."

Instead of taking the elevator down to the cafeteria, she stopped at a coffee machine and paid fifty cents for one in a little playing-card cup. "Want one?"

"I'm good."

I was wondering why she hadn't done this alone, to give me a chance to talk to Nick, who could nod now and grunt when I ran engine scenarios by him. He wasn't doing more than letting me fix the problems—I don't think he really understood most of what I was saying—but he'd lurch excitedly when I pretended to have figured them out with his help.

I was going to tell her about the twenty-five thousand, which I'd had Rod put in with the night's deposit, but first I wanted to hear what she'd brought me out to tell me.

We hadn't gotten far from the coffee machine when she stopped. "You made him try, Justin," she said. "He wanted to fix the cars and he came back."

"It was both of us," I said.

"And now I don't want you here anymore."

I stared at her.

"I don't want him to remember you. He's my husband. He's my baby's father and I love him, and I don't love you." She said this quickly, and before I could respond she said again, "He's my baby's father." For a moment I thought it was true. She didn't know about his vasectomy. Perhaps she had convinced herself that her plan that night had worked, that he had made love to her.

"I'd never say anything—"

"If you come back I'll hate you, Justin. Please. Don't make me hate you."

38.

NICK'S ABSENCE AND THE MANY DELAYED JOBS RESULTED IN A drop-off of business at Out of the Hole. A full day might yield three or four small external engine jobs and a handful of oil changes. Rod even suggested that we park our cars in the upper lot just to look open.

Half asleep one morning I was only vaguely aware of Rod walking around the bays with a tall man wearing an argyle sweater over a shirt and tie. He was in the lobby when I went out for a cup of the road-tar coffee Rod brewed.

"This guy wouldn't be a bad tech," Rod was saying, and in the silence that followed I realized he was talking about me. When I looked up, the sweatered man came forward with his hand out and said his name was Tom Greene. I gave him the mechanic salute—holding up my hand to show him that he wouldn't want to touch it. "How do you feel about repair work?" he said as he lowered his hand.

"How do I *feel* about it?"

"Pretty much about not doing it anymore," Rod said. "Strictly external jobs. Tune-ups, sensors, fuel injection cleaning. You're looking at the guy who just bought the place from Mary Ann."

Greene cleared his throat as if Rod had said something deeply flattering. "I own shops in the Precision Tune franchise," he said. "One in New Britain, one in Meriden. We specialize in the new generation of engines."

"What's the point of getting buried in a fifteen-hundred-dollar overhaul," Rod said, "when you can mash out four grand in little jobs."

"And a significant decline in rechecks," Greene said. "Even the dealerships are moving to a model of replacing engines rather than spending man hours repairing them. The future is customer service."

I couldn't say anything, so I just walked away. "I guess I stand corrected," I heard Rod say as the door was easing closed on its piston behind me.

Half an hour later an old gray-primered panel van backed up to the bays and Bobby got out. He looked terrible, gaunt and unshaven, his hair wild even under a backwards NASCAR cap.

He walked by the lobby window holding his middle finger up to Rod as he passed. He went over to his toolbox and started pushing it toward the van. It was a tall Mac box with loose casters that kept swiveling around, and I went over and pulled the front of it while he pushed.

"That guy out there bought the shop, I guess," I said. "He's going to turn it into a tune-up-only place. Precision Tune."

We got the toolbox outside and Bobby opened the back doors of the van. We pushed it right up against the bumper and then he took out a cigarette and turned around. He folded his arms and looked at the shop. "If I could I'd blow this place up right now," he said. "You ever seen a Precision Tune? They're bright yellow. You staying?"

I shook my head. I didn't know anything else, but of that I was certain.

"Rod?"

"Yeah, sounds like it."

He looked in through the lobby windows where Rod was talking animatedly to the new owner. "They make a good-looking couple," Bobby said. He shook his head and sniffed. "You been back to see Nick?"

"Mary Ann doesn't want me to."

"Me either. I guess she don't want him remembering."

I nodded. Rod had told me the same thing.

"I never told you," he said. "I went out to Chase Street. The Mustang was gone. He must've got rid of it."

I couldn't look at him. I started to open one of the drawers but Bobby pushed it closed. "Don't bother," he said, taking the long steel socket extension off the magnetic bar on the front of the box and setting it by the wheel well. Then he put the cigarette in his lips and started pushing at the top of the box until it tipped, the bumper serving as a fulcrum, and when the weight of the tools inside shifted back it slammed down into the van with the sound of a hundred windows breaking. He pushed at the bottom to slide it in and swore. "Now you can help me," he said, and we shoved it back with everything we had until it was in just past the lip. Bobby straightened, a little out of breath. He looked past me into the parking lot, then back at the lobby. He grabbed the steel extension and strode across the lot to Rod's Duster.

He swung the extension with both hands and hit the back window horizontally, so that when the safety glass popped and turned to pebbles, there was a level slit almost perfectly halfway up. He slammed the extension into the trunk and went to smashing out the driver's window as Rod came running out. He knew to stop, though, which was fortunate for him, and from ten feet away he stood with his hands on his hips watching Bobby destroy his car. Tom Greene stood outside the lobby holding his head. When Bobby was finished he came back around to the van, threw the extension inside, slammed the back doors, and without a word of good-bye to me drove off, baking one of the tires up Wolcott Avenue.

That evening I, too, packed up my tools, and though my box

was only half as tall as Bobby's, I drove home with a bungee cord holding down the trunk lid. I could've watched April, but Mom put her back in day care with the implication that I couldn't be completely trusted anymore. I tried to spend my days out of the house, driving around in the 'Cuda when the weather was nice, catching a matinee at the Watertown Cinema when it wasn't.

One afternoon as I was driving north on Route 6, a green Cutlass swerved at me. There was no question but that he'd done it on purpose—in my side mirror I saw him flip me off over his roof. And then I was getting gas one day at Arco when someone passing yelled out, "Whose car you driving, punk?"

39.

ON THE FIRST OF DECEMBER I LEASED A STUDIO APARTMENT FOR three hundred dollars a month in the West Rock neighborhood of New Haven, not far from Southern Connecticut State University. I just made the enrollment date for the spring semester. I sold the 'Cuda for my asking price of fifteen thousand to a middle-aged man who matched the engine and transmission numbers with a book, and I bought a ten-speed bike as my sole transportation. It was a kind of exile, making the sixty-mile trip to see Mary Ann all but impossible. Sometimes I'd go to the great gothic campus downtown and look at the Gutenberg Bible, one of only forty-eight in existence, or Van Gogh's *Night Café,* which he gave his landlord in lieu of rent, now worth upwards of fifty million, according to the catalog.

But the high points were brief in the expanses of my depression. I was disconnected from people and unsure of how to act in the world. Alone in my apartment I let myself cry, thinking of everything I was responsible for, staring, as all felons must in their cold cells, at the maddening impossibility of going back and changing anything.

I had weekly appointments at the psychology department for a few months, but it wasn't the right time for therapy. I had no friends, and I wanted the psychologist—an older man with kind, dark eyes and the considerate habit of pressing two fingers to his lips as he listened—to like me. I told him half-truths at best and left his softly lit office pretending to have my feet set firmly on the path of self-forgiveness.

On a foggy morning during spring break, while Mom was working and April was at daycare, I rode my bike to the bus stop in downtown Woodbury and took the Eastline out to Waterbury. They had bike racks at the back of the bus, and I got off and pedaled around the city under a cold sun. From across the street I saw Rod hooking up a car to one of the new oscilloscopes. The building was painted yellow, as Bobby had said it would be. I rode by Hog Wild and looked for Bobby's car, but it wasn't there. And then I rode out to Fulton Park, where I locked up my bike and walked down Cooke Street. My old Nova was in the driveway, along with a car I didn't recognize. I saw people in the house moving past the windows, but I didn't get close enough to make out their faces.

I had tried often to re-create that last night in their house. Would she have wanted him to come back after he'd pushed her off? That was the question in its entirety. In my mind, much of the night had distilled to only a few moments: when she asked why he wouldn't touch her, and the dying sounds she made afterward. That was all I'd had for hope, that she wouldn't want him back. That he'd gone too far this time and the pain couldn't be healed.

But another moment that night was on her bed when she took my hand, thinking it was his.

No, there was no doubt she would have taken him back. The questions I was left with were these: Would he have been able to change, to let go of their past and start over? And if not, how much more heartbreak could she have endured?

Not much, I knew. Not much. In my heart I saw the truth. He wouldn't have trusted the new baby not to die. He would have left her. She would have come back to me. That pristine life for us was mine now to mourn, though I couldn't hold this in my mind for very long, a minute or so was all before the thoughts shattered, destroyed by a survival instinct like the one that keeps us from stepping too close to the edge of a cliff, though we want so badly to see. I had betrayed him in a way that is unexplained by love, that I knew couldn't be forgiven or redeemed.

The next time I came to the house, there was a big dual-wheel U-Haul backed in the driveway. Mary Ann came out and walked past the truck toward the street. She had aged considerably, her hair, cut short now and permed, showed gray, and her face was longer and sunken—but then I realized it wasn't her but her sister. She came up to the end of the driveway and took the mail out of the box, and there was an air of kindness in her easy movements and soft expressions that caused me to come out of hiding and hop the chain-link fence. When I saw her again she was frozen, watching me as I walked up the sidewalk.

From ten feet away I introduced myself and said that I had worked for Nick.

She smiled. "They're inside." She turned toward the house and walked slowly until I had caught up with her. "Justin?" she said, and she held her hand to me. "I'm Susan. The oldest sister."

"From Washington," I said.

On the walk, she told me that she and her husband were helping Nick and Mary Ann move back to Oregon. The news, hearing it in words—I'd assumed as much when I'd seen the truck—stunned me only for a second, and then I felt relief because there were times even now, in my new life in New Haven, when I could imagine myself losing control and taking a bus or a train out to see Mary Ann and the baby even after she had warned me not to.

Mary Ann was standing at the kitchen counter with her back

to us when I followed Susan inside. "You've got a visitor," Susan said, and Mary Ann, closing a box, said, "I saw through the window."

Susan dropped the mail on the kitchen table and went off into the living room.

Mary Ann had her hair tied up pirate fashion in a bandanna. I smelled spruce and frankincense. Strength, I thought. Energy. She ran a tape gun over the box three times.

"Rod told me what you did with the engine," she said. "Thank you. We needed the money."

"Do you need more? I sold my car."

"We're okay," she said, her back to me still. "We're moving in with my parents for a while. They've got the room." She was wearing an enormous burnt orange sweater that had elastic sewn in where it came down mid-thigh like the mouth of a sack on her dark blue leggings. She turned finally, and the effect on me was this: a great fist to the gut, and then a stopping of time that allowed me to examine her as if she were a picture. Her face was rounder and lovelier—from the effort of packing and lifting or just from the fact of being late in her pregnancy, there was a blush in her cheeks and forehead—and her breasts were someone else's, and of course the gravity that pulled my eyes down was her belly, and it was true, it was never true until I saw her, and now that it was true, she was carrying a baby that was half my baby, I fell back against the door. I tried to swallow just as all moisture was vacuumed away from my shriveling tongue.

"Are you okay?" she said, walking slowly toward me.

I found my voice again. "You look really good, Mary Ann." It was invigorating to say her name, and I breathed deeply.

She smiled, touched my sleeve for only a second before she stepped back and glanced around. "I can't believe what you accumulate in five years. Not even five years."

Outside I heard Susan talking to a guy, probably her husband, and the shallow thump as they walked up the aluminum ramp of the moving truck. Slowly, against a fading dizziness, I pushed away from the door. Mary Ann looked up and into my face in an intimate way, touching my arm again, and just as I thought we would kiss she pulled back and went to where she'd been at the counter, and I realized that she'd only been checking that I was well.

She wrote KITCHEN on the box with a black Sharpie, and I came up and took the box off the counter. "Just set it by the door," she said.

She was standing at the doorway to the living room when I turned back around. "Come say hi to Nick," she said, and I followed her out of the kitchen.

The futon and the recliner and TV were gone from the living room, and a girl of seven or eight was sitting on the floor, listening to music on a Walkman and writing in a *Mad Libs* book. She didn't look up, and we weren't introduced. I followed Mary Ann down the hallway to their bedroom. This room had been left alone, and it sickened me when I saw the bed in my peripheral vision as I came up to the wheelchair. Nick was wearing a knit cap, under which I could see that his hair was cut short, just longer than a crew cut, it seemed. His head was tilted back so that he was looking at the picture of himself with Buddy Baker in front of Buddy's famous Superbird.

Mary Ann wheeled the chair around. "Somebody came to see you, honey," she said. "This is Justin. He's your friend."

His head seemed to be stretched longer, though it could have been the effect of the snug-fitting cap. One of his eyes wandered as if some of its cords had been severed, and there was a dent in his forehead. He'd lost so much weight I could see his jawbones, where the skin went up like the top of a parachute behind his chin, and his lips were very chapped, flecks of yellow skin peeled up like dried wax. I wondered if he'd lost the part of his brain that reminds us to moisten them.

"Hi, Nick," I said. He smiled gigantically, creasing his face in places that had never been creased before. But I saw through the smile the heavy blanket of the lie. He didn't recognize me. He had been rewarded for recognizing people in the past, and that's all this was. A conditioned response, a knee jerk. He panted out two breaths and then looked down at his hand, and the word I thought he was saying was "ate" until his hand started coming up off the blanket on his lap, and I understood he was saying "shake." And I held his hand, whose strength seemed to be short-circuited, painfully firm between thumb and forefinger and lifeless near the pinkie, the skin as soft and tacky as mine had become. His eyes were dim in the moment before they started darting away.

And where does it go? I had a professor Monday and Wednesday mornings who said that energy cannot be destroyed, so where in the universe does a mind go, a brilliant mind, and can a baby in the womb somehow sponge it up?

Mary Ann walked me out toward Cooke Street.

"We're leaving tomorrow," she said. "Nick and I are flying. He couldn't do a cross-country drive, I don't think. Susan and Jessie are taking my car, and Frank is driving the truck."

"I wish I could help," I said.

She smiled, looking ahead as she slowly walked. "It's going to be a good life," she said. She drew her open hands up to the sides of her belly. "We're just going home."

"I'm in school," I said. "Computer science."

"That's good. That's where you belong."

"Could you send me a picture?" I said. "After he's born? Him or her."

Ten feet before the end of the driveway, Mary Ann stopped and turned to me abruptly. "This is his baby," she said. There was a moment of tightness in her face before she breathed and lifted her thick brows, entering a calmer place. She clasped her hands in front of her belly. "He's suffered enough for this baby."

"I'm sorry," I said, and I hoped she understood that I meant it for everything.

"Good-bye, Justin," she said. "Be well."

"God, it hurts," I said, the words just suddenly there. She closed her eyes, resisting a moment before she sighed and looked at me again. Then she opened her arms and I stepped into them. I felt the mound of her stomach, both soft and firm somehow, and eased back as if it were the result of an injury, as if it were tender. But she pulled me against it, and I thought I felt something. "Tell us good-bye," she said, and just for a second I died. Crushing every self-protective impulse, I found my voice and told them.

40.

ON THE FIRST SUNDAY OF SUMMER BREAK MOM PULLED UP IN front of my apartment, and I loaded in my bike and a week's worth of clothes while April talked nonstop in her car seat. At home she showed me pictures she'd hung in my room and helped me put away my clothes. "I like your room a lot," she said. Her face had lost its roundness and she was starting to look like Mom in the nose and eyes. But the dramatic changes were on the inside. She had dry humor and sarcasm now. She was at the stage of planting expressions in every sentence: "No doy." "Gross me out." "To the max." Five years old, she was trying on personalities to see which one fit, much the same as I was. But I had to work at keeping the sense of loss I felt to myself. I wanted, as I imagined parents did, as Mary Ann would one day want for our son, for her to stay uncomplicated and to never be burdened with wanting opposite things at the same time.

I picked up one of her air-filled bouncy balls in the corner. Then we lay side by side on my old bed, and I tossed it up in an easy loop with some back spin. She caught it and threw it too far forward, and I retrieved it, and pretty soon we had a regular back-and-forth, the ball looping a few feet over our bodies as if we were the sing-along words to a song.

"You know what Dad said we could do in the winter?" she said. With my tiny bead of side vision I saw how big her eyes were. "Maybe go *skiing* in *Vermont*."

"Just maybe?"

"Or probably."

We threw the ball.

"Tell him Stratton," I said, "not Bromley. In the lodge they have chocolate-chip cookies as big as your head."

"Whoa. That's rad."

"He probably won't want to bring you back," I said. "He told me you're really, really hard to leave." I looked at her in between throws, and she was nodding.

"Oh, you knew that?"

"To the max."

I threw the ball so that it hit off the ceiling and came down so fast she didn't even get her hands up. It bounced off her chest and came down gently in my hands.

"Do it again," she said, and this time she caught it and rolled it over to me. "Again," she said. "Again."

My mother was seeing someone new, an orthodontist ten years older, who with his patient eyes and caring smiles reminded me more of Don than any of her boyfriends from Levi. While they played Boggle or watched VCR movies in the living room, I'd go in the basement and light the woodstove. It was a cool, wet May, and in the stove's itching warmth, I'd sip airline bottles from behind the fence, enjoying the half hour to myself.

The fire would hiss and snap, webs of steam lifting from the iron stockpot to a small box fan in the kitchen floor vent that blew the heat up. One of the fan blades was bent or loose, and the soft thump of that imbalance lulled me into my imagination.

We're together again, Nick and I, in the ZL1, that outrageous promise of a car, as Billy Motts raises the bet money as a flag. With two quick throttle snaps Nick clears the exhaust, and I look at him expecting to see the awareness we both have that the car is unbeatable. But his eyes are wide and ambivalent, as if this time he might have to push the tremendous engine for all it's worth. I don't understand, but then I do—he's freeing himself, if only for these thirteen seconds, from the laws that define him, the certainties of math and physics and even time—which he hoped to undo—and submitting to the proposition that anything can happen. I find myself submitting as well, and for an instant the world has possibilities it will never have again.

Then in a quick lever motion he dumps the clutch and drops the hammer, and for entire seconds the nose of the car lifts skyward, Nick our pilot leading us bravely on that flight from everything we know to untouched infinity, reaches of space and time only dreamed of.

ACKNOWLEDGMENTS

I'm deeply grateful to the following people for their advice and edits: Martha Bayless, J. T. Bushnell, John Groves, Betsy Hardinger, Caye Harrison, James Hausman, Andy Kifer, John Larison, Paul Martone, Patricia Moran, Diane McWhorter, Rosalind Trotter, and Jeff Voccola. Thank you to the English Department at Oregon State University for encouragement and support, and to Literary Arts for a generous fellowship. And this book would not have been possible without the tireless efforts of my agent, Seth Fishman, and my editor, Yaniv Soha, two of the very best in the book business.